Her fingers were gentle when she pressed around his stitches. Then she placed her other hand flush against the center of his chest, and he stopped worrying about his shoulder.

He closed his eyes, enjoying the comforting weight of her palm above his heart. Could she feel it beating, the way it sped up when she was near? Did hers do the same?

Her hand slipped away as she _____ opened his eyes to find _____ naked yearning on _____

"Well?" he croaked.

"I do believe you'll live _____ day," she said, her own voice dee_____suous.

"Glad to hear it."

"Me, too," she whispered.

"You know, Doc, I just noticed something."

"What's that?"

"You're a bit overdressed for this party."

She cocked her head, considering him for a long moment. "You know what? I do believe you're right." She stood and peeled off her shirt, dropping it to the floor to join his own.

Dear Reader,

As a native Texan, I have an ingrained fear of snow. Growing up, it was never a part of our regular winter weather, so when I moved to the DC area for graduate school, I packed a ridiculous number of coats and jackets in preparation for the coming cold.

My first real winter was an eye-opener. True to my roots, I abandoned the lab as soon as I saw flakes falling from the sky. There were many days I walked into work (yes, in the snow, uphill both ways!) because I was too scared to drive. And let's not forget my lack of a windshield ice scraper, which meant I had to use a credit card (something I do not recommend). Nevertheless, I survived, mainly because of the kindness of my friends. They had all grown up in states that celebrated winter, so they taught me a lot of the tricks of the trade. I've since made my peace with snow, although we'll never really be friends.

When I started this book, I knew Alex and Jillian were going to face a lot of difficulties. His cover has been blown, she's been kidnapped, and a murderous gang is after them both. How could things get any worse? You guessed it—snow.

So grab a warm beverage and make yourself comfortable. I hope you enjoy reading their adventures as much as I enjoyed writing them!

Lara

LETHAL LIES

Lara Lacombe

HARLEQUIN® ROMANTIC SUSPENSE

Recycling programs
for this product may
not exist in your area.

ISBN-13: 978-0-373-27900-5

Lethal Lies

Printed in U.S.A.

HARLEQUIN®
www.Harlequin.com

Lara Lacombe

I earned my PhD in microbiology and immunology and worked in several labs across the country before moving into the classroom. My day job as a college science professor gives me time to pursue my other love—writing fast-paced romantic suspense, with smart, nerdy heroines and dangerously attractive heroes. I love to hear from readers! Find me on the web, or contact me at laralacombewriter@gmail.com.

Books by Lara Lacombe

HARLEQUIN ROMANTIC SUSPENSE

Deadly Contact
Fatal Fallout
Lethal Lies

This one is for Adam, with love.

Thanks as always to Jessica Alvarez
and Rachel Burkot.

Chapter 1

"The National Weather Service has issued a severe winter storm warning for the DC metro and surrounding areas..."

"You should get going."

Dr. Jillian Mahoney glanced up from the computer screen and blinked. Her friend Carla stood in front of her, wearing neon-green scrubs that were bright enough to land planes at Dulles airport. It was a color Jillian could never wear, thanks to her Casper-the-Ghost-like coloring, but it looked good against Carla's café-au-lait complexion.

"You're very green today," she observed, turning back to the computer screen.

"I was feeling festive this morning," Carla replied dryly.

"Christmas is still over a week away. Besides, I'm pretty sure neon is not a holiday color."

"It is in my book." Carla leaned across the desk, casting a shadow over the keyboard. "I'm serious, Jilly. You need to get out of here before the storm hits. We're supposed to get twelve inches of snow. That's a foot." She held her hands out in an exaggerated approximation of distance, her expression earnest.

"I know," Jillian said, typing faster. "I just need to finish up these charts."

"Got enough food to last you a couple of days?"

Jillian huffed out a breath. "For God's sake, Carla, it's just a bit of snow. It's not the end of the world or anything."

Her friend cocked an eyebrow and narrowed her eyes in a gimlet stare. It was an expression Jillian had seen before, one used to great effect with uncooperative patients or egotistical doctors. She'd never had it directed at her, though, and she ducked her head, feeling chastened.

"Sorry," she muttered, clicking through to the next page of the chart.

"I'll let it go, because I know you're tired," Carla said. "But I worry about you. I know you've been too busy to go to the grocery store, but with this storm coming, you don't want to have to get out in the next couple of days. You need to take the time to relax and recharge, maybe get some sleep."

"I'll order in," Jillian said, entering the final notes with a flourish.

"There's no delivery when the city has shut down," Carla said, her tone reproving.

Jillian pushed back from the desk and stood, reaching for her coffee. "I'll be all right," she said with a smile, knowing her friend was only trying to help. "I'll stop at the store on my way home, pick up the essentials. You don't need to worry about me."

Carla nodded, apparently satisfied with this plan. "Be careful getting home," she said. "And try to enjoy the next few days off."

"Thanks," she said, rounding the desk and setting off down the hall. "And good luck," she called back, remembering that tomorrow was a full moon. Carla gave her a mock glare and Jillian chuckled. She shook her head, thanking her lucky stars that she was off for the next seventy-two hours. A full moon and a winter storm? The ER would be crazy, and she'd had enough crazy this week to last a lifetime.

She retrieved her coat from her locker in the doctors' lounge, not bothering to take off her white coat before shrugging into the outer layer. The puffed black jacket came down to her knees, long enough to cover the telltale fabric. Normally she didn't like to wear the white coat when out in public because it attracted too much attention, but today, she was too tired to care if anyone saw the hem of her coat.

Keeping her head down, she walked quickly through the hall, wanting to make it out of the hospital before anyone stopped her. She'd been on for the past three days straight, and though by all rights she should have left an hour ago, it was all too easy to get caught up in the eternal rhythm of the emergency room. All it would take was one question from a medical student or an interesting case from an intern, and she'd be sucked back into the vortex. Given the coming storm, she had no desire to be waylaid, as it would likely result in her being stuck until the weather passed. As much as she loved her job, she did not relish the thought of sleeping on the stained, lumpy couch in the doctors' lounge, subsisting on cafeteria food and bad coffee for the next three days.

She made it to the entrance without incident and she breathed a sigh of relief as she walked out into a blast of arctic air. Huddling into her coat, she pulled it closer to her body while she made her way to the parking lot. She didn't have a car, but the employee lot was much closer to the Metro station, so she frequently cut through it on her way to and from work.

It had already begun to snow. Small flakes drifted down, landing on the exposed skin of her face and melting into her hair. She was damp within a few paces of the entrance, her nose and ears already going numb as the wind picked up. Great. The grocery store would likely be packed, if the shelves weren't already bare. She'd probably have to be content with frozen dinners, and she could forget about fresh milk and vegetables. In the face of any winter weather, city inhabitants descended like a plague of locusts on the grocery stores, stripping the shelves of supplies and leaving dented cans and ripped packages in their wake. Given the dire predictions of snow, Jillian would be lucky to find any type of food. It was almost enough to send her back into the hospital to scrounge up some pudding cups from the cafeteria.

Almost.

The streetlamps cast an eerie yellow glow over the parking lot and she picked up her pace, her mind already focused on the comparative warmth the Metro station would provide. With her head down, she didn't see the man step out from between parked cars, would have never known he was there had he not spoken.

"Doctor?"

She turned reflexively, stopping out of habit. Encouraged, the man stepped closer, emerging into the light. She wished he hadn't. He was big, tall and broad through the chest and shoulders. Scruffy, too, with several days' worth of beard on his face and dark hair that was a bit on the longish side, curling over his ears and at the nape of his neck. She couldn't tell the color of his eyes, but she felt the intensity of his gaze like a brand.

Jillian took a small step back, alarm bells jangling in her mind. He didn't seem overtly threatening, but he wore only a hooded cotton jacket against the chill. Hunched though he was, she could see his muscles were drawn tight, tense with cold or withdrawal, she couldn't tell which. It wasn't unusual for junkies to patrol the neighborhood surrounding the hospital, although she wasn't sure what they thought they would find. Occasionally violence would erupt when one desperate soul tried to rob another in a bid to get the next fix.

The man standing in front of her didn't appear to be an addict, even though the burned-plastic smell of meth smoke clung to his clothes. He was too big, too healthy-looking, for one thing. He lacked the gaunt, haunted look that was so common among users, although he did have the same fierceness to his gaze. He reminded her of a coiled snake, ready to strike, and she had no desire to be in the vicinity when he did.

"If you're injured, the emergency room is right there." She withdrew her hand from her coat pocket to point. He didn't seem hurt, but it was hard to tell in the shadowy light of the parking lot.

"It's not me, it's my friend. Can you please help me?"

Jillian bit her lip, feeling torn. As a doctor, it was her duty to help people, even if they gave her the willies. She glanced around, searching for his companion. There was no one else in the lot, and she took another step back, suddenly feeling very alone.

"Let's find an orderly. Then we can get your friend inside." *And you away from me.*

She turned to head back to the hospital, but the man moved quickly to stand in front of her, blocking her path. She stepped back, a strangled yelp dying in her throat.

"There's no time for that. He needs help now."

Jillian stared up at him, her mind racing. She could try to scream an alarm, but the hospital entrance was at least a hundred feet away and, with the doors closed, it was unlikely anyone would hear her. She glanced around, hoping against hope that someone was just arriving, late for their shift, but the parking lot was still and silent. There was no one around, no one to help her.

"Please, you're a doctor, right? Can't you please help him?"

She halted her slow retreat, the need to help warring with her desire to get away. *Don't be an idiot*, she chided herself, knowing the right thing to do was to return to the hospital. There was no telling what kind of injuries his friend had sustained, and she couldn't exactly treat him in a dimly lit parking lot. No, better to retrieve a wheelchair and bring it back to collect the injured man.

But she couldn't exactly do that with this man standing in front of her, blocking her path to the emergency room entrance.

"I'm just going to get a wheelchair," she said, speaking calmly as if trying to soothe an angry dog. "It'll be easier to move your friend into the ER if we can put him in the chair, and I'll be able to examine him better once we get him inside."

The man let out a huge sigh, his shoulders slumping further when he dropped his head. Jillian stepped to the side, intending to skirt around him. He muttered something that sounded strangely like, "I hoped it wouldn't come to this," but before she could process his words, he moved, his hand shooting out of the darkness to grip her arm with painful strength.

This time she did yelp, but he hauled her up against his broad chest so quickly the breath whooshed out of her before she could gear up to scream. She kicked and clawed at him, but he grabbed her other hand and tugged both arms behind her back, braceleting her wrists with one hand and effectively restraining her. Desperate, frantic, she jerked her knee up, hoping to land a crippling blow between his legs. He swerved to the side, easily deflecting it, so she brought her foot down hard, aiming for his instep. Another miss.

Just as she sucked in the air to scream, he flipped her around and clamped a hand over her mouth. He released her wrists to band his arm around her torso, locking her own arms by her hips and effectively rendering her helpless.

He picked her up and hauled her between the rows of parked cars, pulling her into a dark corner of the lot. Part of her brain screamed at her to resist, to make noise, to do *something*! She kicked furiously, her legs windmilling in the cold air but missing him completely. Her foot made contact with a car and a sudden numbing pain shot up her leg. She blinked back tears and bit down on the hand clamped over her mouth. She was rewarded with a mouthful of leather, the taste so foul it made her gag.

The man ignored her attempts to escape, maneuvering her easily through the lot, as though he did this kind of thing all the time. Maybe he did. He stopped next to a dark, four-door sedan and removed his hand from her mouth so he could open the back door. He quickly pushed her inside before she had a chance to scream, but took care to keep her from bumping her head against the frame.

A considerate kidnapper.

The burned-plastic smell that clung to his clothes was even stronger in the car. Habitual drug use had saturated the upholstery, and she dimly wondered if she would get high just from sitting on the fabric. He released her wrists and shut the door. She waited until he rounded the hood to scrabble at the handle—if she could get the door open, she could run. She had a head start; she could make it back to the ER.

But the door wouldn't open. She threw herself against it, hoping it was just stuck, but it remained stubbornly closed.

She heard the driver's door open and the man slid inside. "Gotta love child locks," he said, eyeing her in the rearview mirror. She glared back, defiance and anger quickly replacing the numbness in her limbs as she began to thaw out.

A soft moan next to her made her jump. She shrank against the door in a bid to get away. What she had thought was a shapeless pile of clothes was in fact a person. One who was in bad shape, if the pitiful sounds coming from the opposite side of the back seat were any indication.

"That's Tony," the man said softly. "He's been shot."

So the friend really did exist.

"I don't know what you want me to do about it," she snapped. "If you really wanted to help him, you'd let me take him inside instead of kidnapping me like this."

The man shook his head as he started the car. "That's not an option."

"How do you expect me to treat him when I don't have any medical supplies?"

He reached across the front passenger seat and lifted a paper bag, which he handed back to her. It was rather heavy, in a bulky, awkward way. Jillian glanced inside, surprised to find a large collection of vials, syringes and bandages. She lifted one out, straining to read the label as they drove. Ketamine.

"Where did you get this?" She picked up another vial. Acepromazine. Controlled substances, both of them, and neither of them routinely used in human medicine. Veterinary medicine, on the other hand…

"Does it matter?"

She shrugged. "Not really, but I typically don't work with these drugs."

"Keep digging."

She did, pulling out a vial of Buprenex. The amber glass shone warmly in the glow of the streetlamps, the liquid inside turbulent as they hit a deep pothole.

"You can work with that."

She glanced up to find him staring at her in the rearview mirror. "Oh?" He sounded so sure of himself; she couldn't resist poking him just a little. Who was this man and why did he think he knew what she needed to treat his friend?

His eyes narrowed briefly before he returned his focus to the road. "You know that's a morphine derivative. It'll help calm him down so you can dig the bullet out."

How the hell did he know that? Did he have some kind of medical background? But if that was the case, why did he need her? She glanced over at his friend, who was leaning against the door, his body limp. The sound of his labored breathing let her know he hadn't died, but neither was he unconscious, as evidenced by the faint moans he released every time they hit a rough patch of road.

"Where were you shot?" She scanned his body, searching for blood, but it was too dark to see anything. No way was she going to touch him without gloves— she was a doctor, but she had her limits.

The man didn't respond, but his eyes flickered open in response to her question. He stared at her for a beat, then leaned his head against the window and closed his eyes again.

"The chest," the driver responded. "I think he punctured a lung."

Jillian clenched her jaw, frustration mounting. "If that's the case, then we really need to get to a hospital. He'll need a chest tube, scans and quite possibly surgery to remove the bullet."

"No."

"He could die!"

The driver spared her a glance. "Make sure he doesn't."

Jillian leaned back against the seat, her heart kicking

into high gear. Great. Not only had she been kidnapped, but she was expected to treat a man with serious injuries, without the benefit of a hospital. It belatedly dawned on her that if this man died, her kidnapper would have no further use for her, and he didn't seem the type to drop her off on the corner with a wave goodbye.

Fear trailed a cold finger down her spine and she shivered, her stomach roiling. "Can we at least stop moving?" she asked, knowing she couldn't do much for the injured man in a moving car. "And you can't expect me to treat him in the dark. I'll need light. Lots of it."

"We're almost there." His voice was grim, determination underlying every word.

Jillian took another look at her patient. His condition hadn't obviously changed, so she decided not to risk examining him until they had arrived at their destination, wherever it was. He seemed stable enough, and she didn't want to make things worse. She returned her focus to the bag in her lap. There were several suture kits, additional vials of drugs and antibiotics, and at the bottom, a chest tube kit. Her kidnapper had come prepared.

But who was he, and why was he so insistent they stay out of a hospital?

Was it the nature of his friend's injury? The law stated doctors had to report gunshot wounds to the police. Maybe he was on the run and didn't want to reveal his whereabouts. Still, she knew there were back-alley clinics that would stitch up bullet holes for a price. He could have easily taken his friend there, gotten the job done without having to resort to kidnapping. *Or theft*, she thought, glancing down at the bag of medical supplies in her lap. It was clear the hospital hadn't been their first stop tonight, and she was willing to bet all the toilet paper in the city that her kidnapper had broken into a vet clinic to steal supplies before grabbing her.

He took a corner hard, the car sliding a bit as the tires fought for purchase on the slick street. The snow was coming down in earnest now, a thin layer of flakes dusting the sidewalk white, as if someone had spilled a bag of powdered sugar over the city. She didn't know where he was taking them, but if the weather continued in this fashion, it was likely they'd be stuck, at least for the foreseeable future. If his friend took a turn for the worse, or she was unable to treat him, that meant they'd be cut off from help. While the driver didn't appear to be too concerned about her lack of resources, she shivered at the thought of his reaction if his friend didn't make it.

They pulled into a small parking lot riddled with potholes and puddles. A squat, plain building that may have once been white sat at one end of the lot, looking like a deflated soufflé. She caught sight of a red-neon Vacancy sign as they circled to the back of the building, but she didn't see a name for the place. She cursed herself for not paying attention to street signs and landmarks along the way—the kidnapper hadn't bothered to conceal their route, so if she'd had half a brain, she could have easily called for help and led rescuers to them, or run away herself.

Jillian stared at the back of his head, considering. He didn't seem to be a very good kidnapper. He'd let her see his face, which, according to all the movies she'd seen, was a big no-no. Either he didn't care about being caught or…

She swallowed hard, her stomach cramping in warning. It was possible he wasn't going to let her live long enough to be caught. Why else would he let her see his face or see the route they'd taken to his hideaway? Was he going to have her treat his friend, then kill her?

He parked next to a stained blue Dumpster and turned around to face her. "Are you going to give me any trouble?"

She shook her head, her mind desperately churning. She had to come up with something—she couldn't just let him lead her like a lamb to slaughter.

Her fingers curled around the bag in her lap and she felt the faint stirrings of an idea. The man had given her several vials of sedatives—enough to fell an elephant, if her hasty calculations were correct. Maybe she could use them to incapacitate him, giving her enough of a chance to run.

"I can see the wheels turning in your head," he said, frowning at her. He glanced down, understanding dawning on his face as he saw the way she clutched the supplies. "Oh, no," he said softly, reaching out to take the bag. "Don't get any ideas."

She forced her fingers to relax their hold, knowing that if she put up a fight he'd be even more suspicious. Besides, she'd get it back eventually. She had to have access to the supplies if he wanted her to help his friend.

"Time to go inside."

He got out of the car and opened her door, letting in a blast of cold air and snow. She instinctively shrank away when he reached for her, but he grabbed her easily enough, pulling her from the car and pressing her against the trunk as he slammed the door. The cold metal bit through her coat and she ground her teeth together to keep from crying out.

"Why are you doing this to me?" she asked as he hauled her up to a door. She stared at the faded black numbers, which grew blurry as tears pooled in her eyes. She blinked them away and shook her head. Crying wasn't going to help her. Not now.

If her captor noticed her emotion, he didn't show it, ignoring her question as he gently but firmly pushed her inside. It was warm compared to the car, and she had a moment to register that the room was surprisingly clean, if rather spartan. He marched her past two beds and guided her into the bathroom, closing the lid of the toilet and gesturing for her to sit. She did, and he reached into the pocket of his jacket and withdrew a length of plastic. She recognized the temporary cuffs, having seen them used before when the police needed to restrain a patient.

Jillian pulled her hands away, but her captor merely stared at her, his hand extended patiently as he waited for her to accept the fact that she was well and truly at his mercy. She glanced up at him, expecting to see anger at her defiance, but he regarded her with a flat, bored expression. Slowly, she returned her hands to her lap and he slipped the plastic loops around her wrists, taking care not to tighten them to the point of pain. Another length of plastic was used to secure her to the plumbing of the sink, effectively trapping her in the bathroom. Then he turned on his heel and walked out, shutting the door behind him with a click that echoed off the tiles in the small room.

Now that she was alone, Jillian didn't try to stop the tears.

* * *

Special Agent Alexander Malcom was having a bad day.

Deep undercover ops were not all they were cracked up to be. It had been hard enough infiltrating the 3 Star Killers, as the gang was inherently distrustful of outsiders. Still, he'd managed to worm his way into the organization, starting as a low-level runner and working up the chain until he'd become part of the trusted inner circle. It helped that gangbangers had a short life expectancy, which meant a vacancy had opened up at just the right time.

He'd been feeding his Bureau case manager a steady stream of information for the past two years, which had further strengthened their case against the group. The gang specialized in drug trafficking, serving as the main meth distributors for the mid-Atlantic region. They weren't above a little human trafficking and gun running, though, and so the FBI, ATF and DEA had worked together to establish a plan to take them down. It was a shining example of inter-agency cooperation, and the higher-ups couldn't stop patting themselves on the back for a job well done.

Except it had all gone to hell.

Tonight was supposed to have been a smooth takedown. Alex had been told a shipment of drugs was arriving at an abandoned warehouse on the outskirts of the city. It was a commonly used location for the gang; an ideal site for an operation since there was only one road leading to the building, which made it easy to control traffic in and out. He knew that such a big load would include guns as well, along with a few of the unfortunate women the gang moved from state to state, prostituting out to the highest bidder as a way to augment their earnings.

The alphabet soup had decided tonight's shipment would be a perfect cherry on top of their case, and that bringing it down would not only cripple the 3 Star Killers, but send a message to the other groups who might think to take their place. It was a decent plan, and it should have worked.

But it hadn't.

He ran a hand through his hair, cursing at the memories. The semitrailer, opening to reveal not the expected shipment of drugs, but a veritable army of gang members who jumped out, guns blazing… The government operatives, firing back but being forced to retreat in the face of the gang's overwhelming force… The screams of the wounded, as they lay bleeding out in the crossfire…

And the horrible realization that his cover had been blown.

Tony had turned to him with a sneer. "Not what you expected was it?"

Alex had swallowed hard, not wanting to believe the carnage in front of him. "How did you know?"

Tony lifted one shoulder in an eloquent shrug. "You have your sources. I have mine."

The realization that there was a double agent at work filled Alex with a potent rage. Not only had the bastard outed him, but whoever it was, they were also responsible for the deaths of the agents tonight. Without stopping to think, he grabbed Tony, intending to arrest the man and haul him in for questioning. Tony wasn't about to go quietly, though, and in the ensuing scuffle, managed to shoot himself in the chest.

"Damn moron," Alex muttered.

He wanted nothing more than to let the man die, but he needed Tony to reveal the name of his mole. So he had shoved him into the back seat of his POS car and set off, intending to get him patched up.

And that's when the evening had gone from bad to worse.

Now he stepped out into the cold night air, his case manager's words ringing in his ears. "Why'd you do it, man? Why did you betray us?"

"I didn't."

Alex pulled open the door to the backseat, eliciting a moan from Tony as the movement jostled him. Too bad. Any pity he might have felt for the man was gone, washed away in the blood of the operatives who had died tonight, all because of his actions.

He stooped and got an arm around the injured man. "Let's go. Time to move."

"No, please. No more. Leave me alone."

Alex ignored his request, pulling with a steady pressure until Tony slid from the car. He was a skinny guy and Alex had no trouble carrying him to the door of the motel room. He deposited Tony on one of the beds and stepped back, staring down at the man. His shirt was saturated with blood, and Alex could feel the sticky wetness on his own hands. Repulsed, he wiped his palms on his pants, needing to remove the stain of Tony's blood from his skin. God, would he ever be clean again?

Feeling old beyond his years, Alex walked to the bathroom door and paused. He hated himself for having kidnapped this woman, this doctor who held his life in her hands. Hated terrorizing her, threatening her, hurting her. He'd tried to be careful with her, but given the ferocity of her struggles in the parking lot, he'd had to use more force than he'd intended to subdue her. He hoped she wasn't too bruised from their encounter, but did it really matter? He'd kidnapped her, and he was going to force her to treat Tony's injuries in a bid to keep the scum alive. In the grand scheme of things, a few bruises were the least of his worries right now.

He opened the door and she jerked, shrinking back from him as he entered the tiny bathroom. Her eyes were huge brown pools in her pale face and he had to look away, unable to stand her hunted expression as she studied him warily.

Alex stepped forward, pulling out his knife so he could cut through the plastic cuffs. She gasped and shoved away, her feet scrabbling wildly as she kicked at him in self-defense. He closed his eyes, sucking in a breath through his nose.

Idiot. What did you think she would do?

"Please," she whimpered.

Her pitiful plea hit him like a punch to the gut. He was driven to find the mole to protect innocent people, but at what cost? The woman in front of him was completely blameless; her hands were clean of any wrong-doing. Her only mistake was being in the wrong place at the wrong time, and now her life was forever changed. It pained him to admit it, but she was one more casualty in this war. One more life, irrevocably altered, by the actions of a few bad men.

And one more mark added to his personal tally of destruction.

"I'm not going to hurt you," he said quietly. She stopped kicking and stared up at him with a look of profound distrust. Not that he could blame her.

He gestured to her wrists with his free hand. "I want to cut the restraints off. I won't cut you, I promise."

She held his gaze for a long moment. He remained still, waiting for her to give him permission to approach. It wouldn't change things, but he wanted her to understand, even if only on an instinctual level, that he truly wouldn't hurt her.

Finally she nodded once. He knelt and reached for her wrists, trying not to notice how fragile the bones felt in his hands. *Like a bird's wing*, he thought. *All graceful lines, perfectly formed.*

The skin of her inner wrist was so pale as to be almost translucent, and he could see the dark blue lines of the veins that snaked from hand to forearm. He caught her shudder as he brought the blade close to that vulnerable skin, and was struck by the sudden urge to gather her in his arms, press her to his chest and rock her, to convince her with his body, if not his words, that he would keep her safe.

The knife sliced cleanly through the thin plastic. Once free, she snatched her hands away from him and wriggled to put more space between them. He felt an odd hollowness in his chest at the loss of contact, but quickly shoved it aside as he stood and returned the knife to his pocket. Time to check on Tony.

"My—" he almost choked on the word "—friend is on the bed. I need you to fix him."

She stared up at him, her light brown eyes narrowing as he towered over her. "What if I can't?" She thrust her chin out in defiance, but he caught the flicker of fear that danced across her face.

"You can."

He'd meant the words to be reassuring, but her face

blanched, losing the little color she had. Not wanting to scare her further, he elected to keep his mouth shut. He gestured with his arm and she slowly rose.

"He's on the bed."

She kept her eyes on him as she moved, reminding him of a watchful cat. She inched around him, pressing her back to the wall, careful to keep space between them. He caught a whiff of vanilla as she passed, and resisted the temptation to haul her close so he could bury his nose in her hair. The warm scent reminded him of home, but he knew she wouldn't welcome his touch. Not now.

Not ever, he told himself firmly. In another life, she would have been his type. With her dark blond hair pulled back in a no-nonsense ponytail, soft brown eyes and gently curving mouth, she was just the kind of girl-next-door he preferred. Pretty but not intimidatingly so. A woman who could hang out with the guys in the afternoon then put on a ball gown and knock his socks off at night. And since she was a doctor, he knew she was smart, to boot. In other words, she was the perfect woman, the embodiment of all his fantasies.

And totally off-limits.

With a soft sigh he followed her into the main room. While he didn't think she'd try to run before treating Tony, he couldn't give her a chance to call for help. With the 3 Star Killers and the FBI after him, his life depended on staying off the grid. The last thing he needed was a 9-1-1 call revealing their location. His case handler already thought he was a traitor—if he discovered Alex had kidnapped a woman, he would never believe the truth, and Alex would be dead before the next sunrise.

I just need a few hours.

That's all. Just a little bit of time to make sure Tony was going to survive. Once he was sure the bastard wasn't going to die on him, he'd make his move and clear his name.

Chapter 2

Jillian kept her eyes on the man lying on the bed as she shrugged off her black coat. She'd entertained a brief but vivid fantasy of kicking her kidnapper in the face and bolting from the room, but logic told her she wouldn't get far. Besides, she couldn't leave this man alone to die. It wasn't in her nature to ignore a person in pain, not if she could do something to help.

She dropped the coat in the chair and scooped the bag of medical supplies off the chipped table. Fishing out a pair of gloves, she pulled them on as she walked over to her patient.

He was young, impossibly so. No older than twenty, she guessed. Another kid caught in the crossfire. Moving carefully, she unzipped his hoodie and peeled it away from his chest. Now that she had light, the blood from his wound was obvious. It had soaked into the fabric, making it cling to his skinny frame.

She felt rather than saw her kidnapper enter the room. He didn't make a sound, but she sensed a change in the air, a charge that told her he was there. She could feel his gaze on her as she bent over his friend, heavy as a touch. It made her uncomfortable to be the focus of his attention, so she decided to distract him.

"Scissors?"

"What?"

"Do you have scissors?" she asked.

"No."

"Then give me your knife."

She felt him hesitate and turned to face him. "I need to cut his clothes away so I can access his injury."

He stepped forward. "I'll do it."

Jillian rolled her eyes, but let him approach. Like she was going to stab him and make a run for it. She wouldn't get far, not in this weather. And while she didn't know precisely where they were, she did know they were in the kind of neighborhood where people minded their own business. It was unlikely anyone would offer her assistance, even if she did escape. No, she was stuck here, at least for the next little while.

The man loomed over his friend, blade in hand. He held the knife above his friend's abdomen for the space of a few heartbeats, and Jillian could have sworn she saw a flash of anger cross his face. But then it was gone and he quickly sliced through the young man's shirt, taking care not to cut him in the process. He peeled back the ruined cloth, making additional cuts to remove it completely.

He's so gentle. Shocked at the errant thought, Jillian shook her head. No, he wasn't gentle. Not at all. He'd attacked her in the parking lot, gripping her arm so tightly she could feel the bruises his fingers had left behind. He'd shoved her into a car, then yanked her out and pushed her into this godforsaken room. Those were not the actions of a gentle man.

But…he hadn't slapped or hit her when she'd fought him, just used enough force to restrain her. He had kept her from bumping her head as he'd put her in the car. And his touch in the bathroom had been very light, his hand cupping her bound wrists with a softness that surprised her. Now he'd removed the shirt from his injured friend, trying not to jostle the man too much in the process. He didn't seem like a violent man, but she couldn't reconcile his behavior with the fact that he had forcibly kidnapped her.

"What's your name?"

He glanced back at her, his brows lifted in surprise. She could have bitten her tongue off for asking the question—if she knew his name, she'd start seeing him as a person, not the enemy. But it was too late to take the words back, so she held his gaze as he stepped away from his friend, giving her room to stand next to the bed.

He didn't answer right away and she turned her focus back to the young man, her brain already clicking over into doctor mode. That was what Carla called it anyway, having learned not to attempt a non-patient-related conversation with her when she was engaged. Jillian couldn't exactly explain it, but it was an almost trance-like state in which her entire consciousness was aimed at the person under her hands.

With his clothing gone, she could see the small bullet hole in Tony's chest. It was on the right side, more lateral than central, which was likely why he was still alive. It had missed his heart and while it looked a little too high to have affected his liver, she couldn't be sure. "Help me roll him."

"You want him on his stomach?"

"No. I want him on his side so I can check for an exit wound and determine the trajectory of the bullet."

She placed the kidnapper's hands on the young man's body, one on his shoulder and the other on his hip. When he was in position, she walked to the other side of the bed, pulling out her penlight as she moved. The lamp on the bedside table didn't provide as much light as she would like, but it was better than nothing. The man waited for her nod, then pulled in a fluid motion, rolling her patient to his side and triggering a groan from the young man.

Jillian ran the light along his back, noting the hole the bullet left behind when it had exited his body. It was fairly small, indicating he hadn't been shot by hollow-point ammunition. It was also almost directly in line with the entrance wound, which meant the bullet hadn't taken any detours on its way out. Both were good indicators, but he wasn't out of the woods yet.

She gave another nod and he lowered Tony to his back. She pulled out her stethoscope and placed it on the man's chest, listening intently. Breath sounds on the left, none on the right. Given the young man's labored gasps for breath, she'd suspected a pneumothorax, and this confirmed it.

"I need occlusive dressing. Two of them." He had air in his chest cavity, which prevented his right lung from expanding normally. The first order of business was to seal the bullet holes to keep more air from getting in. Then she could work on restoring his breathing.

She held out her hand, but the expected supplies didn't materialize. Annoyed, she glanced up to see her kidnapper digging through the bag of supplies.

"Give me that," she said impatiently, snatching it from his hands and dumping the contents on the bed next to her patient. Gauze, Band-Aid bandages, tape… no occlusive dressing.

"Do you have any plastic bags?"

The man shook his head. Of course not. Fabulous.

"Okay," she said, thinking out loud. What else could she use to seal off the wounds? "I need you to cut off two squares from the shower curtain liner. Make them about this big—" She held out her hands to demonstrate. "Can you do that?" It was a long shot, but it just might work.

As he left to procure the requested material, Jillian collected the jar of Vaseline, several gauze squares and the roll of white tape. She spread a liberal coat of the petroleum jelly on the gauze, saturating it completely before moving on to the next stack of white squares. By the time she was done, the man had returned from the bathroom with her liner.

"Lay them on the bed. I need you to roll him again."

Her patient moaned as he was repositioned. The kidnapper grimaced in response, and she realized with a shock that he was upset by the sounds. She was so used to people moaning, crying or screaming that she'd become desensitized, no longer bothered by the sound of a person in pain. In fact, she much preferred it if they made noise—it told her they were still alive and breathing.

"If he's crying, he's still here," she told her kidnapper, uncertain why she offered him such reassurance. Maybe because his unguarded reaction to his friend's pain made him seem more human, not the dark monster she had painted him as after he'd thrown her in the car.

Moving quickly, she placed the soaked gauze over the hole in the young man's back, applied the square of shower curtain liner and taped down three edges. She leaned back, gesturing, and her patient was returned to the bed, giving her access to the chest wound. She repeated the process for his front, studying the dressing with a critical eye. It wasn't ideal by any stretch, but it would have to do. Now to restore his breathing.

A large-bore IV was the safest way to decompress a patient, but she didn't recall seeing those supplies in the bag. Still, best to double check. She scanned the paraphernalia on the bed, clenching her jaw in frustration as she realized she was going to have to employ a more dangerous, and painful, method of treatment. She hesitated, but there was no help for it.

"Give me the chest tube kit." She held out her hand, gratified when the man passed her the bundle right away. "We'll make a nurse out of you yet," she murmured, laying the kit on the bed and ripping open the package. It was slightly different than what she was used to—the diameter of the tube was much smaller, for one thing—but she was pleased to see a valve on the end of the tube. Since she didn't have access to a drainage system, the ability to seal the tube was critical. She put on fresh gloves and picked up the scalpel.

"Hold his right arm above his head."

The man moved forward, grabbing Tony's arm and raising it as instructed. "Keep hold of him," she said, meeting his eyes for a brief second so he would know she was serious. "Don't let go."

Jillian bent to make the first cut. "Wait," the man said. She looked up at him to find his eyes wide and his face pale. "Aren't you going to give him something first? Something for the pain?"

She gritted her teeth, unused to having her actions questioned in an emergency. "I can't," she explained with a patience she didn't feel. "He's lost too much blood and I can't risk sedating him when I don't have control of his airway. You didn't steal me any local anesthetic, so I have nothing to give him to numb the area. Now, hold him down."

Tony's eyes flared open and he grunted as she sliced quickly and cleanly through the skin, making a small cut to insert the tube. She stuck her finger inside, probing through the deeper tissue until she felt the bone of his rib. Keeping her finger in place to hold the incision open, she picked up the plastic tube and positioned the tapered end.

"Now it's really going to hurt," she warned, and thrust the tube through the opening she'd created. Tony let out a guttural scream and writhed on the bed, trying to wriggle away from the pain. "Hold him." She bit the words out, working fast to push past the resistance of muscle and connective tissue until the tube broke into the free space of his chest cavity with a pop she felt in her fingertips.

There was a soft hiss as the air in his chest began to escape through the tube, a sound that always made her think of opening a soda bottle.

Jillian held her breath, looking for a flash of red. If the bullet had nicked an artery and his chest cavity was filled with blood, it was unlikely the man would live. She couldn't treat an internal hemorrhage in a motel room.

Fortunately for him, the tube stayed clear. She kept one eye on the dressing that covered his bullet hole, gratified to see the gauze suck into the wound as Tony's chest cavity decompressed. The shower curtain liner seemed to hold, as well, creating a seal to prevent air from re-entering his body. As the gas left his chest he began to cough, gasping in great lungfuls of air between the racking spasms that shook his thin frame. Jillian bared her teeth in a fierce grin, the familiar rush of satisfaction washing over her as she rode the high that came from saving someone's life.

When the hissing sound stopped, Jillian twisted the stopcock on the end of the tube to seal it off and picked up her stethoscope. Normal breath sounds on the left and the sweet sound of slightly labored, but functional, breathing from the right. His heart sounded good, too, the frantic cadence settling into a steady rhythmic pulse as his breathing evened out. Excellent.

She leaned back, looping the stethoscope around her neck. "We'll leave the tube in place for a few hours, make sure the dressings don't leak. If he still looks good, we can take it out." She taped the tube in place to keep it from moving too much, then picked up the gauze and petroleum jelly. Time to make another dressing. It wouldn't do to have air re-enter his chest through the hole she'd just created.

"I need another square of the shower curtain."

The man didn't move right away and she looked up, wondering if he'd heard her request. He was staring down at his friend, his expression a mixture of anger and hope, almost as if he couldn't bear to believe the young man was going to make it. While Tony was stable for now, he wasn't out of the woods yet, and Jillian knew there were many things that could still go wrong. It would be so much better to get him to a hospital where his condition could be properly monitored, but since that wasn't going to happen, she'd just have to make do as best she could.

"Hey," she said again, waving her hand to get her kidnapper's attention. "It's not time for a break yet. I need another square of curtain liner."

He blinked at her, as if he was coming out of a trance. With a short nod, he rose from the bed and disappeared into the bathroom.

Jillian pressed the saturated gauze over the incision she'd made and allowed herself a brief moment of rest. Treating patients always brought an adrenaline rush, and tonight was no different. If anything, she was even more on edge, given her current circumstances. Still, she had done her job, and done it well. She had saved this kid's life, and if he cooperated, nothing else would go wrong. Maybe the kidnapper would even let her go—after all, she'd done what he'd asked her to do. Surely there was no need to keep her now?

That thought made her shudder as she circled back to the realization she'd had in the car. While she didn't know his name, she had seen his face. He wasn't just going to let her walk out of here—no way.

That didn't mean she had to make things easy for him. She heard him stir in the bathroom and knew she didn't have much time. Glancing quickly over the supplies on the bed, she grabbed a syringe and a vial of sedative and shoved them both in her pocket. When she was finished with Tony, she'd ask to use the bathroom and draw up a dose of the drug while she had privacy. It was a risky defense, since she'd have to get close to the man to administer the drug, but it was the only option she had.

She wasn't going down without a fight.

God, he was actually going to make it.

Alex sagged against the wall of the bathroom and shook his head at the realization, relieved beyond words. Tony was going to survive, which meant he was one step closer to discovering the identity of the mole who had betrayed him. It had seemed like such a long shot that he had hardly dared hope Tony could be saved. His death certainly would have been the low point of a truly crappy day, but now there was a chance he could make things right.

And all thanks to her.

She'd been amazing, he reflected as he bent to his task. So totally focused and intense, as though she could heal Tony through the sheer force of her will. It had certainly made him sit up and take notice, and he could only imagine what her patients thought when she brought that energy to them. He couldn't have asked for a better doctor, and felt a fresh wave of guilt at the knowledge he had forever changed her life.

He wanted to let her go, wanted to return her to the nice, safe life she'd led before. But now that he'd pulled her into this mess, he couldn't leave her until he knew she'd be safe. With the 3 Star Killers after him and the FBI thinking he was a traitor, he had to clear his name and make sure she had protection before walking out of her life. Hopefully she'd forgive him for what he'd done, once she knew why he'd done it. He paused, wondering why with everything else going on, the thought of her anger upset him. Not like he didn't have enough to worry about right now.

He cut the plastic square free and stood, folding his knife and putting it back in his pocket as he returned to the bedroom. She was still sitting on the side of the bed, her hand pressing a square of gauze to the place where the tube entered Tony's body. A small part of him felt a perverse satisfaction at the memory of Tony's reaction as she'd inserted the tube—he deserved all the pain he could get.

The doctor glanced up as he neared, but quickly looked away when she took the square from him. Interesting. She'd never had trouble meeting his eyes before. He watched as she taped it into place with brisk, efficient movements. Then she sat with her hands in her lap, as if at a loss for what to do next.

He could relate. When he geared up for an operation, adrenaline was a palpable rush in his limbs, coursing through his veins in a powerful rhythm. During the operation was no different, his body seeming to move of its own accord, his actions perfectly choreographed thanks to endless hours of training. But afterward, when the danger was gone and there was nothing left to do, it was hard to come back down to earth. He imagined emergency medicine, with its life-or-death stakes, was much the same way.

Without stopping to question his motives, he decided to distract her. "Alex," he said softly in answer to her earlier question.

She looked up at him, confusion in her eyes.

"Before, you asked me my name. It's Alex."

"Oh," she said, her gaze sliding away from him again. She removed her gloves with fumbling fingers and tossed them into the trash can by the desk. He gave her a moment to respond, but she didn't say anything.

"When someone offers their name, it's customary for you to offer yours in exchange."

She glared at him then, a flash of temper darkening her brown eyes in the dim light of the room. He fought to keep a smile off his face, knowing it would only anger her further. "It's the polite thing to do," he pointed out reasonably.

"Polite?" she huffed. "You manhandled me in the hospital parking lot, shoved me into a car, threatened me and forced me to treat your friend with stolen veterinary medical supplies, and now you want to lecture me about manners?" She shook her head, her ponytail dancing with the movement. "As if this night couldn't get any stranger," she muttered.

"I did do those things, yes," he said. "But there's no reason we have to be rude to each other now."

"Is this some kind of Hannibal Lecter thing?" She tilted her head, leaning away as she studied him. "Because I'm really not in the mood for games."

He frowned at her. "What are you talking about?"

"You know, the bad guy from *Silence of the Lambs*."

"Never seen it."

"Well, he always insisted on being uber-polite to his victims before he killed them. You should know that's not going to work on me."

He'd tried to keep her from bumping her head as he'd put her into the car, but maybe the stress of being abducted had caused her to snap. "I'm really not following," he said, sitting on the second bed and trying to appear non-threatening. At least she'd saved Tony before going insane. That was something.

She sighed, the action pulling her white coat tight across her chest. He swallowed hard, keeping his eyes glued to her face. No way was he going to let her catch him ogling her, especially when she was clearly delusional. She seemed calm right now, but if she thought he was going to assault her, there was no telling how she'd react.

"Being nice to me won't make me trust you," she said, speaking slowly, as though he were a small child.

"I don't expect you to trust me," he replied truthfully. "I just want to know your name."

"Why?" Her expression was wary, like she thought he could use her name against her somehow.

He spread his hands, palms up, in a gesture of supplication. "So I know what to call you."

"Oh." She bit her lip, as if that possibility hadn't occurred to her. "Maybe I don't want to talk to you."

He clenched his jaw, biting back the retort that sprang to mind. It was his fault she was so jumpy, and snapping at her for it would get him nowhere.

"Fair enough. But we're going to be stuck together for the foreseeable future, so I thought it might be nice if we were on speaking terms. Unless you think you can ignore me for the next few days?" He raised a brow in challenge.

"Days?"

The color drained from her face and for a second he thought she was going to faint. Alarmed, he half rose from the bed, but she held up her hand to keep him in place.

"No, it's fine. Stay there. I just… I need to go to

the bathroom." She bolted up and dashed off before he could do so much as nod.

Poor thing. He'd worked with guys who threw up before an op, the stress and nervous energy settling in their stomach where it couldn't do any good. He'd never had that problem himself, but he knew she'd be fine once she got it out of her system.

Wanting to give her a bit of privacy, he stood and stepped closer to Tony's bed. The medical supplies were still strewed across the other half of the mattress, a jumbled mess of syringes, gauze and glass bottles. He could tidy this up, at least, so she wouldn't think he'd been sitting here listening to her the whole time.

He tossed the wrappers from the supplies they'd used and then set about collecting the items and putting them back in the paper bag. He moved methodically, gathering all the supplies of one type at a time in an effort to keep the bag somewhat organized, to make it easier to find what was needed in case there was another emergency. He hoped they were done for the night, but he couldn't be sure.

His hand paused as he began collecting the vials of medication. There were only two bottles on the bed. He closed his eyes, thinking back to his frantic search through the cabinets of the vet clinic. Most of the medication had been locked away, but he distinctly remembered finding three bottles that had been left out. He'd grabbed them along with fistfuls of other supplies and run, not bothering to stop to read the labels of what he'd taken.

Where was the third bottle? He felt along the bed, checking to make sure it hadn't rolled against Tony. It wasn't under the pillows, and a quick search of the floor didn't turn up anything. He paused, suspicion making the hairs on the back of his neck prickle. Had she taken it?

He silently moved to the bathroom door, listening for any noise that would indicate what she was doing in there. It had been disturbingly quiet since she'd entered the bathroom, with no sounds of retching or water running. Almost as if she was trying to be *too* quiet, so he wouldn't suspect anything.

Alex grasped the door handle, hesitating only a second. If he interrupted a private moment, he'd apologize. But he doubted she was in there trying to regain her composure.

With a twist and a tug the door opened, making her shriek. She jumped and he heard the musical tinkling of breaking glass as the third vial of medication hit the tiled floor. Just as he'd thought—she had taken it. Probably thought to drug him and make her escape. It wasn't a bad plan, all things considered, and a small spark of admiration flared to life in his chest.

He leaned a shoulder against the door jamb, crossing his arms and legs as he studied her. She glowered at him, a half-filled syringe in one hand, her other clenched in a tight fist.

"I'm curious, Doctor," he said conversationally, striving to keep the amusement from his tone. "What would you have done if the first dose didn't knock me out?"

Chapter 3

He wasn't dead.

The bastard must have been born under a lucky star, because by all rights, he should have been killed tonight. That had been the plan. That was how things should have gone.

Alexander Malcom, former golden boy of the Bureau, turned traitor and killed by the very gang he had infiltrated. Pity the Bureau hadn't gotten to bring him to trial, but everyone knew you didn't cross an organization like the 3 Star Killers. Street justice was bloody and swift.

Or at least it should have been.

Dan Pryde pasted on a somber expression, shaking his head over the loss of life. Yes, it was a shame that so many promising young men and women had been injured or killed tonight. Even more shameful that they had died in vain, since the primary target was still alive.

He'd checked and double-checked the identity of the bodies, called all the hospitals to make sure Alex hadn't slipped through the cracks. There was no sign of him. While some of the casualties were still being collected, he knew in his gut that Malcom wouldn't be among them. The man had vanished like a ghost.

Nodding to the other agents around the table, he wheeled out of the room and down to his office. Let them point fingers at each other and rant about operational security—he had bigger things to deal with.

Such as finding Malcom before the man had a chance to expose him as a double agent.

Dan paused just inside his office to shut the door behind him. He needed privacy for this call, and although it was late and the halls were empty, he couldn't take a chance that someone walking by would hear him. He motored to his desk, the whir of his wheelchair a soft hum in the otherwise silent room. It was a nice chair, provided by the Bureau, but after all, they owed it to him to provide the best in wheelchair technology, seeing as how it was their fault he was in the damn chair in the first place.

No, he corrected silently, *not their fault.* Not the faceless entity that was the FBI. One man was responsible for the paralysis that had rendered his legs useless and made him a prisoner in this chair, and now, after too many years, Dan had decided to enact his revenge.

I set the wheels in motion.

Shaking his head at the awful pun, he dug into his jacket pocket and retrieved his burn phone. Time to check in with his friends on the other side; find out just what the hell had happened out there tonight.

He hesitated a brief second, debating who to call.

That punk kid Tony or someone a little higher on the food chain? Tony was his eyes and ears on the ground, but he was always a little too brash, too cocky for Dan's liking. Although he provided good intel, he was still just a seventeen-year-old kid with a big mouth and a hot head. Like all teenage boys, Tony thought he was immortal, a testament to the power of denial, since he saw his friends gunned down on a regular basis. He was on his way to a gang leadership position, but he wasn't there yet. If he'd managed to keep himself alive during tonight's fiasco, he'd be one step closer to the position he craved.

No, Tony wouldn't provide him with the information he sought. If he really wanted to know what had happened tonight, he needed to go all the way to the top.

He dialed quickly, loosening his tie as he waited for someone to pick up on the other end of the line. Hopefully his contact hadn't been killed in the shootout. He frowned at the thought, but dismissed it quickly. Despite their reputation, the leaders of the 3 Star Killers were not brainless thugs. They were too smart to get in the middle of a firefight between the government and the gangbangers. But as the phone continued to ring, cracks of doubt began to mar his conviction. Why weren't they answering?

Finally someone picked up. They didn't speak, but he could hear the raspy sound of their breath on the other end of the line. "What happened?" Dan didn't bother with preliminaries, nor did he offer any kind of identification. He thought of the gang as a tame beast—under his control for now, but capable of turning on him in a heartbeat. He wasn't stupid enough to give them the ammunition they'd need to ruin him.

There was a scratching as the phone was passed and then a familiar voice greeted him. "Mr. Hoover."

It was the gang's pet name for him, something he'd suggested they use. It was nice being called by the same name as the father of the FBI. He usually got a small thrill out of it, but tonight he was too wound up to notice.

"Why'd you call? We're busy."

Dan bit his bottom lip, refusing to give voice to his thoughts. *I know you are, you little shit. And the only reason you're busy is because I saved your ass tonight.* Instead of pointing out that they should be thanking him for the fact they were still alive, he silently counted to five before he spoke again. "Did you take out Malcom?"

There was a pause, which made him grit his teeth. He started counting again. One… Two… Three…

"Haven't seen him yet."

"Which means he's still alive."

"Nah, man, it means I haven't found him yet. I'm pretty sure he's dead."

"You'd better hope he is, because that was the price for the information I gave you." When there was no response, he hardened his voice. "Do I have to remind you of the terms of our deal?"

"Nah, I got it. Look, he's probably dead. We're out looking for him and Tony now, to make sure."

Tony was missing, too? That was disturbing news. Although the kid couldn't identify him, Malcom could still get information from him. Information that would have him asking questions and stirring up trouble.

Why couldn't you just die?

"I'll call back in an hour. You'd better have good news for me." He hung up before the man on the other end of the line had a chance to respond. Things were even worse than he thought.

Dan tucked the phone back into his pocket with a sigh. He knew better than anyone that life didn't always go as planned. While he hoped the gang would turn up Malcom's body, he had to prepare for the very likely possibility they would not. It was a setback, but he wasn't about to let Alex go that easily, not after all these years.

Not when he was so close to getting his justice.

Jillian stared up at him, her heart pounding so hard she felt as though it might beat right out of her chest. So much for her grand escape plan. She'd only managed to fill the syringe halfway before he'd barged in. She glanced down at it now, still clutched in her right hand. With a sigh, she set it on the sink. It wouldn't do her much good, and she didn't want to antagonize him further.

He was already intimidating enough, taking up the width of the doorway as he leaned against the jamb. He blocked her exit, but he didn't seem threatening. His stance was casual, arms and ankles crossed, like they were having a normal conversation and he hadn't just caught her making preparations to drug him. His expression was open and curious, and as she watched him, she could have sworn the corner of his mouth twitched. She focused on his lips, caught the movement again. Was he—? He was! The jerk was laughing at her!

"This is funny to you?"

He sobered at that, his gaze sharpening as he regarded her. "Not at all. But I admire your determination. Not many people would be so resourceful." His eyes cut to the syringe, then back to her. "Or so brave."

"If you'd just let me go, I wouldn't have to resort to such desperate measures."

He shook his head before she'd even finished speaking, which had her temper flaring.

"Why not? I've done what you asked. I saved your friend, and now I want to go home." Her voice broke and she bit her lip, blinking furiously. She would not cry, especially in front of *him*.

"Not yet." His voice was flat, his jaw clenched. She could see that he was upset, but she pressed on, hoping she could get through to him.

"Is it money? Is that what you want?" When he didn't respond, she took a deep breath. He needed to know the truth, even though it would probably upset him. "You should know I don't have any money. Residents don't make much, and most of what I do make goes to paying off my school loans. I can barely afford my apartment, much less pay you."

"Don't you have family?" There was a flash of something in his eyes—Interest? Calculation?—but then it was gone, making her wonder if she was imagining things.

"No." She didn't like to talk about her brother on the best of days, and she certainly wasn't going to discuss him now. "So if you were hoping to use me to get rich, I'm sorry to disappoint."

He smiled then, a brief curve of his lips. It transformed his face, making him look friendly. In other circumstances she would have found a smile like that on a man like him attractive.

"I'm not interested in money," he told her.

"Then let me go."

He shook his head, shifting slightly. "Can't do that. It's not safe."

"What do you mean?" She felt a chill on the back of her neck and reached up to rub the sensation away. What could be worse than this?

He ran a hand through his hair, mussing it even further. "There are some bad guys after us," he said, uncrossing his feet and scuffing the toe of his boot on the stained linoleum. "We need to lay low for a while."

"Bad guys?"

He nodded. "Have you heard of the 3 Star Killers?"

Heard of them? Oh, yes. She saw the results of their handiwork on a daily basis, treating gunshot wounds, stabbings and overdoses with a regularity that broke her heart. They were a major presence on the streets of DC, and the news that they were after her kidnapper did nothing to alleviate the knot in her stomach.

"You have a gang after you?" She should have known—the smell of the car alone should have tipped her off. The 3 Star Killers were the major meth suppliers for the city, and the heavy, cloying stench emanating from the upholstery wasn't due to casual drug use. She'd probably been riding around in a mobile meth lab, a thought that made her skin crawl.

Watching her captor now, she was struck again by the thought that he didn't look like a typical user or dealer. How was he associated with the gang and what had he done to bring their wrath down on his head?

"Something like that." He ducked his head, the gesture of a little boy in trouble. His refusal to meet her eyes made her stomach clench. He was hiding something.

"There's more." It wasn't a question and he knew it.

"You don't need to worry about the details now."

She considered his statement, wondering if he was right. It would be easier to remain ignorant of the danger facing them, but what good would that do in the long run? Better to know, so she could be prepared for the worst. Maybe there was a chance she could slip away before the gang even realized she was with him. The 3 Star Killers weren't known for their subtlety, and she knew that if the gang found them, they wouldn't distinguish between the one who had wronged them and the one who was in the way.

"Please," she said, her voice quiet. "If you're not going to let me go, at least tell me what's really going on."

He looked at her then, his dark blue eyes sharp and focused, glinting like twin sapphires in the dull bathroom light. "Why should I tell you? How do I know I can trust you?"

Jillian felt her eyes grow round with the question. Trust her? He had doubts about trusting her? After everything he'd done to her? She fought down a wave of exasperation and tried to see things from his perspective. She'd probably be a little paranoid if a gang was after her, but still. Who was she going to tell?

"Seeing as how you kidnapped me, and not the other way around, I don't know why you'd have trouble trusting me."

He raised a brow, regarding her skeptically. "Seeing as how I just found you filling a syringe with a whopping dose of sedative I can only imagine you meant for me, you can see why I'm a little worried."

She felt her cheeks heat with a blush, but refused to look away. "Can you blame me?"

He smiled again and she couldn't help but return the gesture. "No, not really. I'd probably do the same thing."

"But you'd probably be successful," she muttered.

His smile broadened as he dipped his head in acknowledgment. "I appreciate the vote of confidence."

"Please tell me," she whispered.

The smile faded from his face as he regarded her, his expression sad. "I don't think that's a good idea," he said softly.

How could she get him to talk? What could she say that would convince him she needed to know what was going on? She deserved to know—her life was in danger too, dammit!

She wanted so badly to yell and scream, to rail at him until he gave in. But she knew he wouldn't respond; if anything, her temper would only cause him to shut down. No, if she wanted answers, she would have to extend some kind of olive branch. What did she have that he wanted?

When someone offers their name, it's customary for you to offer yours in exchange.

Did he still want to know? Would that be enough?

"Jillian," she blurted, breaking the silence between them.

He tilted his head, studying her like she was some kind of talking monkey.

"My name," she clarified. "You asked me before. It's Jillian."

* * *

The name fit her, Alex thought as he watched her draw herself up, as though she was preparing for battle. He knew why she had finally told him—she was hoping he'd give her some information in exchange. Tit for tat. One of the oldest interrogation tricks in the book; a tactic he'd used with varying degrees of success throughout his career. He'd never been on the receiving end before and was surprised to realize how susceptible he was. Her confession, her peace offering, made him want to explain things, to lay it all out for her. He was sorely tempted to tell her the truth, not just about why he'd taken her, but about everything.

It was a heavy burden he carried. He wanted badly to share it with someone.

But he didn't want to put her in any more danger.

Needing time to think, he stuck his hand out in a bid to buy a few seconds. She stared at it warily, as if he offered her a stick of dynamite. When he didn't move, she grudgingly slid her hand into his and gave him a perfunctory shake. "Nice to meet you, Jillian," he said.

She pulled away quickly, no doubt repulsed by his touch. He wished he could say the same, but her small, strong hand had felt nice in his own. It was so easy to think of her as fragile, because of her porcelain skin and delicate bones, but he had only to touch her to be reminded of her hidden strength.

His resolve weakened with the contact, the words building up on the tip of his tongue. Why not share the truth with her? Who could she tell? After all, he was going to keep her by his side until the mess died down. He should be able to make contact with his case handler soon, explain everything. Now that Tony was stable, he had evidence to support his claim. He'd get things straightened out with the Bureau, find the mole in the organization, and then his nightmare would be over. He'd make sure Jillian had a protective detail, so if the gang got wind of her involvement tonight, she'd still be safe.

The more he considered it, the more he realized that if he told her the truth, things could only get better. Since they were going to be stuck together, he needed her to trust him. Besides, he couldn't stand the way she looked at him now. The combination of fear, determination and hurt that shone in her eyes just tore him up inside. The way she flinched every time he moved broke his heart. He'd never hurt a woman before, never given one cause to be afraid of him, and he didn't like the slimy sensation he felt in his gut every time she jumped in response to his actions.

His mind made up, he straightened from the door jamb. Jillian watched him move, her stance reminding him of a feral cat, ready to run at the slightest provocation. Alex took a deep breath, gearing up to say the words. After so many years as an undercover agent, it was hard to overcome his ingrained reluctance to reveal his identity. But it had to be done.

"I'm undercover FBI. I was involved in a sting that went south tonight. A lot of government agents died because of a mole in the organization who told the 3 Star Killers about the takedown. Tony knows the identity of the double agent, which is why I needed you to save his life. I couldn't take him to a hospital, because the FBI and the gang would know, and they would send people to either arrest or kill me. I can't let that happen."

She watched him, her eyes growing round as he

spoke. "You're an FBI agent?" Her voice was barely more than a whisper, but he thought he detected a note of doubt. Not that he could blame her—he hadn't exactly acted like an upstanding lawman tonight.

He nodded. "I infiltrated the 3 Star Killers almost three years ago. I've worked my way up the chain of command, passing on intel to the FBI so they could build a case against the gang. Tonight was supposed to be the big operation, the one that crippled the gang and effectively took them out. But it all went wrong."

"I see." She nodded mechanically, and he had the distinct impression she was humoring him. As though he was a mental patient and she was agreeing with everything he said so as not to provoke him.

Biting his lip in frustration, he thrust his hand into his back pocket and pulled out his identification. He normally didn't carry his badge and ID, but since tonight was the big op, he'd brought it along so he could identify himself to the other agents. Jillian jumped and shrank back as he shoved it forward for her inspection, but when she realized he wasn't going to hurt her, she reached out to take the leather case from his outstretched hand.

Her brows pulled together as she studied the badge and card. "This looks real," she said, sounding confused. "How is that possible?"

"Because it's the truth?"

She glanced up at him, her brown eyes shining with an emotion he couldn't name. "But you kidnapped me."

"I had to. I couldn't let Tony die."

She took a step forward, evidently growing braver in the face of his confession. "Why didn't you tell me who you were before?"

He shook his head. "There wasn't time. I couldn't stand there in the middle of the parking lot and explain the situation to you. We had to move. I made a command decision, and while I'm sorry you were scared, I'd do it again."

She stood in front of him now, a breath away. "You idiot," she seethed. She slapped his badge against his chest and he raised his hand to keep it from falling. "I would have helped you. I could have admitted Tony as a John Doe, bought you some time. But you didn't think of that, did you?"

Actually, no, he hadn't considered that possibility. He'd figured the FBI and the gang would comb the area hospitals looking for him, and he'd wanted to get away as soon as possible. Besides, while the FBI would be careful not to harm any innocent bystanders in their quest to arrest him, he knew the gang wouldn't be so circumspect.

"I couldn't risk other people getting hurt. You know the 3 Star Killers wouldn't hesitate to mow down everyone in the ER if they knew I was inside."

Some of the anger in her eyes dimmed at that. "You still could have told me the truth."

"When?" he asked, his temper flaring to life. "In the car on the way here, as you were looking through the supplies? When you were treating Tony? When you were sneaking off to drug me? When, exactly, do you think I should have had this conversation with you?"

"I don't know!" She took a step back, throwing up her arms as she moved. "But don't get mad at me for being upset at the fact that you kidnapped me and brought me here under false pretenses."

Alex opened his mouth to reply, but stopped as he

caught the hitch in her breathing. She was terrified, and trying hard not to show it. The knowledge doused his anger like a cold shower. "I'm not the bad guy," he said softly.

Jillian stared up at him a long moment, considering. He watched the emotions play across her face—anger, frustration, fear, denial. And acceptance. Finally she spoke again. "I know."

"But the bad guys are out there. And they are coming for us. So we have to decide—are we going to work together or are we going to argue over all the crap that's happened tonight?" He reached out to rest his hand on her arm, squeezing gently. For the first time, she didn't flinch at his touch. He felt like whooping in celebration, but kept his voice quiet. "For what it's worth, I'm sorry about the way things went down. I'd give anything to keep you out of this."

The corner of her mouth hitched up in what might have been a smile. "Woulda, shoulda, coulda," she said wryly. "You're right about one thing—if we waste time arguing, we're as good as dead. But don't think I'm going to forget about the fact that you kidnapped me and shoved me into a car."

He nodded. "Fair enough. You can punish me later. For now, let's get some rest."

"I need to check on Tony first."

He leaned back so she could walk out of the bathroom. As she brushed past him, he put a hand on her arm, stopping her. She glanced up, a question in her eyes. "I was never going to hurt you," he said softly. "I know it's asking a lot, but please believe me—I would never deliberately hurt you."

Her expression softened and she reached up to rest

her hand on his shoulder. "I know that now," she said, giving him a reassuring pat.

He released her, the tension in his chest loosening with her words. "Good."

He watched her walk into the bedroom, a curious sense of relief making him feel almost giddy. She knew. She knew all about him, about what had happened tonight. And now she could help, as his partner, not his hostage. He wasn't alone any longer—he was part of a team.

Alex moved to the second bed and folded down the scratchy spread. Jillian glanced up from her examination of Tony, and he gestured to the empty bed. "You should get some sleep."

She looped the stethoscope around her neck as she stood. "What about you?"

He nodded to the chair on the other side of the room. "I'll take first watch."

"Promise you'll wake me in a few hours?" She was already stripping off her white coat and shoes. He heard a thunk as she set her pagers on the bedside table before climbing in.

"Promise," he said, but he doubted she heard him. Her breathing was already the deep, even cadence of a person sleeping. She was probably a pro at taking advantage of the odd stolen moment; a skill he imagined came in handy in her line of work. He watched her for a moment, envying the peace she'd found and wanting nothing more than to lie next to her and rest for a few minutes. Or a few years.

Shaking off the errant thought, he flipped off the lights and settled into the chair, positioning himself in the dark corner. He had a good angle of the window and

door, but was out of the direct line of fire, should anyone burst into the room with guns blazing. He checked
his Glock, then his backup weapon—a snub-nosed .38
Special. Both were in good working order, loaded and
ready for use. Just in case.

He'd been careful to make a clean exit tonight and
knew they hadn't been followed. The gang didn't know
about this room at the no-tell motel. Neither did the
FBI. It was his personal bolt hole, a place to retreat
and regroup when things went bad. In the three years
he'd been with the gang, he'd never once had to use it.

Until tonight.

Sighing quietly, he reached up a hand to rub his eyes,
trying to scrub away the images from tonight's attack.
The screaming. The smell of cordite and gun smoke on
the wind. The blood.

Watching the attack unfold tonight had made him
feel helpless. It was a sensation he hadn't had in years,
not since the day of that horrible training accident when
he'd reached out a hand to help Dan make it to the top
of the obstacle wall. Dan's grasp had been solid and
sure, until suddenly it wasn't, and Dan was scrabbling
for purchase as he slipped. The screams of the injured
tonight were a haunting echo of Dan's cry as he'd fallen.
Even now, Alex had only to close his eyes to see the man
lying at a terrible angle at the base of the wall, the image
as clear and perfect as a photograph. It had been almost
ten years, but he hadn't forgotten any of the details.

Probably never would.

Jillian sighed and shifted on the bed. He focused on
her, using the distraction of her presence as a lifeline to
pull himself out of the sea of memories. It wouldn't do
to get bogged down in things that couldn't be changed.

He had to stay focused on the job at hand—he owed her that, after dragging her into this mess.

It was the only way to make sure they survived.

Chapter 4

Jillian wasn't sure what woke her. She opened her eyes to unfamiliar surroundings, a heavy blanket of disorientation clogging her senses until her brain logged on and she remembered.

The parking lot. The car. The motel room.

And Alex, the undercover FBI agent.

It was quite a story he'd told her. If not for the badge, she wouldn't have believed him. Even with the proof of his identity, it was hard for her to accept the truth of his words. Things like this didn't happen to people like her. She worked her shift, went home and slept. If she was feeling really crazy, she'd have a glass of wine with dinner. But getting kidnapped by a Fed and held for her own safety so a bloodthirsty street gang didn't kill her? She wouldn't have imagined this, even in her wildest dreams.

Or her worst nightmares.

She stared at the ceiling, wondering if she should offer to relieve Alex. There was no way to know how long she'd slept—the room was dark, save for a faint rim of light showing around the drawn curtains. Even that didn't tell her anything, since it was the artificial light of a streetlamp. She couldn't tell if dawn was approaching or if it was still the middle of the night.

A faint wheeze interrupted the silence and she was up and out of bed before her mind fully registered what she was hearing. Time to check on her patient.

She flipped on the lamp on the bedside table. The bulb appeared to be on its last legs, sputtering out a weak yellow glow that wasn't much of a match against the darkness. Still, it was better than nothing.

Tony stared up at her, his eyes dark shadows in his thin face. She plugged her stethoscope into her ears, blew on the drum to warm it and placed it on his bony chest. "Having trouble breathing?"

He nodded, his chest heaving with effort. One of the bandages must have gotten loose, breaking the seal to allow air to sneak back into his thoracic cavity. She checked the dressings on his chest, but they appeared fine.

"Can you roll for me? I need to check your back."

Tony braced himself and pushed, grunting with effort. A quick glance at his back confirmed her suspicions—the bandage had come loose, probably as he shifted on the bed. Jillian quickly re-taped it, adding a bit extra to make sure it stayed in place. Then she guided Tony back down to the bed.

"One more second," she said, twisting the stopcock

to open the chest tube. The air hissed through the tubing, and he gasped and coughed.

"Thanks," he said after his breathing evened out again.

"No problem," she said automatically.

He studied her for a moment, as if she was a puzzle he was trying to piece together. Finally he spoke again. "You saved my life."

Jillian shrugged, unsure how to respond. "Just doing my job."

Tony shook his head. "Nah. You coulda let me die. But you didn't."

"I don't like any of my patients to die."

"I wasn't your patient."

She stared down at him, struck by a sudden urge to laugh. "Is that what you think?"

He was quiet for a moment. "You're a good person."

Confused by the sudden change in topic, she searched for something to say. "I try to be."

"I try to be, too. That's why I'm gonna help you now."

Jillian sat on the edge of his bed, wondering where he was going with this. How could he help her? "Oh?" she said.

"You saved my life, now I'm gonna return the favor. You need to leave."

"Why is that?"

"My boys are on the way. They're gonna be here soon, and you don't want to be around when that happens."

A cold finger of fear trailed down her spine, but she tried to keep her voice steady. "How do you know that?"

"I saw the name of this place when we pulled in, and

I texted them. When you were in the bathroom with him." He placed a special emphasis on *him*, heaping all his scorn and disgust onto that one word.

She glanced over her shoulder, searching for *him*, but the chair was empty. Where had he gone? Had he really just left her here with Tony?

"I don't know where he is," Tony said, following the direction of her thoughts. "But you can be sure my boys are gonna find him." Satisfaction rang in his voice, a promise of violent retribution that made her stomach turn.

"Look," Jillian said, wetting her lips with the tip of her tongue. "I'm sure your friends are looking for you. But I don't think they can move in this weather." She gestured in the direction of the window, its mustard-yellow curtain billowing slightly as the heater kicked on. "We were supposed to get a foot of snow tonight."

"Lady, you ain't hearing me," Tony said, an edge creeping into his voice. "They're on the way. And if you're here, you're gonna regret it. I can keep 'em from killing you, but I can't stop them from having a taste."

"A taste?" she whispered. Fear clawed at her throat, making it hard to breathe.

Tony must have sensed her horror. "You look like a nice girl," he said, his voice softer now. "You don't need to be used like that. Get out of here while you still can."

She leaned back, her mind racing. Could she really leave, with Tony clearly still needing care? The idea of abandoning a patient went against every principle she held as a doctor, but a small, instinctual part of her recognized that she couldn't help people if she was dead. Perhaps it was better to go—she could call the authorities to make sure Tony got the help he needed, and the police could arrest any gang members who showed up. The idea of leaving this mess for someone else to deal with was distasteful, but in the long run, it was probably for the best.

She rose, her legs shaking only slightly as she shrugged into her white coat and dropped her badges and pagers into the pockets. She stepped over to the window, tugging the corner of the rough curtain aside to glance out. A sea of white greeted her, the parking lot and street beyond coated in a thick blanket of snow that glittered prettily in the moonlight.

Her heart sank at the sight. Not only would she have trouble walking in that, her tracks would be visible for miles around. Easy work for the gang to go after her, if they were of a mind to. But what other options did she have?

She turned back to the bed. Tony watched her quietly, his eyes tracking her every movement. "Tick tock," he said, the innocent words taking on a new, terrible meaning for her.

Determined to ignore him, she glanced around the room, looking for any sign of Alex. Where the hell was he? Had he really left her alone with Tony? But why? He'd made such a big deal about keeping her out of danger—had he really abandoned her to face that danger on her own? He didn't seem to be the type to just run away, but she hadn't known him very long. Still, she remembered the intensity of his gaze, the total focus as he'd tried to convince her he wanted to keep her safe. He'd seemed almost desperate for her to believe him, as if the thought of her doubt caused him physical pain. Surely he wouldn't drop her after she'd decided to trust him?

She glanced back at Tony as a new thought struck

her. Had something happened to Alex? She dismissed the possibility almost immediately. She knew there was no love lost between the two men, but Tony could barely sit up, much less do anything to incapacitate Alex. Furthermore, she would have heard something if Alex had been injured. No, wherever Alex had gone, he'd done so willingly.

And she couldn't wait around for him to return.

Jillian pulled on her heavy black coat, glancing around the room to make sure she wasn't leaving behind anything the gang could use to identify her. If she was lucky, maybe she could make it to a main road before they showed up so her tracks would disappear. It would be tough going, but she could do it. She had to, if she wanted to survive the night.

Her gaze caught on the brown bag of medical supplies and she paused, remembering the bottles of controlled substances. No way was she going to leave them behind for people to abuse or sell. She made a quick detour to the bathroom to grab the half-full syringe, then recapped it and shoved it into the bag. Tucking the bag under her arm, she moved to stand over Tony.

"If you have trouble breathing, open the valve at the end of the tube to let the air out of your chest. Try not to move around too much, and keep the bandages on your bullet holes for a few more days, until they start to heal. That tube needs to come out soon. You should really go to an emergency room."

He nodded at her, even though she knew he wouldn't follow her instructions. Oh, well. He wasn't going to be her problem anymore, and she'd done all she could to help him.

She glanced past him, noticing for the first time what

appeared to be a door in the back corner of the room. It was hidden in the shadows, so she'd missed it before, being more focused on treating Tony than anything else. She walked around the bed and quietly pulled it open, pressing her ear against the door of the neighboring room. As far as escape routes went, it was preferable to hiking through the snow, but if the room was occupied she couldn't very well burst in.

It sounded quiet, but then again, it was the middle of the night. Most people, if they had any sense, would be asleep, so the lack of sound didn't fill her with confidence. Still, she had to try.

Straining to hear the slightest noise, Jillian slowly turned the knob, holding her breath as she eased the door open. A shaft of moonlight spilled across the floor, but otherwise the room was dark. And empty. She breathed a sigh of relief and pulled the door to Tony's room closed before shutting this door and flipping the lock. No sense making it easy for them to follow her.

She started across the empty room, intent on finding the door that connected this room with the next. She needed to put distance between herself and Tony, needed to get as far away from him and his gangbanger friends as possible. If she could make it to the office, she could use their phone to call the police—her cell phone had died hours ago, before she'd even left the hospital.

Stepping lightly, she crept toward the opposite wall. The curtain billowed as she moved, making the silvery light in the room shift and bringing the shadows to life. It was an unsettling illusion, one that made her increase her pace.

She was a few feet from the door when a shadow detached from the wall and moved in front of her. Jillian jerked back, a scream lodged in her throat as a hand wrapped around her upper arm.

"Just where do you think you're going?"

Alex knew the moment she recognized him by the way she relaxed. The tension left her muscles and her shoulders slumped slightly as she exhaled, her head dipping to land against his chest with a gentle thud.

The simple gesture of trust reverberated through him, the act more powerful than any words. Her acceptance of his protection lit a spark of warmth in his chest—a bright spot in this otherwise horrid night. He wanted nothing more than to wrap his arms around her, to bring her closer so he could hold her. To savor the contact. It had been so long since he'd truly enjoyed the touch of another person that the idea of embracing her was almost too much to bear.

It took almost all of his willpower, but he kept his distance, knowing that if he did touch her further he wouldn't want to let go. Even though he was desperate, he realized that he'd scared her enough for one night. For one lifetime, really.

Still, he couldn't help but drop his own head, his nose hovering close to the tantalizing scent of her hair. Warm vanilla and something else, subtle and familiar. He took in a deep breath, part of him hoping Jillian wouldn't realize he was sniffing her, the other part not caring if she did. It had been months since he'd been around people who didn't smell like drugs or booze, far too long since he'd encountered the delicacies of a woman's perfume. The indulgence of her scent brought some measure of comfort, made him feel almost human again.

She raised her head from his chest to stare up at

him, her eyes glossy in the dim moonlight of the room. "What are you doing in here?" she whispered.

Her breath flowed warm across his lips and chin, a soft caress. Alex closed his eyes as sensations swept through him, battering his control. It had been too long since he'd kissed a woman. Too long since he'd been around a woman he was tempted to kiss, one who wasn't a user or a dealer, one who wasn't reduced to selling her body in a desperate bid for survival. He opened his eyes to stare down at the shadows of her face, her lips dark and indistinct. No matter. He filled in the details from memory—the perfect bow of her upper lip, the fullness of her lower lip and the way she bit down on it when she was concentrating. No doubt about it—her mouth was sexy as hell, and he wanted to taste it.

Drunk on her scent and the nearness of her in the dark, he dipped his head. It was only when she said his name, this time with urgency in her voice, that he re-called his senses.

Releasing her, he stepped back and took a deep breath to clear his head. Now was not the time to scratch an itch. He had to find out why she was here and not in the room with Tony. Had something happened to him?

"What happened to Tony? Why aren't you with him?"

She shuddered, making the hairs on the back of his neck stand up. Had the bastard said or done something to her? He looked her up and down, but it was impos-sible to see if she was physically hurt. He'd been so sure Tony was incapacitated—it was the only reason he'd left the room. God, had he misjudged the situation? He'd never forgive himself if Tony had harmed her...

"Tony's fine. But we have to go."

"What?" His relief at her assurance must have messed with his hearing. "Did you say go?"

"Yes. The gang is on the way here."

Alex shook his head. "Impossible. They have no way of knowing where we are."

"Tony texted them our location. When we were in the bathroom."

A cold fist gripped his stomach as he digested her words. He'd taken a cell phone from Tony before stuffing him in the car, but he hadn't conducted a thorough search. It was entirely possible the kid had another phone stashed away, one Alex had missed.

He cursed, long and low. A rookie mistake, in a night filled with them. And one that had cost him a safe place to wait out the storm.

"Let's go." Jillian tugged on his arm, clearly anxious to leave.

"Wait," he said, resisting her pull. "We can't just run out of here. We need a plan." She paused, but he could tell she wasn't happy about it. He appreciated her instinct to run, but leaving in a panic was a good way to get killed.

He mentally reviewed his options, wondering how much time they had before the 3 Star Killers showed up. The snow was still coming down, but that wouldn't stop them. They were fueled by vengeance, and no amount of winter weather would douse those flames.

The car was parked out front, in clear view of the road. The vehicle was no match for the icy roads, and it would take too long to clear the snow from around the tires so they could get enough traction to leave. Besides, the car was on its last legs, likely to stall even if he did manage to get it started. Not exactly an ideal getaway.

One thing was certain—they couldn't stay here. The gang wouldn't give up when they found Tony in an otherwise empty room. No, they'd search the entire motel, methodically going from room to room as they hunted their prey. He was just glad the motel was otherwise empty, as his conscience couldn't handle any more innocent deaths.

A car rolled into the parking lot, the flash of its headlights brightening the room and interrupting his thoughts. Time to move.

Alex grabbed Jillian's hand and tugged her toward the connecting door, pulling her into the next room and locking it shut behind them. Quickly and quietly, they made their way through several rooms, putting more and more distance between themselves and Tony. He had no way of knowing if the newly arrived car held gang members, but it wasn't worth the risk of sticking around to find out.

As if she'd read his mind, Jillian whispered, "Do you think that's them?"

"Not sure," he whispered back. Muffled shouts and the thud of a slammed door urged them forward. "But I'd say it's likely."

Jillian made a soft whimpering sound that hit him like a punch to the gut. "I'll keep you safe," he said, pushing her ahead and drawing his gun. "Keep going—I'll watch your back." He turned around to face whatever danger might lie behind them as she moved forward.

He heard her grab the handle of the connecting door and twist, but nothing happened. She cursed and tried again, rattling the door with her efforts. "It's locked," she hissed. "What do we do?"

By now Alex could hear the gang members as they approached, kicking down the connecting doors and searching each room. They had maybe half a minute before they were found, and with only his two guns for protection, he didn't like their odds.

"Oh, God, they're coming. Should we hide?"

He shook his head, pulling her over to the window. They were close to the office and from this angle he could see an older model pickup parked at the end of the lot, half hidden by the hulking form of the Dumpster. Probably the attendant's car—and their best shot at getting out of here.

"See that truck?" He pointed it out to her, careful to keep his voice low. "That's where I want you to head. I'm going to open this door and make sure there's no guard, and when I give you the signal, I want you to run like hell for the truck. Get around to the passenger side and wait for me."

She nodded mechanically, eyes wide. Alex caught her gaze. "Listen to me, Jillian. No matter what you hear, I want you to stay hidden. If I'm not right behind you, stay crouched by the truck until you hear them leave. Then go to the motel office and call the police. Do you understand?"

"Why wouldn't you follow me? You can't leave me!"

He laid his free hand on her shoulder and shook her gently. "Tell me you understand. Stay hidden, stay safe."

"Okay," she whispered, blinking hard. She threw herself into his arms, squeezing him tight in a brief embrace. "Be careful," she said, her voice low and thick with emotion.

Alex nodded, stunned by her apparent concern for him. Her touch stirred up emotions he didn't have time to examine now, so he shoved them aside and focused on the task at hand. Staying low, he eased open the door, gritting his teeth against the blast of frozen air. He peeked out, looking back toward Tony's room for any sign of a gang member monitoring the parking lot. It was empty, no doubt too cold for any kind of foot patrol. The windows of the car were heavily tinted, so he couldn't be sure there wasn't someone inside watching, but it was a chance he'd have to take.

Motioning Jillian forward, he kept his eyes trained on the car as she ran for the truck. There was no sign of movement, so he decided to make a break for it. Keeping as low a profile as possible, he plowed through the snow, trying to stay in her footprints to make it look as though only one person had crossed the lot. Tony had clearly tried to save Jillian by warning her about the gang, which meant he might not tell his friends about her role in all of this. If Alex could keep her hidden, so much the better.

He made it to the truck and tested the door, relieved beyond measure to find it unlocked. He quickly climbed inside to find Jillian already in the cab, hunched down in the front seat.

"You made it," she breathed, clearly happy to see him. He spared her a quick grin as he began a search for keys. Anyone stupid enough to leave their vehicle unlocked in this neighborhood probably didn't have the brains to take their keys with them. He hit the jackpot when he flipped the sun visor down, releasing a small bundle that landed in his lap with a metallic *clink*.

"You didn't really think I'd leave you here all alone?" he said, stabbing the key in the ignition and cranking the engine. It groaned and the truck shuddered, but the engine didn't turn over.

He heard a muffled shout and glanced over to see two gang members staring at the truck from the doorway of the room they'd just left. In unison, they drew their guns and started across the parking lot.

Crap.

"Get down," he said to Jillian as he turned the key again. Still no response.

By this time the manager of the motel had stepped out, no doubt drawn by the noise of the struggling engine and the taunting shouts of the gangbangers as they drew closer. When he saw his truck was occupied, he moved forward, his face contorted with rage.

Everything seemed to happen in slow motion. Alex watched as the taller of the two gang members raised his arm and fired a shot at the motel manager. It went wide, but just barely. The man stopped walking toward the truck, swiveling to focus on this new threat. When he saw the two young men approaching with guns drawn, his expression morphed from combative to terrified in the blink of an eye. Apparently deciding the truck wasn't worth it, he beat a hasty retreat back to the relative safety of the office. Good—one less person to worry about.

"What's happening?" Jillian asked from her position on the floorboard of the passenger seat.

"Nothing," Alex lied, pumping the gas pedal. "Stay down."

He twisted the key again, the engine whining for an endless second before turning over with a beautiful roar. Throwing the gearshift into reverse, he skidded backward out of the spot, making a wide arc in the snow. Realizing their quarry was about to escape, the two gang members broke into a run in an attempt to close the distance. They fired several times, shooting wildly at the truck without really stopping to aim. The bullets pinged off the frame of the truck, but a few hit the windshield with a sickening crunch. Alex grunted as something—bullet or glass, he wasn't sure—hit his arm. It felt like a red-hot poker had been jammed into his shoulder, but he didn't have time to take care of it now. Peering through the spider-webbed windshield, he put the truck into drive and lurched forward.

The gangbangers didn't have time to get out of the way. There was a satisfying thud as he sideswiped them, their soft bodies no match for the steel of the truck. "Whoops," he muttered, feeling no remorse. "Gotta look both ways, boys."

He checked the rearview mirror as he pulled onto the street. They were lying in a crumpled heap in the snow, clearly hurting from the impact. He didn't think they were dead, but they should be out of commission for a while. Served them right for shooting at him.

Alex reached up to touch his shoulder, hissing when the contact sent a fresh burst of pain down his arm. His hand was wet when he pulled it away, the blood looking almost black in the streetlamps.

"Doc?" he said, steering as best as he could on the slippery streets. He hadn't seen the gang car pull out behind them yet, but it was just a matter of time. He needed to make it to a main road, and fast, so they could blend in with the other cars.

Jillian didn't respond, which kicked his heart into overdrive. Had she been hit, too?

"Doc?" he said again, this time louder. He scanned

the road, looking for a place to pull over in case she was hurt. He wasn't sure how much he'd be able to help, but no way was he going to keep driving if she was bleeding out on the floorboard.

"Is it safe to come up now?" Her voice was muffled but steady, and he exhaled in relief.

"For now. Better for you to buckle up than stay crouched down there."

She unfolded herself with a wince and slumped into the front seat, pulling the belt across her torso. "What happened back there?"

"There was some objection to our leaving."

She snorted at that. "I suppose that's one way of putting it. Did you hit something? It felt like we ran into something."

Alex kept his gaze on the road. "I may have clipped a couple of guys who were shooting at us."

"Oh, my God. Are they dead?"

He narrowed his eyes at the concern in her voice. "No. But would it matter if I had killed them? Are you honestly worried about the health of two guys who were trying to end us?"

"Yes. No. I don't know!" He saw her glare at him from the corner of his eye. "I'm a doctor—I don't like to stand by while people are hurt. It goes against everything I believe in."

"Well, I believe that if someone is shooting at me, I get to defend myself. Even if that means hurting them."

"I suppose," she muttered.

"Speaking of hurting," he said, sliding around a corner. "Do you still have that bag of medical supplies?"

"Yes. Why?"

"I need some gauze."

"Why? Where are you injured?" She pulled the bag into her lap and began rooting inside.

"My shoulder. It's no big deal, but I'm bleeding a little bit."

He reached for the gauze she held out, but she jerked it away when she saw his hand. "Is that blood yours?"

"Yes. Would you please give me the damn gauze?"

She scooted across the bench seat until she was pressed up next to him, her hands roving over his chest in a search that made him grit his teeth with the effort of staying in control. "Were you hit anywhere else?"

"No. Now stop molesting me." *Before you find out just how much I like your hands on me.*

Ignoring him, she tugged at the collar of his shirt, exposing his right shoulder. "Just this one?" she asked, probing the injury with cold fingers. Pain flared in the wake of her touch, burning away the arousal her earlier search had brought to life.

"That's the spot." He gritted the words out.

She pressed the gauze to his shoulder, and he couldn't hold back a grunt of pain. "Sorry," she muttered.

"It's okay," he assured her. He slowed a bit as they approached Massachusetts Avenue, glancing in the rear-view mirror as he navigated the turn. So far, no sign of the boxy sedan from the motel parking lot. Maybe they had gotten lucky, after all, and the gangbangers were too busy licking their wounds to follow.

"Where are we going?"

Alex glanced over at Jillian, who was watching the road with her hand against his shoulder. It felt nice to have her next to him, even if she was trying to torture him by pressing hard on his injury. "I'm not sure," he admitted. Fresh snow began to fall, fluffy and delicate.

He flipped on the wipers to brush the flakes away, leaving short streaks of water that blended with the cracked lines of the windshield.

"We need to find someplace where I can examine you," Jillian said. "I think that bullet is still inside your shoulder."

"We're not going to a hospital," he began, but she cut him off.

"I know," she said a bit impatiently. "I wasn't going to suggest it. I have another location in mind."

That got his attention. "Oh, yeah? Where?"

"My place."

Chapter 5

"Absolutely not." Alex turned his head to scowl at her before returning his focus to the road. "Out of the question."

"Why?" she said. "Have you got a better idea?"

He was silent for a moment, his jaw tense as he guided the truck over the slick roads.

"No one but you knows who I am," she pointed out. "So they don't know where to look. It'll buy us some time."

"I don't like it," he gritted out

"Yeah, well, I don't like a lot of the things that have happened tonight, but I haven't complained. You need to suck it up and deal."

He gave her a sidelong glare and tightened his grip on the wheel. The gauze she held to his shoulder had grown soggy under her fingertips, so she added some fresh squares and pressed harder against the wound, eliciting a grunt from Alex.

"You're still bleeding," she said unnecessarily. "I need to patch you up, and I can't do it in a moving truck. I have no desire to do it in a dirty gas station bathroom, either, so please just take me home."

He opened his mouth to respond, but a loud gurgle rose from the direction of his stomach. Her own stomach rumbled in response, breaking the tension and making them both smile. "I have food," she said, the words a proverbial carrot she dangled in front of him without apology. If she couldn't convince his mind, perhaps she could win over his stomach. It was said to be the way to a man's heart, but could she use it to break down his resistance, as well?

Apparently she could. After a long silence he nodded. "All right," he said quietly. "I suppose it's as good a plan as any right now."

Sensing her victory was fragile, Jillian resisted the temptation to roll her eyes. She gave him directions to her apartment and he followed them without comment. She didn't try to make conversation, just kept her hand pressed to his shoulder. Worry rolled off him in waves. She could practically *feel* it, as though it was a tangible thing, another passenger in the truck with them. She wanted to reassure him that they would be all right, that things would turn out okay, but she kept silent. Her words would be hollow promises at best, and he didn't seem the type to take comfort from platitudes.

Alex pulled into the parking lot of her apartment building, finding a spot at the rear of the lot, away from most of the other cars. Hopefully the truck wouldn't attract attention from the other residents. They tended to mind their own business, and the winter storm should keep them indoors. It would buy them some time.

He turned off the truck, but made no move to get out. Instead he sat there, staring ahead at the bank of trees that bordered the lot. Jillian could tell by his vacant expression that he was lost in thought, and she was torn between a desire to give him a moment to process and the need to stitch him up. The longer she waited to tend to his shoulder, the more it would hurt.

"Alex?" She spoke his name quietly, not wanting to startle him into jumping. When he didn't respond, she tried again.

He blinked, then turned to look at her as if just now remembering she was there. She caught her breath at the unguarded look on his face—desolation, despair and guilt danced across his features in rapid succession before a neutral mask dropped into place. It happened so quickly she almost missed it—would have, had she not been watching him closely. It was the first time she'd seen him as anything but confident, and the knowledge that he was hiding doubts and insecurities should have worried her even more.

Instead it made her want to gather him in her arms, to hold him close and stroke his hair the way her mother used to soothe her when she was upset. She knew he would reject the gesture—a tough undercover federal agent like Alex wouldn't want to admit he needed comforting. He would likely see it as a weakness, but she knew differently. As a doctor, her focus was primarily on the physical bodies of her patients, but she had seen too many people on the verge of death rally, and too many people with recoverable injuries wither, due to an abundance or lack of human contact to dismiss it as unimportant.

But that was a conversation for another day. "We should go inside," she said quietly, her breath forming faint clouds in the rapidly cooling cab of the truck. "I'll fix us something to eat and patch you up. We can rest for a few hours."

He nodded. "That sounds great," he said, relief plain in his voice. He offered her a weak smile and she took his free hand and placed it over the gauze on his opposite shoulder.

"Hold this for me until we get inside?"

"Yeah."

Jillian slid out of the truck, her serviceable clogs making a soft crunching sound as she dropped into the snow. A lump of fabric caught her eye as she turned to shut the door and she reached back to find a dark jacket. The denim was crumpled and smelled strongly of fried fish and cigarette smoke, but it was better than nothing. Rounding the truck, she met Alex as he climbed out of the cab. With an apologetic smile, she reached up to drape the jacket around his shoulders.

He reared back, wrinkling his nose as he caught the scent wafting from the fabric. "What the hell is that?"

"It's cover for your shoulder. Just until we get you inside."

"Is it really necessary?"

"Seeing as how you have a large bloodstain on the front of your shirt, I'd say so."

Alex glanced down and winced. "Fair enough. But can we please get going? This thing stinks."

She guided him to the back door and swiped her card, ushering him into the warmth of the building.

"It's just a little farther," she murmured, leading him down the hall and around the corner. She held her breath when they arrived at her door. Hopefully Mrs. Rodriguez was asleep—technically, it was still the middle of the night, but the old gal seemed to get up earlier and earlier every time she saw her.

Jillian withdrew her keys from her pocket, taking care not to jingle them. As quietly as possible, she twisted the dead bolt open and then moved to insert the key into the doorknob.

There was a rattle from behind the neighboring door, the sound of a chain lock being unhooked. Mrs. Rodriguez opened the door a crack, poking her nose out into the hall like a mouse scenting cheese. With her gray hair wrapped in pink foam rollers and her large plastic-framed glasses obscuring half her face, she was the very picture of a nosy neighbor.

"Is that you, Jillian?" She squinted into the hall, peering near-sightedly at them. Jillian swore silently, knowing she was caught.

"It sure is, Mrs. Rodriguez. What are you doing up so early? You should still be in bed."

The old lady pressed her lips together and shook her head. "My bones hurt something awful. The weather, you know. Cold gets me every time."

"I know." Jillian clucked in sympathy. "Have you been using your electric blanket?"

Mrs. Rodriguez nodded. "And drinking that tea, like you told me."

"Good. Just remember, don't lie on the blanket, put it on top of you. And be sure not to turn it up too high."

"Oh, yes."

Jillian turned back to her door, hoping her neighbor would take the hint. No such luck.

"And who is this young man?" Mrs. Rodriguez eyed Alex up and down, her lips forming a perfect *O* as she took in his size. "Is he your boyfriend?" She sounded mildly scandalized at the prospect and leaned forward with a sudden gleam in her eyes.

Before Jillian could respond, Alex spoke up. "I'm her cousin. Jillian was kind enough to pick me up at the train station. She's letting me stay with her overnight so I don't have to pay for a hotel room."

Mrs. Rodriguez nodded, her hand going up to pat her hair before she pushed her glasses up on the bridge of her nose. "I see. Well, if you get hungry, be sure to come over. Your cousin is a lovely lady, but she can't cook to save her life." She shook her head and tsked quietly over this gross character defect. "I make a wonderful meat loaf. It was my Harold's favorite, God rest his soul."

Alex smiled indulgently and Jillian watched in fascination as twin spots of pink appeared on Mrs. Rodriguez's lined cheeks. Jillian couldn't blame her—the flash of dimples in his stubbled cheeks made something flutter low in her belly, even though she wasn't the direct target of his smile.

Ignoring the inconvenient spike of attraction, Jillian tore her gaze away from his mouth. Alex was looking a bit pale under the harsh lights in the hall, faint lines of strain feathering from the corners of his eyes. It was clear he was in pain but putting on a brave front for Mrs. Rodriguez. Time to get him inside.

"Try to get some rest, and stay warm!" Jillian told her neighbor, pushing open the door to her apartment and reaching in to flip on the light.

"Ah, yes. You, too, dear."

Mrs. Rodriguez retreated into her apartment as Jillian ushered Alex inside.

She shut the door and twisted the lock before turning to him with an apologetic grimace. "Sorry about that," she said, shrugging off her coat. "She's a nice lady, but I had hoped to avoid talking to her."

"She seems harmless," Alex observed, removing the dirty jean jacket and holding it away from his body with a look of distaste.

"She is," Jillian agreed. She motioned him into the kitchen and stuffed the jacket in a trash bag in a bid to seal off the stink. "But I didn't want to have to explain your presence. I don't want her to get hurt, if people come looking for us.

"They won't." His voice was hard.

She glanced over at him as she washed her hands. His muscles were bunched and tense, but whether with pain or determination, she couldn't tell. His hands curled into loose fists, as though he was prepared to fight at the slightest provocation. His expression completed the picture of a warrior—mouth pressed shut, eyes narrowed to thin slits as if he could bend the world to his will with the force of his gaze alone.

If only it were that simple.

She turned back to the sink to rinse the suds from her skin. "Um, no offense, but things haven't exactly gone according to plan tonight. Better safe than sorry."

From the corner of her eyes she saw him look down, his scowl relaxing as he silently acknowledged her point.

Jillian dried her hands on a few squares of paper towel, then turned to face him. "Let's get you patched up." She gestured to the small table at the end of the room, indicating the lone chair that wasn't piled high with mail. He sat, eying the detritus across from him with interest.

"Have a lot of guests, do you?"

"Oh, yeah," she said, carefully peeling away the fabric of his shirt. "I love to throw lavish dinner parties. Gotta keep my Cordon Bleu training fresh."

His eyes widened as he looked at her, clearly trying to gauge the truth of her words. "But your neighbor said you couldn't cook…"

She snorted, unable to keep the farce going. "I can't. But if you're going to be snarky about the state of my apartment, I'm going to give it right back to you."

"I wish," he murmured.

His words sent a delicious thrum through her limbs, making her skin tingle and her chest warm, as if she'd just taken a sip of hot tea. Deciding it was too dangerous to acknowledge the feelings he stirred up so easily, she studiously ignored him, deliberately looking anywhere but his face as she continued to probe the wound, her gaze unseeing.

Stop overreacting. He probably didn't mean anything by it.

After a few seconds her body got the message and her brain cleared enough to register what was in front of her.

It wasn't bad, as far as gunshot injuries went. A small dark hole marred his skin, the margins a bit jagged and starting to swell. She pressed gently at the edges and was rewarded with a fresh welling of blood, oozing red in small, bright beads of color that made her think of holly berries. She stepped around to check his back for an exit wound, biting her lip as she saw the smooth expanse of skin, unmarred by injury.

"The bullet is still inside your shoulder," she informed him, straightening. It felt safer to look down on him, as if she was actually in control rather than at the mercy of her hormones. *I shouldn't have hugged him*, she thought. It had been an impulsive move, born of nerves and adrenaline. She'd been terrified; sure they would be caught at any moment. She'd wanted a connection—however brief—to ground her, to keep her from falling down the rabbit hole of fear. So she'd pressed her body to his, felt his heart beat against hers.

And now she couldn't stop thinking about it.

His lips moved and she realized with a sudden jolt that he was asking her a question.

Get it together, Mahoney.

"I'm sorry, what did you say?"

Alex cocked a brow while he studied her, like he was evaluating her sanity. "Can you get the bullet out?" he repeated slowly.

She nodded, feeling her cheeks warm at being caught distracted. "Yes," she said simply. She turned away and reached for the paper bag of supplies on the kitchen table. She'd seen a suture kit earlier, which would come in handy if she had to dig around for the bullet...

"Do I get any drugs?" he asked, his tone half joking. "Surely I haven't lost too much blood, right?"

Jillian set her supplies on the table, considering. "I think I have some lidocaine around here somewhere. Sit tight—I'll be right back."

She returned a moment later, syringes in hand. Alex shook his head as she set them on the table and resumed prepping his shoulder.

"As a Federal agent, I should report you for having controlled substances in your home," he said, his tone dry.

"Is that right?" she asked, slipping on a pair of gloves. "Should I stop what I'm doing and turn myself in? I'd hate to put you in an awkward position, professionally speaking."

He chuckled. "Touché. No, I think under the circumstances, I'll look the other way."

She swiped his shoulder with Betadine, the chill making him suck in a breath. "Very kind of you," she murmured.

"That's just the kind of nice guy I am." He paused then spoke again. "Seriously, though, why do you have random syringes lying around your apartment?" His tone was light, but she could tell by his slight frown that the answer was important to him.

"Working in the ER, I stitch a lot of people up. If I don't use all of the syringes, I put them in my pocket while I'm cleaning up. Sometimes I forget I have them, especially if I get called to another emergency soon after." She shrugged. "I make a pile at home, and take them back to work when I remember."

"Ah." He relaxed at her words, clearly relieved at the innocent explanation.

"Did you think I was some kind of addict?" She spoke quietly, giving him the option of ignoring the question.

He was silent for a long moment, making her think he wasn't going to respond. She focused on his shoulder, injecting the lidocaine in a ring around the entrance wound. She'd give it a minute to work, then start digging.

"No," he said softly. He cleared his throat and spoke again. "No, of course I don't think you're an addict. It's just…" He trailed off, looking down at his hands. "I've spent too much time around bad people and it's made me question everything. I'm sorry."

Jillian leaned back against the table, considering him. "Don't apologize. I can't imagine the things you've seen—it must be hard for you to trust anyone." She was careful to keep her voice even and calm, sensing that he didn't want platitudes and eager reassurances.

"You have no idea," he murmured.

She kept still, waiting to see if he would continue, giving him the space to explain—if he wanted it.

He didn't. After a few seconds he shook his head, physically shrugging off the darkness that had settled over him at the mention of his undercover work. He looked up and gave her a wry smile. "I can't feel my shoulder anymore. I suppose that's a good thing?"

Jillian recognized his attempt to change the subject, nodding in response. Part of her was disappointed— she'd quickly become fascinated by Alex, and found herself wanting to know more about him, what he'd been through. The rational part of her brain recognized this was a foolish desire. They'd been thrown together by desperate circumstances—he wasn't exactly going to stick around after the danger to them had subsided. Better for him to remain a mystery than for her to learn too much and get drawn into wanting more. Everything about him practically screamed "stay away," and she would do well to heed the message.

She poked experimentally at his shoulder, checking to make sure the area was fully numb before she started.

He watched her, shaking his head slightly. "It's the

strangest thing," he said, tracking her progress with his eyes. "I can see you poking me and I know I should feel it, but I don't."

"That's the idea." The corner of her mouth quirked up as she turned back to the table to pick up the forceps. "Better living through chemistry," she muttered.

"Beats the alternative," he agreed.

He was silent while she worked; a fact for which she was grateful because it meant she wasn't distracted by the rumble of his voice. Fortunately for him, the bullet wasn't embedded too deeply in his shoulder—she was able to grasp it with the ends of the forceps, and a steady pull was all it took. It came free with a faint pop, a squishy, wet sound that made him wince.

She held the bullet up to the light, checking for any cracks or splinters that would indicate it had fragmented inside him. The small bit of metal shone dully, a red gleam coating the surface. Jillian turned the forceps to check from several angles, breathing out a sigh of relief when she confirmed it was whole and undamaged from its foray into Alex's shoulder.

"Hold out your hand," she instructed, dropping the round into his open palm when he complied. "A souvenir for you," she murmured, turning her attention back to the operation at hand.

"Thanks," Alex said, sounding somewhat dubious.

Jillian spared him a glance, smiling at his expression of distaste as he studied the bloody metal in his hand. "I once took three bullets out of a gangbanger," she said, using the forceps to probe the wound in search of the small bit of fabric from his shirt that had inevitably traveled with the bullet. She had to remove it, or it would cause the wound to fester. "He asked for them after I was done, and since the police said they were too destroyed to use for ballistics, I handed them over."

"Wonder what he wanted with them."

"I wondered that myself." She pulled the forceps out slowly, grinning when she saw the bit of cloth trapped between the prongs. Success. "Saw him a few months later, for another gunshot wound. He'd made rings out of the bullets." She shook her head and set the forceps on the table, picking up some gauze to blot at his shoulder, which had begun to bleed again.

"Rings?" Alex shook his head. "I've seen guys wear them on a chain around their neck before, but I've never seen them made into rings."

"It was quite the fashion statement." She lifted the gauze, frowning at the trickle of blood that showed no signs of stopping. She'd need to put in a stitch or two to close up the hole. "He had soldered each bullet onto a metal band. The finished product looked like a misshapen solitaire."

"Sounds classy."

"Definitely. And now you, too, can have your very own bullet ring!" She spoke in the voice of an As-Seen-on-TV announcer and felt a small flush of pleasure at his laugh.

"Let me guess—just three easy payments of $19.95?" She felt his eyes on her while she worked and had to force herself to keep her gaze on his shoulder and the stitches she was placing. She could look at him later, when there was a safe amount of distance between them. This close to his lips, it would be all too easy to lean over and kiss him.

"That's the idea." Her voice sounded a little shaky to her ears, but fortunately Alex didn't seem to notice.

He shook his head. "Thanks, but if it's all the same to you, I think I'll save this one for ballistics."

Jillian dabbed at his shoulder, mopping up a few residual drops of blood. "Okay," she said, leaning back and stripping off the gloves. "You're all set here."

She began to gather the debris into a tidy pile as Alex rolled his shoulder experimentally. She watched him while she cleaned up, noting that the pinched lines of strain around his mouth and eyes had eased. Signs of fatigue had taken their place, though—his lids were heavy and dark smudges under his eyes testified to his general state of exhaustion. When was the last time he had slept?

Or bathed, for that matter? His hair hung in limp, greasy strands across his forehead, and now that her adrenaline had faded, she could smell him—unwashed male mixed with the potent chemical stench of drugs.

"Why don't you get cleaned up while I fix us something to eat?"

He blushed, a faint pink that colored his cheeks and the tips of his ears. "Sorry about the stink," he muttered. "Part of the job."

"I understand. But we have some time before morning, so let's put it to good use. Sit tight for a minute—I think I have some clothes that might fit you."

She left him at the table and headed for her bedroom, pulling down a dusty gym bag from the top shelf of her closet. Her brother Jason had left it here after his last visit.

He'd come to stay with her for a few days after completing his latest bout of rehab. Her throat grew tight as she pictured him as he'd been then—painfully thin, his eyes burning bright with the zeal of the recently converted, the set of his bony shoulders conveying hope and determination.

"I mean it, Jilly. This time I'm going to stay clean. I'm not going back—never again."

His resolve had lasted three days. She'd taken a few days off from work, and they'd spent the time playing tourist in the city, going to museums, monuments, the zoo—all the things they'd never made time to do before. It had been wonderful, and Jillian had started to believe her brother had truly turned a corner.

But when she'd returned home from work on the fourth day, Jason was gone. He'd given her no warning, no explanation other than the scrap of paper left on top of the pile of neatly folded bedding.

I'm sorry.

She pulled the note out now, running her fingertip across the strong, bold writing. It had been two years since that visit. Two years since she'd seen her brother. Where had he gone? Why hadn't he come back, or at least contacted her to tell her he was okay? Not a day went by that she didn't think of him, feel a stab of guilt that she hadn't seen any signs of his impending slide back into darkness. As a doctor, she knew she couldn't save everyone, but the rules were different for family— she should have known.

Ignoring the hollow feeling in her chest, Jillian tucked the note back into the side pocket of the bag, then unzipped the top. Neatly folded stacks of clothes greeted her, and she rummaged through the collection until she found a pair of boxer shorts, a T-shirt and some red-and-black-plaid flannel pants, which she eyed critically. They looked a little short, but they would do for now.

Grabbing the bag with her free hand, Jillian returned to the living room. "Here you go," she said, setting the bag by the couch. Alex turned when she entered the kitchen, accepting the clothes from her with a look of mild surprise, as if he hadn't expected her to return with men's clothes. She could see the question in his eyes and spoke quickly to distract him.

"Let's get you some towels." She pivoted on her heel and led him down the hall, stopping at the linen closet along the way.

"Are you sure I can take a shower with these stitches?" Alex gestured to his shoulder with his chin as he followed her into the bathroom.

Jillian shook her head. "You need to keep them dry, if possible." She set the towels on the counter and then turned to face him. "Which is why you'll be taking a bath." She grinned at the expression of distaste that spread across his face at this news.

"I haven't taken a bath since I was a kid," he protested. "Can't you put a bandage on my shoulder so I can shower?"

"Nope." She pulled out a fresh razor and placed it on the counter alongside an extra toothbrush. She always kept a spare set of toiletries in case Jason ever returned. She knew it was naïve, but a small part of her believed that as long as she had the things he would need, there was a chance he would come back to use them.

She slipped past Alex into the hall, leaving him standing in the bathroom looking bereft. "I'm going to heat up some soup and make some toast. Come out when you're ready." With that, she shut the door, grateful for the barrier between them. It was hard to think straight when she was close to him, and the night had already been a roller coaster of events and emotions. She needed a few moments to herself to regroup and catch her breath. Then she could start thinking about what to do next.

"He's not here."

Dan tightened his grip on the phone, refusing to give in to the urge to hit something. Preferably the man on the other end of the line. "Any sign of where he might have gone?"

"Maybe. But that's where you come in."

"Excuse me?" Like he hadn't already done enough for these punks—now they wanted him to do their jobs, as well?

"We found Tony. He's been shot."

"Oh?" If Tony died, it would mean one less link between him and the gang, one less thread tying him to their illegal activities. He tried to muster up some sympathy for the thought of such a young kid meeting a violent end, but his own sense of self-preservation won out.

"Yeah. Seems Malcom took him to a motel just on the other side of the river, had some lady doctor treat him." He rattled off the address and Dan typed it in, pulling up the location on a city map.

Dan felt his anger rise again as he stared at the screen. How had Malcom managed to escape? And how had he found a woman to help him so quickly? "Did Tony catch her name?" Maybe he could use this to his advantage—if he knew her name, he could use her to track down Alex.

"Nah."

Of course not. That would make things too easy.

"I'm beginning to wonder why I help you," he said,

his voice dangerously low. "I asked you to do one thing, and you failed. Tell me why I shouldn't use what I know to end you and your pathetic organization."

"Tony said Malcom kidnapped her from a hospital parking lot. If you call around, you can find out who she is, where she lives. We'll take it from there."

"I don't think so," Dan replied, knowing all too well what the gang would do if they found the woman. "I'll find out her name, but you won't be the one to question her. You've already made too many mistakes tonight."

"Fine. But at least let us have some time with Malcom. He shot Tony and hit two of my guys with a truck tonight, broke their legs. He needs to answer for that."

"And he will." Dan smiled as he imagined Alex's treatment at the hands of the gang. They didn't take kindly to traitors, and their revenge would be long and painful—just what Malcom deserved. "You can take as much time as you want with him. But you have to keep him alive. I get the pleasure of killing him."

"Whatever you say."

Dan ended the call and turned back to the computer screen. DC had several hospitals, but he was willing to bet Malcom wouldn't have gone far from the motel to find help. That made his search a little easier.

Enjoy your freedom, he thought while he typed. *It won't last.*

Alex slowly lowered himself into the tub, biting his lip to stifle a groan at the sheer luxury of soaking in the steaming water. It had been ages since he'd felt truly clean. No matter how many times he showered or washed his clothes, a thin layer of sweat and drug residue constantly clung to him, as though it had been baked into his pores. It was just another aspect of being undercover, one that he hated. And after everything that had happened tonight, he'd figured it would be days before he'd see a bar of soap. Now, he almost couldn't believe his luck. If not for the nearly painful heat of the water, he might have thought he was hallucinating, like a man in the desert imagining an oasis.

His body was taken care of, but as Alex leaned back, he had to wonder if his soul would ever feel clean again. After what he'd seen, what he'd been forced to do… Shaking his head, he quickly corralled his thoughts before he fell into an abyss of regret and recrimination. No sense in diminishing the pleasure of a soak in the bath with bad memories—there would be time to punish himself later. Now, he was going to enjoy this particular indulgence, because God only knew when he'd get to experience something like it again.

Never, if the gang has its way.

He reached for the shampoo and took a cautious whiff. Vanilla. He'd smelled it on Jillian before, but the scent that had wafted off her body had seemed somehow warmer, the natural perfume of her skin mixing with the homey aroma to create a new, complex odor that both tantalized and soothed him.

She'd been so close, leaning in to focus on his shoulder with a startling intensity. And lucky for him, too, because it meant she hadn't caught him staring at her, hadn't seen the growing desire he felt for her shining in his eyes. He had no business entertaining such feelings—there was no chance of a relationship between them, and any attraction was due to the stress of the moment. Besides, he'd kidnapped her. Even though he'd tried to be gentle, he had physically forced her into the backseat of a car, using his strength to overwhelm her defenses. The memory of it made his stomach turn. Not exactly his finest moment.

He massaged the shampoo into his scalp, frowning slightly as the movement pulled his shoulder. The drugs were beginning to wear off, and while his shoulder didn't exactly hurt, he could tell the pain was coming. Maybe the good doctor had some aspirin she'd share, just to take the edge off. He wasn't afraid of pain—he welcomed it, in fact, as it would help keep him awake—but too much would dull his senses, making him an easy target.

The bathwater turned scuzzy as he washed, and he felt a flash of guilt over the fact that he was getting Jillian's nice clean bathtub dirty. He'd have to rinse it out when he was finished—the thought of her cleaning up the residue of his filth was too shameful to contemplate. She'd already done enough for him. He wasn't about to insult her by leaving another mess for her to deal with.

Not wanting to soak in his own grime, he finished bathing quickly. He stood as the water drained, eyeing the towels she'd stacked for him. Clean, fluffy and soft. Not something he should use to dry his still-dirty body. He glanced around for an alternative, but didn't see anything. Although he hated to ruin her towels, he couldn't stand there and drip dry. That would take all night.

With a sigh, he grabbed one off the top of the stack and began to pat himself dry. Maybe if he didn't rub, the grime wouldn't smear onto the fabric. He made a mental note to buy her new towels when this was all over. It was just another item on his growing list of things he needed to do to put her life back to normal.

While he shaved, he eyed the clothes she'd provided.

Where had they come from? They were clearly men's clothing, but he hadn't seen any sign of a male presence in her apartment—no shoes, no stray jacket, no toiletries to suggest a man lived with her, or even stayed over on a regular basis. Furthermore, no man had stepped from her bedroom demanding to know where she'd been. He felt an odd sort of pleasure at the conclusion that Jillian was single, even though he had no right. She would never look twice at a man like him, especially after the way he'd treated her tonight. Still, he couldn't deny the primal satisfaction washing over him—although he didn't have a chance with her, he didn't like the thought of another man's hands on her body.

Perhaps the clothes belonged to an ex-lover? That made more sense. But why would she have kept them? Did she still have feelings for the man? Did she secretly hope he would one day return and they could pick up where they'd left off? Alex shook his head and splashed his face to rinse off the residual shaving cream. He was spending way too much time pondering the relationship status of his hostess when he should be working on a plan to keep her safe. Relationships and undercover work did not go together. Hadn't he already learned that lesson the hard way?

A familiar pang pricked at his heart at the thought of Shannon. They'd met at the Academy, and had hit it off right away. He'd thought she was the one, until he'd gotten his undercover assignment.

"Won't you wait for me?" he'd asked, gripping her hand as if to keep her from flying away from him.

Shannon had blinked back tears and offered him a watery smile. "You don't need the thought of me hanging over your head while you work. It's better this way."

And so she had been the one to walk away. It had hurt like hell, but looking back on it, he could understand why she had left. It wasn't fair to ask her to put her life on hold for the years he would be on assignment. And now that he knew how much he had changed, he was glad she had ended things. He wasn't the same man he'd been, and their relationship probably wouldn't have survived the challenge. Better to have fond memories of their time together.

He'd seen her once, about a year later. He'd been standing on the sidewalk, eating a hot dog with Tony. Just another normal day, on the way to intimidate another low-level dealer. Then Tony had tapped his arm.

"You know her, man?"

He nodded, and Alex followed his glance. His heart moved up into his throat when he saw Shannon, standing a few feet away. She was staring at him, her expression a mix of pleasure and confusion.

"Nah," he replied, hoping he sounded casual.

Tony eyed him suspiciously. "Why's she staring at you then?"

Alex shrugged. "Maybe she wants to know me." He turned back to Shannon, who hadn't moved. "Whaddaya say, sexy? Want to spend some time with me?" He winked at her and grabbed his crotch in a lewd, suggestive gesture. Shannon's mouth twisted into a grimace, her face going pale. She shook her head, turned and walked quickly away.

Alex took another bite of his hot dog, trying to ignore the greasy feeling coating his stomach. *Chew and swallow*, he told himself sternly. If he puked now, Tony would know something was up.

Tony laughed. "Hey, come back, sweetness!" he

called to Shannon's retreating form. He took a step forward and Alex raised a hand, ready to restrain him if necessary. But the young man stopped, apparently satisfied to just yell after her. "I'm much cuter than he is!"

Alex tried to play it off, laughing along with Tony. But he couldn't shake the profound sadness that dropped over him like a heavy coat. How would his life have been different if he'd refused this assignment and stayed with Shannon?

A few days later he checked his personal cell phone. There was a new message waiting. A two-word text: I'm sorry.

He stared at the screen for several long minutes, debating with himself. Should he reply? What could he say? There was too much distance between them now, too many new experiences that they didn't have in common. How could he explain his life to her? Why would he even want to? Bad enough he had to deal with the darkness.

In the end, he'd said nothing.

He shook himself free of the memories and pulled on the flannel pants, amused to find they were a few inches too short and just a little too tight. It was the same for the shirt. Although he looked ridiculous, his pride was gratified by the knowledge that he was bigger and more muscular than her ex. He recognized he was being vain, but after the crappy night he'd had, he'd take his pleasure where he could find it.

And while he still could.

more guns, no more threats. She could go back to her
normal, safe life and pretend that this had all been a
bad dream.

She ran her fingers over the phone in her pocket,
sorely tempted to dial the three numbers that would
bring help to her door. The only thing stopping her was
her memory of Alex's face as he'd told her his story.
The haunted, defeated look in his eyes, like he was so
beaten down by it all that he didn't dare hope he could
fix things.

He could be lying, she thought. Sure, he had a badge
and identification, but how hard was it to obtain coun-
terfeits, especially for someone with his kinds of illegal
connections? Maybe he carried them around to evade
the authorities—if he ever did get caught, all he had
to do was to flash the badge and tell them he was an
undercover agent and they'd let him go, no questions
asked. It was the perfect strategy for a gang member, a
nice way to ensure he stayed out on the streets, direct-
ing the flow of drugs through the city.

Except…he didn't strike her as a dealer or a user.
Even from the beginning, he'd seemed somehow different from the gangbangers she was used to treating. And
although he had manhandled her in the parking lot, he'd
taken care to keep from hurting her, using just enough
force to subdue her but not enough to cause her pain.
From what she'd seen tonight, the 3 Star Killers didn't
appear to operate with that kind of subtlety.

Jillian shook her head. *He didn't hurt me, so that
makes him a good guy?* She must be suffering from
some kind of rapid-onset Stockholm syndrome. How
else to explain her sympathy for her kidnapper?

But he did save my life tonight. It was another mark

in the pro-Alex column, even though she never would have been in danger in the first place if not for him. He could have easily left her to the mercy of the gang, but he hadn't. He'd gotten them out of that run-down motel, and been injured doing it. Those weren't the actions of a traitor or a liar. They were the actions of a good and honorable man. Was she really going to repay him by turning him in to the very people he said he couldn't trust?

The problem was that his story seemed so far-fetched. A mole in the FBI? Could it really be true? Maybe Alex had misread the situation—he said himself he'd been around bad people for so long, he felt as though he couldn't trust anyone anymore. But surely there was someone who knew him, someone who could explain what had happened tonight. Maybe he could call in the morning and get some answers, after everything had settled down. That was probably the best thing to do.

Jillian pulled her hand from her pocket to take the soup off the stove. She'd hold off on calling the police—for now. Although she didn't like the situation, Alex had kept her safe tonight, and she felt like she owed him a few hours' rest before sending him back out to face the unknown. Besides, he was her patient now, and she wanted to check his shoulder in a bit to make sure it looked okay.

She heard the bathroom door open and turned to greet him. Her breath caught in her throat as she watched him walk down the hall toward her. As she'd suspected, Jason's clothes were on the small side. What she hadn't anticipated was the way they clung to him like a second skin, giving her a delightful view of his muscled thighs and broad shoulders. There was a small gap between the hem of the shirt and waistband of the pants, providing her with a tantalizing glimpse of lean stomach bisected by a thin line of dark hair.

She'd seen him without his shirt on earlier while she'd stitched up his wound, but she'd been in clinical mode then, seeing his body as something to be repaired, not admired. Now she looked at him the way a woman looks at an attractive man, and she couldn't deny she liked what she saw. The too-small clothes should have made him appear ridiculous, but instead he seemed almost larger than life, as though he was too much man to be contained by mere clothing.

Get a grip, she told herself. She tore her gaze away from his body, hoping he hadn't noticed her staring. She was a doctor, for crying out loud! He didn't have anything she'd never seen before. Although, truth be told, she didn't usually get to see such a nice example of masculinity. She entertained a brief fantasy of stripping off his clothes and exploring his body—purely for medical reasons, of course. It was entirely possible he'd sustained additional injuries tonight, and she would be remiss as a doctor if she didn't fully examine her patient.

"Smells good." His voice was a low rumble that she felt as much as heard. She tore her gaze from his chest, taking in his freshly shaved cheeks and slicked-back hair. His skin appeared shiny and smooth, and now that his beard was gone, she had a better view of his high cheekbones and full, sensuous mouth. A mouth that she suddenly wanted to spend some quality time exploring.

"Do you need any help with that?" He gestured to her waist, and for a second, she was torn between embarrassment and arousal at his directness. Then she remembered the pot of soup she held, and her face heated.

"No, that's okay. I just need a second to clear the table." She put the soup back on the stove and stepped toward the table, contorting her body to avoid bumping into him as he moved to enter the small kitchen. He raised a brow at her acrobatic avoidance, his expression questioning her sudden reluctance to touch him after pulling a bullet from his shoulder.

It was silly of her, she knew, but touching him before had been a necessity, something she'd had to do to treat him. She'd been a doctor and he'd been her patient. Even when she'd hugged him at the motel, the bulky padding of her coat had prevented her from really feeling the contours of his body. Now that only a few thin layers of fabric covered each of them, she had no doubt that touching him would be an entirely different prospect.

"Why don't you fix yourself something to drink?" Hopefully giving him something to do would distract him and give her a moment's relief from the intensity of his dark blue gaze. "Cups are in the cabinet next to the sink, and you're welcome to anything that's in the fridge."

She left him to it while she quickly gathered up the mail and other debris on the dining room table, depositing everything in the corner so it was out of the way. She frowned at the thin layer of dust on the table surface, casting a covert glance at the kitchen. If she went back in for a towel, she'd have to reach around Alex, a prospect that was disturbingly appealing to her libido. Given her exhaustion, it would be all too easy to give in to the temptation to press herself against his strong back and wrap her arms around his lean stomach. The episode with Tony and his fellow gang members had shaken her more than she cared to admit, and she wanted the reassurance that came from holding someone and being held in return. Since Alex was her only company, he was the prime candidate for her affections.

Not willing to risk it, she pulled her shirt sleeve over the heel of her hand and used it to wipe the table clean. Good enough. She straightened and looked toward the kitchen just as Alex stepped into the doorway, holding two glasses.

"I took the liberty of fixing you some water," he said, holding up one of the glasses with a small smile. "There wasn't much else to choose from."

Jillian shrugged. "I'm not home much. I was planning on going to the grocery store tonight after work, but that didn't happen."

Alex looked down, the tips of his ears turning a dark pink. "Sorry about that," he muttered.

She moved around the table, coming to a stop a step away from him. "Let's not worry about that now. We need to eat before the soup gets cold."

He looked at her then, gratitude shining in his eyes. "Thank you," he whispered.

She waited a beat for him to move out of the doorway, but he stayed in place, forcing her to twist to the side to slide into the kitchen. She caught a whiff of him when she moved past, the familiar vanilla scent of her shampoo and body wash taking on a darker, warmer note that overwhelmed her senses and made her want to step closer. *Keep moving*, she told herself. Now wasn't the time to get distracted.

Why was she so rattled? She'd had men in her apartment before, of course. Well, one man. And that had been a long time ago.

Mark had been a fellow doctor at the hospital, an anesthesiologist. They'd seen each other on several occasions when he'd been paged to stabilize the airway of particularly difficult patients. After one such call, he'd asked her out. A few dates later and they'd fallen into a comfortable, if slightly boring routine: dinner when their schedules allowed, and then he would stay at her place. "My apartment isn't fit for company," he'd explained. "I only use it for sleeping and showering—I live at the hospital." As the months passed with no indication that things were changing between them, Jillian had asked him the question despised by men everywhere.

"Where do you see us going?"

Mark had set down his glass, his brows rising slightly as if he hadn't expected her to bring up the topic. "What do you mean?"

"I mean, what do you see as our future, long-term? It seems like we haven't really grown as a couple, and I want to know if you feel the same way, and if you see that changing for you."

He reached for his wine again, a puzzled frown pulling down the corners of his mouth. "I'm quite happy with the way things are. I don't understand why you want to change that." He reached for her hand, squeezing gently. "Why mess with a good thing?"

Unsatisfied with his response, Jillian had pulled away. Things had fizzled between them after that and a few weeks later she'd discovered that Mark was already married and she'd been nothing but the other woman. He'd fed her a steady diet of lies, and the sad thing was she'd believed every last one of them. The betrayal had rocked her to her core, but before she could confront him, he'd taken a position in California and was gone.

She hadn't really seen anyone since. A few dates here and there, but nothing serious. Mark had left her feeling shaken and foolish, and she couldn't get over the irrational suspicions that plagued her whenever she interacted with men. Then Jason had disappeared and she couldn't even think about dating. It became something she filed into the category of "someday," along with those cooking lessons she'd always wanted to take, and the trip to Paris she'd been dreaming about for years.

So she was surprised and a little disturbed to feel those tingles of attraction again, when she'd been so sure a relationship wasn't in her future.

Shrugging off the bad memories, she stepped back into the dining room with soup in one hand and bowls in the other, and found Alex studying her bookshelves. She placed everything on the table and frowned slightly when he didn't turn around. She walked over to stand beside him, wondering what he found so fascinating. There was a limited collection of fiction and some books from her childhood, along with a smattering of family photos and knickknacks. Most of the space was occupied by texts from college and medical school—interesting reading to her, but boring to most everyone else.

He was staring at her battered copy of *Gray's Anatomy*, the one her grandfather had given her when she'd gone off to med school.

His face was pale and she could tell by the emptiness of his gaze that he was miles away. "Alex?" When he didn't respond, she laid her hand on his arm. "Ready to eat?"

He turned to face her, his eyes so full of pain she immediately thought he'd done something to his shoulder. "What's wrong?" she asked, guiding him to the chair and tugging at the neck of his shirt to get a better view of the wound. Had he moved wrong and ripped the stitches out? Was the injury more severe than she'd originally thought?

"I'm okay." His voice came out as a croak. He cleared his throat and tried again. "Really, I'm fine. I just moved wrong and it set my shoulder on fire."

Jillian leaned back, letting her hands fall away from his body. "Okay," she said, her adrenaline fading with the knowledge that he wasn't taking a turn for the worse. "I'm out of lidocaine, but I do have some ibuprofen. Let's get some food into you, and then you can take something. I'll fix you an ice pack, as well, which should help keep the area numb and the swelling down."

Alex nodded, the color already starting to return to his face. She dished up the soup and placed a bowl in front of him, pleased to see it was still steaming. Although she'd eaten her share of cold soup over the years, she would never force it on someone else.

They ate in silence for a few moments. Jillian had a dozen different questions racing through her mind, but she wanted to give Alex a chance to eat in peace. She focused on the hot, salty tang of the chicken noodle soup, using the familiar, comforting flavor as a distraction. Her mother had never been much of a cook, so anytime Jillian had been sick as a child, she got soup from a can. Now she associated the taste with her mom, and was startled to realize she had defaulted to fixing the same meal in an effort to provide Alex with some relief.

"I've always wondered," Alex said, pulling her out of her thoughts. "Is chicken noodle soup really the best medicine?"

Jillian smiled. "It certainly doesn't hurt. It's got lots of good stuff—protein, vegetables, carbs—and the broth helps keep you hydrated." She swallowed another mouthful and reached for her water to wash it down. "Well, maybe not this broth," she amended. "But the homemade stuff doesn't have nearly as much salt."

"Doesn't bother me," he said with a smile. "It's hot and filling, which is better than I expected after tonight."

Seeing her opening, Jillian decided to ask the question weighing heavily on her mind. "About tonight…" she said, putting down her spoon and folding her hands on the tabletop. "What do we do now?"

Alex dabbed at his mouth with the napkin, stalling for time. She said "we," he marveled. "We" implied they were a team; that she was going to stick with him, help him face whatever came next. How could she feel that way after everything that had happened tonight? Surely she hadn't forgotten how they'd met? He allowed himself to bask in the warm glow of her "we" for a few heartbeats, even though he knew it was just a turn of phrase, something she'd probably said without thinking about what it actually meant.

They would never be a "we." And once she knew the truth, she would want to get as far away from him as possible.

He couldn't believe his eyes when he'd seen the photograph on her bookshelf. The picture was a few years old, but he'd recognized her immediately. And the guy standing next to her. He had to be her brother—the resemblance was too strong for the guy to be a friend or her boyfriend. His heart had dropped into his stomach when he'd seen the image, and he was powerless to stop the rush of memory that assaulted him.

He'd been working with Tony, making contacts with mid-level drug dealers. The 3 Star Killers were an up-and-coming producer and distributor of meth, and the more dealers they supplied, the bigger their territory and power grew. Alex had gone into a stairwell to talk to Billy, leaving Tony outside to watch his back. He'd just gotten Billy to agree to use the gang as his source of meth when the sound of angry voices drifted into the concrete alcove, followed by the telltale pop of a gunshot.

"What the hell, man?" Billy had said, pulling out a switchblade and taking a step back.

Alex had put his hands up and tried to look non-threatening. He never carried a gun to these meetings, not wanting the dealers to get the wrong idea. It generally wasn't an issue, because most dealers were unarmed themselves. It would be bad enough to get busted on a drug charge; carrying a weapon only made things worse.

"Alex?" Tony stuck his head in, squinting in the darkness of the stairwell. "Where you at?"

"I'm here," he said, keeping an eye on Billy. Evidently deciding he wanted no part of this, Billy turned and ran up the stairs. Alex heard the echo of a door slam from somewhere above and put his hands down. "What the hell is going on?" he said, turning to Tony.

"Guy out here in the alley got a little aggressive. Had to put him down."

Alex felt his stomach drop. "Did you really have to shoot him?" He'd had to do a lot of distasteful things for the gang, but he'd never had to kill anyone, and he hated the fact that Tony had shot someone while with him. It would be tough for him to explain this to his case handler—Jim understood that Alex sometimes found himself in a sticky situation, but he tended to frown on murder.

Tony thrust out his chin and jerked up a shoulder, moves Alex had seen him make a hundred times before when the shorter, younger man was trying to look tough. "Boy tried to get physical with me. I can't have people disrespecting me like that."

"Boy?" *Oh God, please not a child...* Surely not even Tony would stoop so low?

Alex stepped around him, emerging from the dark stairwell into the brightness of the alley. Since it was the middle of the afternoon, there was little relief from the sun, and it felt like an oven in the narrow corridor. The stench nearly knocked him over—rotting garbage from the Dumpster at the end of the alley, stale vomit and urine mixing to create a singularly terrible miasma. And over it all, he detected the heavy, metallic scent of fresh blood.

He saw the feet first. A pair of stained tennis shoes sticking out into the alley, attached to feet that were splayed apart. Alex moved quickly, holding his breath as he approached.

The victim wasn't a child, but he wasn't that old, either—no more than twenty-three or so, unless he missed his guess. Alex knelt beside the thin body and pressed his fingers to the kid's neck, checking for a pulse he knew wouldn't be there. There was too much blood on the ground, and the light had already gone out of his eyes, replaced by the dull, vacant stare of death. "Dammit, Tony," he muttered.

He could imagine the scene even before Tony started making his excuses. The kid was plainly a user, and he'd come to get his fix from Billy. Tony had tried to stop him, and had gotten angry when the kid hadn't left. One thing had led to another and now the young man was dead.

"Why you wasting time, man? We need to go. Someone will have heard the shot."

Alex cut him a glare before returning his attention to the body. "We need to make sure there isn't any identifying information on this guy. We don't want anything that could lead back to us." That wasn't really his concern, but it was a decent excuse to explain his interest in the nameless victim. In truth, Alex was hoping to find some ID so he could pass the info along to Jim. It broke his heart to picture a mother forever left to wonder about the fate of her missing son. "Besides," he said, staring at the kid's face to commit it to memory, "no one around here is going to call the police."

Tony scoffed. "You think I don't know that? Cops don't scare me. But we're close to MS-13 territory."

He was right. MS-13 was a brutal street gang who controlled part of DC. While he and Tony technically weren't in their territory, the gang wouldn't take kindly to the presence of the 3 Star Killers so close to their turf. And since it was just the two of them, and only Tony was armed, Alex didn't want to wait around for a welcoming committee.

"Then I guess you'd better help me. It's your mess, after all."

Grumbling under his breath, Tony knelt and patted the man down, checking one side while Alex did the same on the other. He was careful to keep his hands out of the guy's pockets—no telling what his drug of choice had been, and Alex had no intention of getting stuck by a dirty needle.

The kid was clean, a fact that was disappointing, but not surprising. Alex stood and took one last look at the latest casualty in his life. Time to go, though he hated himself for leaving.

"Alex?"

It took him a split second to realize it was Jillian talking and not Tony. Shaking off the memory, he ran a hand over his face and looked up to meet her concerned gaze.

"Are you all right?" she asked.

He nodded slowly. "I'm fine. Sorry I spaced out. I was just thinking."

Jillian leaned back, apparently satisfied with his answer. "Do you know what we're going to do next?"

No, but he was certain of one thing. "There is no 'we,'" he said, setting the napkin next to his bowl. "You've done more than enough already, and I can't ask you to keep putting yourself in danger for me."

Especially after what happened to your brother.

Bad enough the gang had claimed one member of her family. He wasn't going to let her fall victim to them, as well.

"Alex—" she began. He raised his hand to cut her off.

"No. I mean it. I don't want you to get any more involved in this than you already are."

"I can't just let you walk into danger by yourself!"

"Why not?" Her concern was puzzling—he was a stranger to her, and one who had abducted her at that. Why would she care about his well-being?

Now it was her turn to look away. "You're my patient," she said, shrugging slightly. "I have to make sure you don't relapse or ruin my handiwork."

It was a poor excuse, but he decided not to press her for a real answer. It didn't matter. He wouldn't see her again anyway.

"I think you can trust that my shoulder will be fine." He stood and picked up his empty bowl, gritting his teeth against the wave of pain that followed his movements. He took the few steps into the kitchen and placed the bowl in the sink. "Thank you for dinner. I should be going."

"Oh, no." Jillian shot to her feet and raced to block the door. "You are not going anywhere."

"Doc—" he began. She clapped her hand over his mouth, stunning him into silence. She smelled strongly of soup and hospital disinfectant, but underneath was the faint vanilla musk he'd come to associate with her skin. He focused hard on her words, pushing aside the arousal stirred by her touch.

"You can't go back out there. Not in your condition."

Alex took her wrist and gently pulled her hand away from his mouth. "You stitched me up," he pointed out. "I'm not bleeding anymore."

She shook her head. "You were, and you need to give your body time to recover. Plus, you're exhausted. You need rest—at least a day's worth of sleep, but since I know you won't do that, a few hours will have to suffice. And," she said, arching her brow when he opened his mouth to respond, "you don't have a coat." This final pronouncement was made in the smug tone of a gambler holding a winning hand of cards, as if the fact that he lacked winter wear was enough to win the argument once and for all.

Alex bit his lip to keep from smiling. The good doctor was feisty, he'd give her that. And she had made some solid points. He *was* tired. The idea of sleep was almost too tempting to pass up. He couldn't remember the last time he'd slept peacefully—in the back of his mind, he was always expecting an attack, always wondering if the gang had figured out who he really was. It was hard to fully surrender to sleep when the threat of discovery and death hung over his head every night.

No one knows I'm here, he thought, considering. How could they? He'd been careful not to call Jillian by her name in front of Tony, and no one had followed them from the motel. He truly was off the grid. It would be stupid of him not to take advantage of that fact.

Plus, if he slept here, it would give him a little more time with Jillian. He absently stroked his thumb over her wrist, catching his breath when her eyes flared in response. Even though he knew he wouldn't be sleeping with her, he couldn't deny that he was reluctant to leave her company. She was a remarkable woman, and he wished he could get to know her better.

"Okay," he said, giving her hand a squeeze before releasing it. "If you're sure you don't mind, I'd love to crash on your couch."

Jillian smiled at him then, the expression making her seem younger and heightening her resemblance to her brother in the photo. Guilt and remorse twisted his gut into a sickening knot, but he forced himself to smile back.

"Great," she said, her voice ringing with relief. "Sit back down and I'll grab some sheets to make up the bed."

"Hold on," he said, reaching out to stop her. "I'm not taking your bed."

She patted his hand. "The couch is a pull-out. It's not the most comfortable spot, but it's not the worst, either. At least, my brother never complained."

His skin prickled, followed by a wave of nausea so strong it made his legs rubbery. It was one thing to suspect the kid was her brother, but to have it confirmed... He staggered over to the recliner and sank down, grateful Jillian was rummaging in the closet and hadn't seen his reaction. Breathing deeply, he forced himself to put the memory of her brother's dead face back in the box where it belonged. He couldn't do anything to help him now, and while it was wrong of him to use his sister, he needed to get some rest so he could figure out his next move.

"I'm sorry," he whispered. "I will make sure your killer pays for what he did." He paused, gathering his resolve and determination.

"And I will keep your sister safe."

Chapter 7

Am I going crazy?

Jillian searched the closet for a spare set of sheets, her thoughts still with Alex in the other room. He was a stranger. A sexy stranger, but a stranger nonetheless. It was a bit unnerving—she didn't go for one-night stands, so she wasn't used to having a man she'd just met in her apartment. And she certainly hadn't ever made up a bed for an erstwhile kidnapper.

There was just something about him, she mused, shoving a pile of sweaters to the side. Even though he was in a fix, he was still determined to make things right. Faced with such dire circumstances, most people would just give up. But in the short time she'd been around him, Jillian had seen that Alex had a core of steel. He would fight until the end, and she wanted to make sure he was prepared for it, at least physically. A few hours of sleep would be a good start.

She just hoped she'd be able to sleep as well. Seeing Alex wearing Jason's clothes had thrown her. After her initial arousal, she'd seen past his body to the shirt and pants. Memories of Jason had hit her then, dredging up emotions she'd buried long ago.

She wasn't a fool. While her heart would always hope to see her brother again, her head realized that two years with no contact—not a call, a note or a visit—meant he was probably gone for good. On her darker days, she figured he was dead. What else would keep him from getting in touch?

"I just hope you're safe," she whispered, pulling the sheets free from the bottom shelf. "Wherever you are, I hope you're okay."

It didn't take as long to find a spare pillow, and a few moments later she returned to the den. Alex was sitting in the recliner, his eyes closed and his breathing deep and regular. She moved quickly to unfold the couch and put the sheets on, then stood, eyeing him thought-fully. While she was glad he was getting some rest, in the long run, he would probably sleep better stretched out on the bed.

"Alex," she said softly, not wanting to scare him. When he didn't respond, she reached out and placed her hand on his uninjured shoulder. She repeated his name, a little louder this time.

His eyes flew open and he jerked away from her, half falling off the chair as he moved to put space between them. His hand fumbled at the waistband of his pants, searching for a weapon that wasn't there.

Jillian took a step back, holding up her hands in the universal gesture of surrender. "It's me," she said, trying to keep the alarm from her voice. *I should have known better*, she thought, kicking herself for startling him. He was an undercover FBI agent, on the run from a deadly gang. Of course he'd assume he was being attacked.

"I'm sorry, Alex." *I should have just let him sleep in the chair.*

He blinked a few times, coming awake with a frown. "What happened?"

Jillian dropped her hands. "You fell asleep in the chair. I figured you'd be more comfortable in the bed, so I tried to wake you. I should have thought it through."

He shook his head. "No, I'm sorry. I forgot where I was and just reacted. It won't happen again." He raised his arm to run a hand through his hair and winced.

"Did you hurt your shoulder?"

He rotated it gingerly, testing. He didn't grimace, but he pressed his lips together while he moved. The gesture told her more than any words just how badly it hurt. "I think it's okay."

"Let me check, just to be sure."

He sat on the edge of the bed and submitted to a quick examination. The wound still looked good—he hadn't pulled out any stitches as she'd feared. It would be hard for him to sleep while in pain, though.

"I'll be right back." She walked to the kitchen and fixed him a glass of water, grabbing the bottle of ibuprofen on her way back to the den. She offered them both to him with a small smile. "It's not very strong, but it's all I've got. You can take four, and that will hopefully dull the pain enough for you to sleep."

"Thanks."

His fingers brushed hers as he accepted the glass and bottle, sending warm tingles up her arms. She cleared her throat, ignoring the effect he had on her. "Do you need anything else?"

He looked up at her, his eyes a deep, clear blue she could get lost in. "You've already done more than enough."

"Promise me something?"

Alex stilled, wariness entering his eyes. "What?"

"Don't leave without saying goodbye."

He frowned slightly, but nodded. "All right," he said slowly. "If that's what you want."

It was Jillian's turn to nod. "It is. Sleep well."

"Thanks."

She turned her back on his questioning look and walked down the hall to her bedroom. How could she explain her feelings? Ever since Jason had left so suddenly, Jillian had become almost fanatical about saying goodbye to the people she cared about. She would never get that closure with her brother, but she made sure she had it with everyone else in her life.

And although she barely knew him, she was beginning to care about Alex. Now that the events of the evening were behind her, she could see he was a good man, forced to do desperate things. The more she thought about it, she had to admit that a large part of his appeal was his undercover work with the 3 Star Killers. Having seen the effects of drugs on her once-vibrant brother, Jillian was a big fan of anyone who tried to stop the flow of narcotics into the city. It was an uphill battle, but thanks to men like Alex, there were some small victories along the way.

There had to be a way for him to make contact with the FBI, she mused, slipping into her nightgown. He had said his case handler thought he was a traitor, but surely he had a friend, someone he knew and could trust? He was probably too overwhelmed and exhausted to think clearly. She'd talk to him about it in the morning, after they'd both had some rest. While she didn't doubt his conviction that things were bad, she was a firm believer in the restorative powers of sleep. This whole mess would be easier to tackle in the morning. They could come up with a plan over breakfast, she decided, climbing into bed.

Because despite what Alex thought, she wasn't leaving him to face his troubles alone.

Jillian sat bolt upright in bed, her eyes wide and searching for a threat that wasn't there. For a few seconds she thought she was back in the motel room with Tony, and she turned automatically to look for the second bed and her patient. She blinked in confusion and then remembered where she was. She lay back down with a sigh, glancing at the clock on her bedside table. Three in the morning. She hadn't been out for very long.

She toyed with the idea of checking on Alex, but didn't want to risk waking him. Given his shoulder injury, he might not be sleeping well, and she didn't want to interrupt what little rest he was getting. Better to just go back to sleep herself, if she could.

She was on the verge of drifting off when she heard a muffled noise in the other room. Pulled back into consciousness, she lay still for a moment, trying to determine if the sound was real or just a figment of her imagination. She was about to dismiss it as nothing when it came again, a little louder this time.

Okay, I'm not hearing things. Was Alex just tossing

and turning on an uncomfortable bed or had something bad happened?

She sucked in her breath as a chilling thought struck her—had the gang found them?

Surely not, she told herself, willing her heart to slow down. *I wouldn't have slept through them kicking down my front door.* Unless they had picked the locks and entered quietly, wanting to take her and Alex by surprise.

It had grown quiet in the den, but the thought of the gang invading her house was too disturbing. Deciding she wouldn't get any more sleep unless she investigated, Jillian climbed out of bed as silently as she could and stuck her feet into the slippers waiting at the side of the bed. She took one step toward the door, then stopped, considering. If there was someone out there, she didn't want to face them with nothing but her nightgown to protect her. She pivoted and grabbed the baseball bat her brother had insisted she keep beside her bed.

"You're a woman living alone, Jill," he'd said in one of his rare, unaltered moments. "Better to have it and not need it than to need it and not have it."

She'd scoffed, thinking him overprotective and paranoid. But she'd accepted his gift and left it beside her bed, never dreaming she'd actually have cause to use it.

The wood was smooth and cold in her hands, and she felt the gritty layer of dust that had built up over the years. *How do I hold this thing?* If she put it over her shoulder like a batter, she might not have room to swing. Holding it in front of her like some kind of walking stick didn't feel right, either. In the end, she settled for gripping the bat in one hand, leaving it lowered by her side as she walked. If she did have to defend herself, she would hopefully have enough time to raise her arm and use the Louisville Slugger as a club.

Stepping lightly, she tiptoed down the hall, pausing at the opening to the den. She closed her eyes for a heart-beat, took a deep breath and then stepped into the den, falling into a batting stance that would make a major leaguer proud. She kept the bat on her shoulder while she scanned the room, searching the shadows for any sign of an intruder. Nothing. Her front door was still shut, the lock gleaming dully in the shaft of moonlight streaming in from the large picture window.

Jillian lowered the bat, feeling mildly foolish at her overreaction. She fought the insane urge to giggle, knowing that if she gave in, she'd never stop. The last thing she wanted was for Alex to wake up to find her standing over him, holding a baseball bat and laughing like a demented clown.

He shifted on the bed, drawing her attention and pro-viding a focus for her fading adrenaline. Was he okay? Had he ripped the wound open?

He kicked out, groaning while he tossed and turned. He stilled for a second and then began to move again. A strangled noise came from his throat and Jillian rec-ognized it as the sound she'd heard before, the sound that had woken her.

He's having a nightmare, she realized.

She debated for a split second whether to wake him or to leave him to fight through it on his own. Given his earlier reaction, he didn't respond well to being woken up. But she couldn't leave him to toss and turn—he might do further damage to his shoulder.

In the end, her concern for his injury won out. She stood at the foot of the sofa bed, considering her options.

Best to stay out of his reach. Earlier, he'd tried to run away, but this time, he might wake up swinging. She considered the bat in her hand thoughtfully—maybe she could prod him gently with it, then back away...

It was worth a shot.

Something was touching his leg.

Alex came awake slowly, shaking off the clinging tendrils of the nightmare to focus on the tapping sensation. Was that a hand? No—not possible. An animal perhaps?

He opened his eyes, focusing on the textured ceiling overhead. He was at the doc's apartment, on her couch. While the apartment was in an older building, he'd seen no signs of rats or mice earlier. But then again, those animals tended to avoid people whenever possible.

He raised a hand to wipe his face and the tapping stopped. "Alex?" came the whisper in the dark.

Reacting instinctively he jerked up in the bed, ready to defend himself against this new threat. A searing pain radiated from his shoulder, but he ignored it, squinting in the dark to identify the speaker.

"Doc?" Was she okay? Had something happened to her?

Or had she changed her mind about letting him stay on the couch?

Alex swung his legs over the side of the bed, reluctantly leaving the warmth of the blankets behind. He'd overstayed his welcome, and now it was time to go. It had been good of her to let him stay as long as she had, and he didn't blame her for wanting him out of her home. No telling what fresh hell he would bring into her life if he stayed.

"What are you doing?" she whispered, stepping forward to stand next to the bed.

He glanced up at her, amused despite himself that she still spoke quietly. "I'm awake," he pointed out, trying to remember where he'd left his clothes. "You can talk at a normal volume." Were they in the bathroom?

"Oh," she said, sounding a bit surprised. "I guess you're right." She stepped back when he moved forward, and it was then he noticed the baseball bat she held in a loose grip by her side. His gut cramped at the sight and he felt about two inches tall. Did she really think she'd have to threaten him with a baseball bat to get him to leave? He wanted to crawl back under the blankets and die from the shame of it, but that would only confirm her impression that she'd have to use force to get him out of her apartment.

It served him right. After the way he'd treated her tonight, he deserved no better. Determined to hold his head high and depart with what little dignity he could, he headed toward the bathroom in search of his wayward clothes. He wasn't going to steal from her, on top of everything else.

"Where are you going?"

He stopped but didn't turn around. "I'm looking for my clothes. Do you know where they are?"

"I threw them in the washer after you went to bed. I don't think they're dry yet. Are you uncomfortable in what you have on?"

"No, but…" He trailed off, at a loss. Why would she wash his clothes if she didn't want him to stay the night? He turned to find her watching him, a confused look on her face. "I thought you wanted me to go."

She scrunched up her nose, as if something smelled bad. "No. Why would you think that?"

"You woke me in the middle of the night with a bat?"

"Oh, that." She looked down, and although it was too dark to tell, he thought she may have blushed. "Well, the thing is…" she began, twisting the bat around as she spoke. "I heard a noise, and I psyched myself out thinking someone was in the apartment. I grabbed the bat and came out here to investigate, and that's when I realized you were having a nightmare."

Now it was his turn to blush. "Ah, I see." He ran a hand through his hair, absurdly touched that she had pulled him from the terrors that stalked his dreams. He swallowed around a sudden lump in his throat. "Thanks for…" He gestured to the bat.

She nodded. "Well, I couldn't let you continue to toss and turn. I didn't want you to rip out your stitches."

Alex laughed at that, imagining all too well her look of indignation at the thought of her handiwork being ruined in such a careless manner. "Well, whatever your reason, thanks."

She grinned, a flash of white teeth in the darkness. "All in a day's work. Now get back in bed, and I'll get you an ice pack for that shoulder. I can tell by the way you're holding your arm that it's bothering you."

Too tired to argue, Alex slid under the covers, searching for residual warmth amid the sheets and blankets. The apartment was chilly, and he was grateful for it; there was nothing worse than trying to sleep while overheated.

Jillian returned a moment later, a bulky object in her hand. "Scoot over," she ordered, standing by the side of the bed.

"I beg your pardon?" Was he still dreaming?

She didn't repeat herself, but merely lifted the blankets and climbed in next to him. Alex shifted over to give her room, stunned into silence by this turn of events. Never in his wildest imaginings had he pictured Jillian sharing a bed with him. "It's too cold to stand there," she explained, arranging the ice pack on his shoulder. After an initial flare of pain, the cold sank in, numbing his shoulder into relief.

He sighed in pleasure, enjoying the absence of pain. Although he'd only been injured for a few hours, he'd already begun to accept the discomfort as something he must live with. His rational mind knew the pain would end as he healed, but his body could only process what was happening in the moment, and dealing with the torment was physically exhausting.

Of course, sitting in bed next to the sexy doctor was a whole new level of torture.

"Want to tell me about your dream?" She sounded so *normal*, as though she sat in bed with men who had kidnapped her and chatted about their nightmares all the time. He mentally shook himself. Maybe she was comfortable in bed with him because she brought home strangers on a regular basis. After all, doctors didn't have much free time to date. There were guys at the Bureau who operated the same way—they engaged in a series of no-strings-attached affairs to scratch an itch. As long as everyone knew the score, no one got hurt.

But Jillian didn't seem like a casual kind of woman. She deserved to be cherished and loved, not used and discarded. He tamped down the irritation that rose at the thought of her with another man, one who would enjoy her body without recognizing her worth. She deserved so much more than that.

But he had no claim over her, and he would do well to remember it.

He steered his mind back to her question. "Nope," he said, cutting off that avenue of conversation. "I'd rather just forget it, if it's all the same to you."

"Fine by me." The ice pack crackled when she shifted it on his shoulder. "Will you tell me about your tattoo?"

He moved automatically to place his hand over the three green stars on his forearm. It was a mark of the gang, a branding he hated. One he couldn't wait to have removed.

Alex cleared his throat. He'd rather not talk about the gang, but he owed her this much. Besides, if he talked about his ink, he wouldn't have to talk about his dreams. "It's a gang tattoo, as you probably guessed."

He heard the smile in her voice. "I kinda figured that much. But guys come into the emergency room all the time with variations of that tattoo. What does yours in particular mean?"

"The three stars come from the gang name, and the DC flag." He traced the outline with his forefinger as he spoke, seeing the marks as clear as day even in the dark room.

"But why are your stars green? I remember Tony's were a different color—red? Or maybe black?"

"Good eyes," he said, impressed by her recollection. "The color of the star indicates your role in the gang. Green is for drugs—that's me. I'm involved in distribution, shipments, that kind of thing. Red is for women. Those are the guys that act as pimps or who are involved in trafficking women. Black is for enforcers.

Those are the guys who carry weapons, the ones who provide protection or the ones who do the wet work."

"'Wet work'?" she repeated slowly. "Do I want to know what that means?"

He shook his head. "You can probably guess. I'm sure you've dealt with the aftermath before."

She was silent for a moment and then asked, "What color were Tony's stars?"

"Black."

"But he's so young!"

"He's seventeen," Alex replied. "To a normal person, that's young. For a gang member, that's middle-aged."

"And what about you?" She poked him gently in the side, a teasing gesture that made him smile.

"Me? I'm practically an elder statesman."

She chuckled, and he felt the brush of her hair when she shook her head.

"It's just so surreal to me," she said, turning to face him. "How did you even get involved with the gang in the first place? I don't know much about how they operate, but I doubt they would have let you in on the basis of your smile."

"No, it took a bit more than that," he agreed. He paused for a moment, debating on what information to share with her. She didn't need to hear all of the gritty details, but he could give her an overview.

"Basically, I posed as a new dealer in the city. A low-level guy who wouldn't be seen as a threat. But I made it known that I was interested in growing my business, so to speak. The gang found me and made me the offer they extend to everyone who tries to operate in their territory."

"Which was?"

He cleared his throat. "Join or die."

"Wow." She whistled softly. "Not much of a choice there."

"No. But it was exactly what I wanted to hear. They initiated me quickly, but kept me at arm's length for a bit, to see if they could trust me."

"What was that like?" Her voice was quiet in the darkness, and Alex closed his eyes, savoring the intimacy that came from talking to a woman in the small hours of the night. Even though their topic of conversation was one he'd rather change.

"My initiation?" She nodded and he shrugged. "It was all very business-like. They took me to a tattoo parlor, watched me get my mark. Then they took me to a member's home and got me drunk. At one point, they showed me pictures of my car, the inside of my apartment. They wanted me to know that they knew where I lived, what I drove. That they could get to me anytime. And then they showed me pictures of what they did to the people who betrayed them." He shuddered involuntarily as the memory of those bloody images rose to the surface.

Jillian adjusted the ice pack then rested her hand on his chest. He covered it with one of his own, focusing on the feel of her soft skin under his rough palm. She was so delicate in comparison to his coarseness—he wanted to gather her in his arms and protect her from the rest of the world. But he knew she wouldn't appreciate the gesture. Underneath her fragile appearance was a core of steel. She was an intelligent, independent woman who probably wouldn't take too kindly to being treated like she was made of glass.

"Enough about me," he said, forestalling another of her questions. "I want to know more about you."

She shifted slightly, as though she was uncomfortable with the new focus. "There's not much to tell."

"I'm sorry, that's not an acceptable answer," he said, using his best game-show announcer voice. "I answered all of your questions. Now it's your turn. It's only fair." He squeezed her hand gently, which earned him a rueful sigh.

"I suppose you have a point," she admitted, sounding rather unhappy about it. Her reluctance to talk only served to heighten his curiosity. What was the good doctor trying to hide? "What do you want to know?"

Everything. Knowing that would only scare her, he settled for a slightly more limited question. "What made you want to be a doctor?"

"That's a long story," she said. "Can't we start with something easy, like my favorite color?"

He laughed. "Okay. What's your favorite color?"

"Blue."

"Me, too. Now, what made you want to become a doctor?"

She didn't say anything and the silence dragged on, growing heavier with every heartbeat. Finally she spoke, her voice so quiet Alex had to strain to hear. "My brother."

His gut clenched, but he kept his mouth shut, knowing that if he spoke, she wouldn't. He began to trace his thumb across her skin, wanting her to know that he was still listening.

"I have a younger brother. Jason. He started doing drugs when we were in high school. He was only sixteen at the time. He started on the 'softer' stuff, but I could tell it was taking a toll on him, and that he was addicted. So I decided to become a neuroscientist. I wanted to study how certain drugs act on the brain, and how addiction can be treated or even prevented."

"I heard they're working on a vaccine for cocaine— it keeps people from feeling the effects of the drug, so they don't become addicted. Is that the kind of work you wanted to do?"

Jillian nodded. "Exactly. Can you imagine how things would be different if all it took was one shot to make people immune to drugs? How many lives that would save?" She sounded wistful and a little disappointed, like a dreamer forced to wake up and contend with reality.

"So what happened?"

"Jason moved on to the harder stuff. Cocaine was his drug of choice for a bit. He overdosed one night and I found him on the floor of his bedroom. He wasn't breathing. I had to perform CPR until the paramedics arrived." She shuddered, clearly recalling the event. "Because he was young, and in otherwise good shape, they were able to bring him back. But I decided then and there that I wasn't ever going to feel so helpless again. I knew it was only the start, and I knew that if he did it again, the paramedics might not get there in time. I wanted to be able to save my brother. So I went to medical school and specialized in emergency medicine when I got out."

"Did you ever have to save your brother again?"

She shook her head. "My parents kicked him out a few months after the incident, when he snuck out of rehab and stole their car to sell for drug money. At first, he was beside himself. Then he discovered meth, and he didn't care anymore. A few years ago he came to me, said he was finally done and was getting clean. I let him stay with me, but he left after a few days. I haven't seen him since."

A wave of nausea hit him as the pieces clicked into place, and he shifted uncomfortably. Tweakers in need of a hit were notoriously unpredictable. If Jason had come looking for Billy while in the throes of withdrawal, it was no wonder he'd been aggressive.

"Damn," he muttered, wishing for the millionth time that Tony hadn't been so quick to fire. *If I'd been in that alley, I could have stopped him...*

"I think that's why I like you," Jillian said, sounding a little shy. "You're doing your best to stop the very thing that took my brother from me."

Guilt was a heavy weight on his chest. He had to tell her about his part in her brother's death. She deserved to know the truth.

"Jillian..." he began.

She turned to face him fully and the words stalled in his throat. Her eyes were glassy with unshed tears, but the look she gave him was full of hope, as if he was some kind of superhero that would make things right in her world. If she knew the truth, she'd hate him. And after everything that had happened tonight, he didn't think he could bear that.

"Sorry," she said, blinking hard. "I didn't mean to start crying on you. But it's the first time I've talked to anyone about Jason."

"It's okay," he said softly, reaching out to run his finger across her cheek. She stilled at the contact and he pulled away, cursing himself for having scared her.

"Alex?" Her voice was barely a whisper, but he heard

it as clearly as a shout. Jillian moved closer and he sucked in a breath when he realized her intentions.

The kiss started out gentle; a slide of lips, the barest flicker of her tongue. *I should stop this.* He'd wanted to kiss her for hours, but given his role in her brother's death, he didn't deserve the privilege. And if Jillian knew the truth, she'd hate him forever for using her like this.

He was on the verge of telling her when she deepened the kiss, sliding her tongue across his with a teasing flutter that sent all the blood in his body to his groin. Conscious thought evaporated in the face of her heated exploration and he surrendered to the flood of sensations, no longer caring what the future might bring. There was only now, only Jillian. Only this moment.

And he would make it count.

Chapter 8

Jillian's head spun as Alex took control of the kiss, tilting her head to change the angle while he explored her mouth with his tongue. Kissing him had been a wild, impulsive move. She usually over-thought everything, considering a situation from all angles before deciding what to do. But being around Alex short-circuited her thoughts and wreaked havoc on her self-control. Now that she knew how he tasted, how he kissed, it would be even harder to keep her hands to herself.

She pressed herself against his chest, enjoying the feel of his solid strength against her softness. His hand found her lower back, fisting in the cloth of her nightgown to anchor her in place. She was all too happy to comply.

He was a fascinating mix of textures. The skin of his face was smooth where he'd shaved earlier, but there was a small rough patch just under the corner of his jaw where he'd missed a spot. His back was warm and strong, a smooth, irregular line along his rib cage a testament to a previous injury. She traced the scar with her fingertips, imagining the shiny pinkness of it as she moved. The dusting of hair on his stomach and chest felt like silk to her questing hand, and she lingered for a moment, wanting suddenly to feel his bare chest pressed against her skin, to luxuriate in the sensations of full-body contact.

His arousal pressed against her thigh and she continued her exploration of his body, her hand moving down to cup him. He hissed in pleasure when she touched him, his unguarded reaction triggering a wave of satisfaction so intense it nearly stole her breath.

The soft flannel of the pajama pants did nothing to disguise the hardness underneath, but she wanted to feel him without a buffer, needed to touch him with no barriers in place. She moved her hand to the waistband of the pants, but before she could do so much as tug, his hand wrapped around both of hers, stopping her efforts.

"Wait," he whispered. He pulled back a little but pressed his forehead to hers, keeping them linked. His breath was warm across her face, a feather-light caress over her too sensitive lips. She closed her eyes, enjoying the sensation as her heart rate and breathing gradually returned to normal.

Unfortunately, as her arousal faded, her brain came back online. Doubts and recriminations filled her mind as she realized the magnitude of what she'd done.

I practically threw myself on him, she thought, mentally chiding herself for being so forward, and with someone who had been her patient, no less. *The poor man had to physically restrain me!* Guilt and shame flooded her and she wanted nothing more than to crawl under the covers and disappear. Since that wasn't really an option, the next best thing was for her to leave. Now.

Alex's breathing had evened out, making her think he'd fallen asleep. And no wonder. He'd had a heck of a night, and that was before she'd climbed into his bed and he'd had to defend his battered virtue. Moving slowly, Jillian pulled her hands from his now-slack grasp. Then she rolled onto her back, intending to scoot out of the bed without disturbing him.

She'd just started to move when his arm came around her waist, pinning her in place. She turned to look at him, but Alex's eyes were closed, his face relaxed. She tried to ease out from under his arm, but he tightened his grip and pulled, dragging her until she was pressed against him. He curved his body to fit around hers, the gesture both protective and possessive. Then he sighed, burrowing his nose into her hair with a little sound of pleasure.

"Mine," she thought she heard him murmur before his breathing evened out again as he sank back into a deep sleep.

Oh, dear, she thought, a small thrill racing through her limbs as the implications of that one little word registered. *You may be right.*

"I just don't understand it. He was always so strong, so honest."

Jim DeWinter sat in Dan's office, looking as though he hadn't slept in days. He ran a hand through his hair, then passed it across the front of his hopelessly wrinkled shirt before slouching back in the chair.

"Money is a powerful motivator," Dan said, striving for a sympathetic tone. As Malcom's case officer, Jim might know where Alex had gone. Dan needed to get him to talk, but if the conversation was going to get anywhere, he'd have to suffer through this inane blubbering first.

Jim shook his head. "Not to Alex. He was never interested in buying things, in living the life."

"Do you think he was addicted to drugs?"

Jim snapped his head up, narrowing his eyes slightly. "No," he said emphatically. "He always tested clean. Besides," he said, sounding thoughtful, "I would have noticed a change in him if he'd been using. You can't do the kind of stuff the gang deals in without showing some physical signs."

Dan merely nodded, pretending to care.

"I just wish I knew why he did it," Jim went on, oblivious to the fact that Dan hadn't responded. "What made him turn against us? Never in a million years would I have guessed he'd give up information like that. Not at the cost of so many lives." He slouched in the chair, deflating like a leaking balloon.

A sharp flare of satisfaction burned in Dan's chest. His secret was still safe. As long as Jim and the rest of the team thought Alex had been the one to betray them, no one would suspect him. And since Alex was missing, he couldn't contradict their assumptions. Now all he had to do was to ensure Malcom stayed gone. Permanently.

He hadn't had much luck searching for the lady doctor last night. He'd checked area hospitals, but no one was missing an employee. He couldn't make further inquiries without raising a few red flags, something he wasn't willing to do just yet. So he was stuck, unless Jim could shed some light on where Alex might have gone.

"We need to find him," Dan said firmly. "The only way we'll know the truth is if we get it from him."

"I know," Jim said, sounding miserable. "But I have no idea where he is."

Damn. That was unfortunate. "You've checked his apartment?"

Jim nodded. "Both of them—his real place and his cover. No sign of him, or that he'd been there recently."

"Did he have a safe spot—a bolt hole of some kind?" Dan persisted.

Jim tilted his head and regarded him with mild suspicion. "I'm sure he probably does. He's too smart to not have a backup plan of some kind. But he never told me where it is, and I never asked."

"You're his case officer, for crying out loud! How can you not know something like that?"

Jim leaned forward, a new light in his eyes. "I don't think you understand the kind of life these undercover guys lead," he said, his voice deceptively quiet. "Alex put his life on the line every damn day. If things went to hell with the gang, he knew there was no way to get backup in time to save him. So yeah, he had a place to retreat and regroup, and no, I didn't press him for details. And, frankly, I'm wondering why you're so interested in his whereabouts."

Dan leaned back in his chair, his thoughts swirling. Jim wasn't as dumb as he looked; he'd underestimated the man. He had to make it seem as though his interest in Malcom was legit, rather than personal.

"I'm interested," he replied evenly, "because I owe it to the men and women who died last night to make sure their killer is brought to justice. Malcom may not have pulled the trigger, but he is responsible just the same. And you need to remember that."

Jim reared back, his face turning the color of putty. "What do you mean by that?" he whispered.

"You're very quick to defend Alex," Dan said, going on the attack. "Maybe we need to extend the scope of this investigation, look into how much you knew, and when."

"I—you—" Jim sputtered, but he was interrupted by the trill of his cell phone. He settled for a glare while he pulled the phone from his pocket and glanced at the display. Then his expression changed, his eyes widening and his eyebrows shooting up. He glanced at Dan. "It's him," he hissed.

Dan leaned forward, excitement and adrenaline boiling in his stomach. This was his chance. "Trace the call," he said. If he had a location, he could send the gang in to collect Malcom before Jim ever got there.

Jim waved a hand in dismissal, and Dan clenched his jaw. Insolent bastard. Not for the first time, Dan cursed his useless legs. If he'd been able, he'd have snatched the phone away from Jim and taken the call himself.

The other man tapped the phone screen and pressed the device to his ear. "Alex?" he said quietly. He reached out to shut the office door, then resumed his seat, curling his body inward like he was cradling something precious.

Dan strained to hear, but he couldn't make out the other side of the conversation.

"You need to come in, man," Jim said, his tone pleading. "We can get this all straightened out—" He broke off, then gasped audibly. "What do you mean? What kind of proof—?" He sounded more urgent now and Dan's ears pricked up at the word "proof." What did Malcom know, or think he knew? Had Alex somehow discovered his role in all of this?

Jim glanced at him, evidently picking up on his heightened interest.

What's he saying? he mouthed to Jim, but the other man shook his head. "All right," he said. "I'll be there."

He hung up and stared at the phone in his hand for a moment, as though he couldn't believe what he'd just heard.

Dan had to bite his tongue to keep from yelling at him, knowing that if he appeared too eager, it would only fan the flames of Jim's suspicions. "What did he say?" he asked, careful to keep his tone even.

Jim jumped, clearly startled by the question. "He said he didn't do it," he replied, sounding a little dazed. "Said he'd been set up."

"Of course he'd say that," Dan scoffed. "He knows every federal agent in DC is gunning for him. Just this morning, I spent an hour on the phone with the DC police, keeping them up to date on our search. Malcom isn't stupid—he's trying to deflect responsibility for this mess so he can save his own ass."

"Maybe." Jim sounded doubtful. "But I still have to investigate what he's saying. You know I can't let allegations like that go unchecked."

Dan nodded, feigning a sincerity he didn't feel. "I understand. Why don't you let me help? I can check into some things while you meet with him."

"That might work." Jim stood, pocketing the phone with a distracted expression. "I'm going to take care of an errand before I head out."

"Where are you meeting him? We need to get a team in place."

Jim was silent for a moment, so Dan decided to press him. "You know we have to bring him in," he said softly. "But they won't kill him."

The other man sighed. "I know. I just… He was my friend. It's hard to stop thinking of him in that light."

"I understand," Dan lied. "Let's take it one step at a time. No one else has to get hurt."

"I hope not." Jim turned to go, stopping at the door. "I'm meeting him at Ben's Chili Bowl in two hours. Let the guys know."

"Will do," Dan said, anticipation building with every step Jim took. When he was sure the other man was far enough down the hall, he wheeled around the desk and shut the door. Then he pulled his burn phone from his pocket and pressed a number.

"Ben's Chili Bowl. Two hours," he said to the expectant silence on the other end of the line. "No survivors."

Chapter 9

"Do you honestly think I'm going to let you walk into an ambush with me?" Alex scowled at Jillian who, despite having just woken up, appeared amazingly sexy with her tousled hair and rumpled nightgown. If he didn't know better, he'd say she had the look of a woman who'd been well satisfied last night. The thought only served to remind him about their kiss, and he quickly shifted his focus before he let *that* distraction take over.

"I don't expect you to *let* me do anything." She smiled sweetly up at him, but he wasn't fooled by her innocent expression. "I'm a grown woman. I'll do what I want, when I want. And I suddenly have a craving for a chili dog."

"Doc—" he began, but she raised her hand to cut him off.

"I'm going with you," she stated. "So you might as well save your breath and your strength."

"It's not safe."

"If it's not safe for me, then it's not safe for you, either. I can protect you."

He shook his head, trying to keep up with her twisted logic. "What the hell are you talking about?"

She sighed, evidently disappointed with his reasoning skills. "You called your case handler because you want to set up a meeting, correct?"

"Yes. But what does that have to do with anything?"

"The way I see it, there are two possible outcomes. One." She held up a finger in illustration. "Your case handler comes to the meeting, along with a team of agents tasked to bring you into custody. Now, they're probably quite pissed at you, since they blame you for the deaths of those people last night. I'm sure any number of those guys wouldn't mind putting a bullet into you as payback, or at the very least, making sure you had a rough time of it during your arrest. If I'm there as a witness, they have to behave themselves, or risk me blabbing to the papers."

Alex shook his head. "If you're with me, they'd just treat you as a suspect, too."

She shrugged. "Probably. That's why I won't be with you. I'll be on the periphery, and when they move in, so will I with my trusty camera." She held up her phone, waving it back and forth.

There were so many flaws in that plan he didn't know where to start. So he settled for asking her about option B. "And what's behind door number two?"

"It's entirely possible the mole in the FBI will find

out about this meeting and send the gang out to intercept you."

"That's exactly what I think will happen."

She nodded. "Me, too. And if I'm there, I can follow them to find out where they take you, then call for help."

"You do realize they're more likely to shoot me where I stand, right?"

She paled a little at that, but shook her head. "No. From what you told me about these guys last night, they won't be happy to just kill you and be done with it. They'll want you to suffer first."

His stomach dropped at the realization that she was probably right. They would want to teach him a lesson, and they would take their time about doing it.

"I still don't want you there. What if they bring Tony? He could identify you, and then they'd take you, as well."

"That won't happen," she said, sounding more confident than he felt. "Tony isn't in any shape to be running around town yet. Besides, even if he was, he saved my life last night by warning me. Why would he have done that if he wanted me dead?"

"Tony has a rather warped sense of honor," Alex said. "You saved his life, so he owed you. As far as he's concerned, that debt has been paid and he doesn't owe you anything else. If he saw you again, he wouldn't think twice about letting the gang take you along, too."

Jillian was silent for a moment, making Alex think she was reconsidering. Although he didn't want to leave her, it was for the best. He was a marked man with a lifespan that could probably be measured in days, if not hours. She had her whole life in front of her. And even if she did want to be with him, once she found out about his role in her brother's death she'd never be able to forgive him. No, there was no way they could be together, and the sooner he left her, the better it would be for his heart. At least he'd been able to spend a few hours with her in his arms...

Finally she stood, giving his chest a pat as she moved past him. "I'm going to hop in the shower," she proclaimed. "And I'm taking your clothes with me. So unless you intend to head out wearing that—" she raked her gaze over the length of him, taking in the too small clothes and his bare feet "—you'll have to wait for me." With a final, smug smile, she left the room. A minute later he heard the bathroom door shut and the lock click into place.

"Damn fool woman," he said, shaking his head. But despite his frustration, he couldn't keep from smiling. She was the only person who believed he was telling the truth—even Jim thought he was lying. Her confidence in him was better than any drug, and made him feel as if he could do anything. Find the mole in the FBI? Absolutely. Take on the 3 Star Killers? Bring it on.

But as much as she helped him, he couldn't, for the life of him, figure out what he did for her. Maybe, when this was all over, he could ask her about it.

"If we even live that long," he said with a snort.

Ben's Chili Bowl was a DC institution, located on U Street near the Metro station. Famous for chili dogs, chili burgers and chili fries, it was a place Jillian generally avoided out of respect for her arteries. As far as meeting places went, though, it was perfect. Everyone in the city knew Ben's, and the place was always busy, which meant witnesses. Lots and lots of witnesses.

Even the winter weather hadn't kept the crowds away, an observation that made Jillian breathe a little easier. While she didn't want anyone to get hurt, she felt a lot safer being around so many people.

She sat in a booth in the back corner, pretending to study the iconic mustard-yellow menu while she watched the front door. Jim should be here any minute…

She let her gaze drift over the other patrons, checking again to make sure she hadn't missed him. Alex had described him, but from where she sat, there didn't appear to be anyone who looked like him in the restaurant. Fortunately, there didn't appear to be any gang members, either, but she couldn't really be sure. Everyone was wearing jackets or long sleeves, which covered any telltale gang tattoos.

She still couldn't believe Alex had agreed to let her come along. She'd stepped out of the bathroom, fully prepared to argue with him again. But rather than insisting she stay behind, he'd told her to get ready. He followed her to the bedroom, standing on the other side of the door to tell her his plan while she quickly dressed.

"That's actually a good idea," she said slowly, tugging a sweater over her head.

His tone was wry. "You don't have to sound so surprised, Doc."

She opened the door to find him leaning against the jamb, ankles and arms crossed. The corner of his mouth quirked up. "I appreciate your faith in me," he said, tapping a fist against his heart. "Means the world."

She shot him a mock glare and walked past him, heading into the den to grab her shoes and coat. "You know that's not what I meant."

He shrugged. "This is my job, you know. You stitch people up, I come up with plans to avoid being captured and killed by psychopathic gang members."

"All in a day's work?"

"Something like that."

Except it wasn't part of her normal routine, and while a small part of her got a little thrill out of the James-Bond-style antics, it was hard to appreciate the novelty of the experience while dealing with the nausea brought on by a severe case of nerves.

It was a new experience, feeling like part of a team. Alex treated her like an equal, and seemed to value her input. Thinking back on it, Mark had never really thought of her as a partner or treated her like one. And why would he? His wife had filled that role. She'd been just a little fun on the side.

Despite their rocky start, Jillian had to admit that she felt closer to Alex than she ever had to Mark. She shook her head at the irony of it. Here she was, putting her trust in a guy who lied for a living. But unlike Mark, she was almost certain that Alex hadn't lied to her. And the fact that he trusted her with his life made her believe in him all the more.

The door opened and a cold breeze swept in, stirring the napkins on the front tables. A man stepped inside, huddled into his coat, his face mostly hidden by a brown knit hat and matching scarf. He glanced around and then took a seat at a nearby table, facing the front of the restaurant.

Jillian craned her head, trying to get a look at his face without being too obvious about it. At this angle, she could make out his profile.

C'mon, take your scarf off...

As if he'd heard her thoughts the new arrival began to unwind his scarf, revealing the lower half of his face after a few tugs. He turned in her direction, and Jillian got her first good look at his face. *That's him*, she realized with a jolt. Time for her to make her move.

Her heart in her throat, Jillian stood and casually walked over to his table. "Jim?" She tried to sound cheerful, but it came out as more of a squeak.

The man glanced up at her, his expression wary. "Do I know you?"

She smiled and pulled out a chair, sitting across from him. "Not yet, but you will."

He held out a hand to stop her. "Actually, I'm—"

"Meeting someone. I know." She leaned forward, lowering her voice. "Let me guess. You're waiting for Alex?"

Jim narrowed his eyes and Jillian swallowed hard when he slid his hand into the pocket of his coat. "Who are you?"

"I'm a friend," she explained, keeping her gaze on his hidden hand. *Please don't shoot me.*

"Where is he?"

"Close. He wanted me to give you this." Keeping her movements slow, Jillian reached into her pocket and removed a cell phone. She placed it on the table and slid it across to him, then pulled her hand back.

Jim stared at the phone for a second, then lifted his eyes to hers. "That looks like his phone."

Jillian nodded. "Yes. Press one and it will call him."

"Why isn't he here?"

"You'll have to ask him that." She held her breath while Jim considered her words. His expression never wavered, giving her no clue as to what he was thinking.

Did he believe her? Or did he think she was connected to the gang and involved in the trouble last night? She did her best to look innocent and non-threatening, willing him to trust her.

Finally, Jim reached out and plucked the phone off the table. "We'll see," he muttered, turning his attention to the phone. Jillian relaxed, the tension leaving her shoulders when his focus shifted off of her. She pushed back from the table and made to stand, but he held up his hand. "Stay there, please." His tone was mild, but there was no doubt he expected her to comply. She froze. This wasn't part of the plan.

She briefly considered making a run for it, but Jim returned his hand to his pocket, his meaning unmistakably clear. Jillian leaned back in her chair and put her hands on the table, trying not to let her fear show. She was supposed to deliver the phone and then leave, getting out of the path of any gang members who came looking for Alex. And while she was confident Tony was still out of action, it was possible one of the guys who'd been at the motel would show up today. And if he recognized her...

A cold chill swept over her, leaving a trail of goose bumps in its wake. She tried not to fidget in her chair, suddenly feeling very vulnerable. Sitting with her back to the door had been a bad move, she realized now. Anyone could walk in and she'd never know. They could walk right up to her, a gun in hand, and she wouldn't realize it until it was too late—

"Where are you?" Jim's question cut through her anxiety, dragging her out of her increasingly frantic thoughts.

He glanced at her. "She's here." He paused, then

spoke again. "I don't see— Fine. Yes." He covered the mouthpiece with his hand and spoke to her. "You can go."

Jillian didn't need to be told twice. She bolted up from the chair and tried not to run from the restaurant, blinking back tears of relief. The blast of cold air that greeted her did wonders to clear her head, and she made it a point to slow her pace as she walked down the street, not wanting to call attention to herself.

She entered a coffee shop about fifty yards away and snagged a seat by the window. The rich aromas of the café wrapped around her, bringing comfort and warmth in equal measure. She simply breathed for a moment, taking advantage of the brief respite before turning her attention to the scene outside.

From this spot she had a nice view of the benches near the African American Civil War Memorial. Alex sat with his back to her, looking like a homeless man in his mismatched layers of fabric. He'd put on most of Jason's clothes, and she'd given him an oversize set of scrubs, several scarves and a blanket in the hope of keeping him warm. He had chemical hand warmers in his pockets, but they were no match for this cold. Still, it was better than nothing.

She'd wanted him to meet Jim in another restaurant, out of the wind and weather, but the stubborn man had quickly shot down her suggestion.

"It's too easy to get trapped if I'm inside. Outside, I can run if I need to."

She settled down to wait, hunching her shoulders in sympathy as another gust of wind blew snow off the memorial statue. Alex had to be freezing, but he didn't move from his spot. "C'mon, move your feet. Move something," she urged him quietly. While she understood his desire to have several escape options available, if his muscles got too cold, he wouldn't be able to run very far or very fast.

The door to Ben's Chili Bowl opened and Jim stepped out, once again wrapped up tight in scarf and hat. He glanced around as if trying to get his bearings and then set off toward the war memorial, his head down. After a moment his long-legged stride brought him to Alex's bench and he sat without looking at the other man.

"Here we go," she whispered.

"Give me one good reason why I shouldn't take you down right here."

Alex glanced at Jim, his eyes tearing up from the biting wind. "Because I'm innocent?"

Jim snorted, his breath forming a white cloud in front of his face. "Can you prove it?"

"Not without Tony's confirmation."

"And where is he?"

"He got shot last night. I had to leave him behind at the motel when the gang found us."

"Us?"

Alex nodded, trying to read the other man's mood. He hadn't sounded tense on the phone, but he also didn't appear to be communicating with anyone. Had he really come without a team in place?

"Is she part of 'us'?"

"'She'?" He decided to play dumb, stalling for time. He wasn't sure he could trust Jim, and he didn't want Jillian's name to get out, especially when he hadn't yet figured out the identity of the mole.

"The woman who handed me your phone. How is she a part of this? Is she with the gang?"

"No. She's an innocent bystander who got pulled in against her will."

"Oh?" Jim arched a brow, staring past him. "Then why is she still involved? And if she's so innocent, why is she watching us from that coffee shop down the block?"

Damn. He should have known Jim would find her. He never missed a trick. "She's trying to help me prove my innocence."

"Uh-huh."

"Listen to me, Jim. Please. We don't have much time."

Jim narrowed his eyes. "What makes you say that?"

"I called you out here because I think the gang is going to show up at Ben's any minute, looking for me."

"Did you call them?"

"No!" Alex thrust a hand through his hair, wishing he could come up with the magic words to make Jim understand what was going on. "They're after me because they know I'm a Fed. Someone in the Bureau told them—the same someone who tipped them off about the operation last night."

"Popular opinion has it that you're the one who betrayed us."

"I'm not—I swear it. Look at me." He waited until Jim made eye contact. "We've known each other for years. We go back to the Academy together. You know I would never do something like this. I'm not that guy."

Jim sighed, then looked away. "It's really hard to believe you, when the evidence suggests otherwise."

"What evidence?"

"The events of last night are pretty hard to ignore," Jim said, his voice rising with anger. "Do you know how many people we lost? And not just us—DEA, ATF. Everyone took a hit."

Alex closed his eyes as the memories assaulted him. "I know," he whispered. "I tried to stop it, but I couldn't."

"So why not just come in? Clear your name?"

"I can't. Not when the mole is still in place. Don't you see? If I come in, he or she will go back into hiding and we'll never know who it is. But if I stay out here…" He gestured with his arm, encompassing the snowy landscape. "They'll keep trying to find me. And eventually they'll make a mistake."

Jim shook his head. "That's some pretty thin logic."

"So bring me in now. Don't you have a team in place? What are you waiting for? If you don't believe me, give them the sign."

Jim frowned and Alex realized his earlier suspicion was right—Jim *had* come alone. A surge of hope filled his chest. Since Jim hadn't brought in a team, that meant he still trusted him.

"You're alone," he said quietly.

"I wasn't supposed to be," Jim said. He sounded distracted, as though he was thinking out loud. "They were supposed to meet me here."

Alex glanced around involuntarily, but he saw no signs of a tactical team. Excitement mixed with dread as the pieces began to fall into place. "Who knows you were meeting me here?"

Jim opened his mouth to respond, but Alex's attention was caught by the arrival of a boxy sedan as it pulled to a stop in front of Ben's. The same sedan from the motel last night.

"It's them," he hissed, grabbing Jim's arm. "Don't move."

Three men emerged from the car, moving with a predatory grace that made him think of lions on a hunt. Even from this distance, it was easy to tell they were heavily armed and well-versed in physical violence. They entered the restaurant and Alex slowly removed his hand, tucking it back into the warmth of his pocket.

"Swear to me you didn't call them," Jim said, his voice low and fierce.

"If I had, wouldn't I be running over there to greet them?" Alex shot back. "Now answer my question— who did you tell?"

Jim was silent for a moment. When he spoke again, he sounded dazed. "Dan Pryde. But I can't believe he'd do something like this. It has to be someone else— maybe he said something—"

"No." Alex cut him off, the name hitting him like a punch to the gut. "It's him." He leaned forward, putting his head in his hands. "Why didn't I see it before?" he murmured.

It all made a sick kind of sense. After the training accident at the Academy, Dan had blamed him for his injuries. A thorough investigation had been conducted and it was determined that the accident was due to a loose hand-hold on the obstacle wall. Both Alex and Dan were cleared of any fault, and the Bureau had assumed responsibility for the accident and had taken care of all of Dan's medical bills and physical therapy. Even now, they continued to provide him with a mechanized wheelchair to ensure his mobility was as good as possible.

He'd spoken to Dan several times after the accident, trying to be supportive. But Dan had ignored every overture, steadfast in his belief that Alex hadn't tried hard enough to save him. No amount of official documentation would convince him otherwise. After a while, Alex had stopped trying to get through to the other man, and he'd lost track of where Dan had ended up in the Bureau.

It seemed Dan had kept tabs on him, though.

"Why would Dan work with the 3 Star Killers?"

"To get back at me. For his accident."

Jim's eyes widened above the scarf. "That's crazy! It wasn't your fault."

"Yeah, well. He's always blamed me for it. And if he found out I infiltrated the gang, he could get his revenge by revealing my identity. The gang would take care of the rest and no one at the Bureau would know he'd ratted me out."

"Speaking of the gang," Jim said, his voice tight. "They've realized you're not inside."

Alex resisted the urge to jerk his head around to stare at Ben's. Quick movements would only attract the attention of the gang enforcers, something he definitely wanted to avoid. Slowly, he turned to face the restaurant, his heart kicking into double-time when he saw the men scanning the street, frowning in displeasure.

"I think it's time to go," he said. He caught Jim's answering nod in his peripheral vision, gratified to see the other man was keeping his movements subtle, as well.

"I'm going to head to the Metro," Alex continued. "I think you should walk in the opposite direction. They're not interested in you, and if you leave the area, they probably won't even notice you."

"Sounds good," Jim said softly. "I'll wait to leave until you're gone. If we both get up at the same time, it'll look suspicious."

"Thanks, man. Keep in touch—you know how to get hold of me." He patted his pocket, feeling the solid, comforting weight of Jillian's cell phone through the fabric. Then he stood and walked toward the Metro station, keeping his head forward and his pace measured.

After a few steps he started to breathe normally again. He'd done it—Jim believed him. He knew the identity of the mole in the organization, and he'd evaded the gang one more time. Maybe it was his lucky day after all.

Right after the thought entered his mind, everything went to hell.

An angry shout behind him and the pop, pop, pop of gunshots signaled that this was not to be a clean get-away, after all. Alex darted to the side and crouched behind a trash can, trying to make himself as small as possible. He looked back in time to see the three gang enforcers approach Jim, their guns out and pointing at him. They needn't have bothered with the show of force. Jim was lying helpless on the frozen ground, his hands pressed to his belly as he tried to staunch the flow of blood that darkened his coat.

The lead man squatted and pulled the scarf from Jim's face. He cursed loudly, then stood and turned to his companions, shaking his head. The three men glanced around, one of them pointing in Alex's direction.

"No, you bastards," Alex muttered, willing them to

walk the other way. He had to get to Jim, to help the man before he bled out. Although…

A new plan struck him while the gang debated their next move. Alex had no idea what to do for Jim from a medical perspective, but Jillian did. And he was willing to bet she'd seen the shooting from her spot at the café window. Although he hadn't known her very long, he was certain she wouldn't turn away from a person in need, and if he could draw the gang away from the scene, it would be safe for her to help Jim. As an added bonus, if the gang was chasing him, they would be certain to leave her alone.

Decision made, Alex took a deep breath and stood, waving his arms for good measure. "Looking for someone, boys?" he called.

The effect was immediate. The three men swung their guns to point at him and after a second's hesitation, took off, running toward him with all the grace of deer on a frozen pond.

Alex waited a few heartbeats, making sure they were committed to giving chase before he turned and started to run. His plan wouldn't work if they gave up and returned to the scene to finish Jim off. He slipped and slid his way down the sidewalk, his shoulders hunched in anticipation of the bullet that was sure to hit him at any moment.

The entrance to the Metro station was about fifty feet away. Alex headed for it with grim determination, his legs and lungs burning with the effort of running in the snow and ice. The sounds of labored breathing grew louder behind him, but he didn't dare look back. Instead he put his head down and pushed himself to go faster. He saw the black metal pole of the Metro sign race by in his peripheral vision. Almost there…

About ten feet from the station entrance, his foot hit a slippery patch and he twisted, wrenching his knee and ankle hard as he flailed to keep from going down. *Don't fall, don't fall!* No way would he be able to recover from that.

By some miracle he managed to stay on his feet, but he wound up facing his pursuers.

The man in the middle met his eyes, his lips twisting in a cruel grin. "Got you now!" he shouted. He kept moving forward, while the guy on the left slowed, raising his gun and bracing himself to fire.

Alex didn't wait to see what the third man was up to. He turned and hobbled toward the escalator, half running, half hopping to accommodate his injured leg. Ignoring the pain, he hit the escalators and began swinging down, placing his hands on the railings and pushing his legs out to land several steps ahead. He was a sitting duck while riding the escalator—any fool could fire in a straight line.

He hit the bottom with a jolt that made him see stars. Plowing ahead, he narrowly avoided barreling into two men heading toward him.

"Whoa, buddy. Slow down there."

Alex glanced up and nearly laughed in relief. A DC patrol cop had his hand up and was frowning, as though trying to decide if Alex was going to be trouble.

You don't know the half of it, mister, he thought.

The cop looked him up and down, his eyes narrowing as he took in Alex's bizarre appearance. "What's your hurry?"

"I'm being chased by three men with guns. They

shot a guy at the African American Civil War Memorial." The words came out in a breathless rush, but the cops understood him well enough.

"Stay here," one of them said. They both drew their weapons and approached the escalators warily, leaving Alex behind. While he wanted nothing more than to watch the bad guys get what they deserved, he'd settle for the highlight reel on the nightly news.

He approached the turnstiles and hiked first one leg then the other over the automated divider. Fortunately the attendant station was empty, so there was no one to protest his actions. He swung down a second, shorter escalator and made it to the platform just as a train came rolling into the station. The cars were mostly empty, so he was able to board as soon as the doors opened. He settled onto a bench by the door and tugged his cap down, sighing heavily when the train began to move.

Pressing his back up against the window, he stretched his injured leg out on the seat, ignoring the twinges of pain that accompanied the movement. His knee and ankle felt tight and hot; it was just a matter of time before the joints froze up completely, which would make it nearly impossible for him to move. Fortunately, Jillian's apartment wasn't terribly far away.

They'd agreed to meet back at her place if anything went wrong. He stuck his hand in his pocket, relieved when his fingers hit the metal of her spare key. He'd half expected to find that it had fallen out while he was running.

Score one for the good guys.

He closed his eyes and relaxed into the rocking rhythm of the train as it rolled along the tracks. He flashed back to his last glimpse of Jim, lying in the snow with his hands pressed to his gut. A wave of nausea hit him, along with the chilling realization that if Jim died, no one in the FBI would believe Dan was the double agent.

Please, Jillian. She had to save him. He didn't think he could handle one more death on his conscience.

He thought back to her actions yesterday, treating Tony in the dimly lit motel room. She'd been calm and collected, her movements controlled and strangely beautiful to watch. It made sense that she would be the same with Jim. Although Jim's injuries seemed worse than Tony's single gunshot wound, Alex's confidence in her abilities didn't waver.

He just hoped his faith in her would be enough to save Jim.

Chapter 10

Jillian stared out the window of the café, her mouth open in a silent scream as the carnage unfolded in front of her.

She'd almost thrown up when the gang enforcers had arrived. But after they'd emerged from Ben's Chili Bowl empty-handed, she'd thought they would just leave. She should have known they wouldn't give up so easily.

From her spot at the window, she could see Alex crouched behind a trash can, out of sight of the gang members. "Get out of there," she muttered, willing him to sneak away with every bit of energy she possessed. The shooters were going to start looking around soon, and a trash can wasn't exactly a great hiding place. If he left now, his head start might keep the gang from finding him…

Keeping her eyes on him, she pulled the phone from

her pocket and dialed 9-1-1 to report the shooting. The operator asked her to stay on the line, but she hung up. As soon as the gang left, she was heading out there to help Jim, and she'd need both hands free.

"Oh, my God, what's happening out there?" One of the baristas appeared by her side, staring out the window with a kind of eager, horrified fascination.

"A man was shot," Jillian replied absently. The young woman pulled out her phone, but rather than using it to call for help, she held it up and began recording the scene.

"No way. This is the worst thing I've ever seen. Look at all that blood—it's so gross! I think I'm gonna throw up. Is that guy dead?" The girl kept up this running commentary, pressing closer to the window to get a better view.

Jillian wanted to scream at her, but was distracted by a sudden flash of movement.

Alex stepped out from behind the trash can, waving his arms to attract the attention of the gang. Time slowed to a crawl and she saw the exact moment each of the three enforcers recognized Alex—the subtle jerk of realization, the jolt of energy and anticipation traveling along their limbs, the eager light sparking to life in their eyes when they glimpsed their prey. Their shouts were drowned out by the rush of blood in her ears and the scene in front of her grew blurry when Alex turned and ran, the men hot on his trail.

"Did you see that guy? Where'd he come from?"

Paralyzing despair clawed at Jillian, keeping her feet rooted to the floor of the café. What had he done? She brushed impatiently at her tears, rubbing her eyes clear. The answer was simple—he'd tried to save his friend. If she'd harbored any doubts about his innocence, his actions had just proved that he was one of the good guys.

Please be safe, please be safe, please be safe...

Alex had done his part to help Jim. Now it was her turn.

She turned and headed for the door, grabbing the bar towel off the shoulder of the still-filming girl as she walked past. Ignoring the girl's startled yelp, Jillian pushed out into the cold and made her way over to Jim, crunching through the snow and ice as quickly as possible.

He was ominously quiet as she approached. Most of the gunshot victims she treated were very vocal about their pain, yelling and screaming for all the hospital to hear. In her years as an ER doctor, she'd developed a kind of mental triage for patients—the louder they were, the less serious their injuries tended to be. It was the quiet ones she worried about. If her patients couldn't make noise, they were in dire straits indeed.

A splash of bright crimson marred the white perfection of the snow, lending an irrationally festive air to the gory scene. Jillian dropped to her knees beside him and yanked on his scarf, pressing her fingers to his exposed neck in search of a pulse. It was rapid and thready, but there.

Jim moaned and stirred at her touch, moving his hands in a weak protest when she unbuttoned his coat. "Don't move," she told him, pulling the folds of his coat apart and pushing up his sweater to expose his belly.

There were two entrance wounds, both in the upper right quadrant of his abdomen. She scowled, imagining the likely path of the bullets as they ripped through skin and muscle, passing through his liver on their jour-

ney through his tissues. There was no way to tell how
bad his internal injuries were just by looking at him—
his liver, intestines and even his kidney were all potentially damaged. It was also possible he would walk
away relatively unscathed. Such were the vagaries of
gunshot wounds.

Still, until she knew for sure, she had to act under
the assumption that the internal trauma was extensive.
The bleeding of his entrance wounds had slowed to a
trickle, but he could be hemorrhaging into his abdominal cavity. She placed the bar towel over the small,
round holes, pleased to find that his abdomen yielded to
the pressure of her fingertips. If the bullets had hit the
hepatic or renal arteries, his abdomen would be filled
with blood and rigid to the touch. She'd need a CT scan
to confirm her hunch, but it seemed that Jim had been
very lucky indeed.

Outside of an emergency room, she couldn't do anything more for Jim. He needed fluids, scans, surgery—
all things she couldn't provide. While she wanted to
check for exit wounds, rolling him by herself was too
risky. Better to leave him and let the doctors examine him fully once he arrived at the hospital. About
the only treatment option left to her was to try to keep
him warm. The frigid temperature may have helped to
slow his bleeding, but it also made him more vulnerable to shock.

Jillian tugged his sweater down and closed his coat,
then pulled off her own coat and laid it over him. She
tucked the ends under him as best she could, wishing
in vain for a blanket.

"Oh, my gosh, is he dead?"

The girl from the café was back, her hand clapped

over her mouth as she stared down at them with wide eyes. At least she wasn't filming anymore.

"No," Jillian said shortly. "But I need your help. Bring me any coats from the store, and I need a box— about this big." She held out her hands to demonstrate. The girl nodded, then turned and scrambled back to the café.

Jillian knelt by Jim's head, feeling for a pulse again. Fast, but getting stronger. "Hang in there," she murmured.

His eyes fluttered open, unfocused and dazed. "Alex?" he croaked.

"He's fine," Jillian assured him.

"No. Not safe." Jim struggled to move, so she put her hands on his shoulders and pressed gently to hold him down.

"Stay still," she said calmly.

"Have to warn him. Dan…have to tell…" He was growing more distressed, which was troubling. Agitation was a common sign of early shock, and it didn't take long for patients to slide into the full-blown, no-coming-back version. If the ambulance didn't arrive soon, she might not be able to keep him stable for much longer.

The young woman returned, carrying two coats and a cardboard box. Jillian placed the box under Jim's feet, raising them about ten inches off the ground. She laid one of the coats across his torso, then rolled up the other and placed it under his head. His breathing and pulse were still steady, but for how much longer?

"What else can I do?" The girl was swaying back and forth on her feet, her worried gaze cutting from Jim to Jillian and back again. Jim was still muttering about the gang and the traitor in the FBI, and although his voice was soft and his words indistinct, Jillian didn't want to take a chance on the girl hearing something she shouldn't.

"Go stand at the curb and wave down the ambulance," Jillian said. She could hear the faint sounds of sirens, and hoped with a fierce desperation that they were headed her way and not part of the normal symphony of city sounds.

It was strange, sitting by a patient and having nothing to do. Normally she didn't stop moving once someone came into her ER—she assessed injuries, ordered tests, probed, prodded and stitched as needed. But without the tools of her trade, she could do little more than offer moral support to Jim. It was unsettling; to be idle when she knew there was so much more that needed to be done for him. A kind of helpless anxiety stole over her, making her stomach churn queasily and her breathing hitch. She reached out to offer Jim a comforting pat, but pulled back when she saw how badly her hand was shaking.

It's the cold, she thought. Now that she had stopped working, she realized just how glacial it was outside without a coat to block the wind. The tremor of her hand extended up her arm, then took over her whole body in violent, racking shivers.

It's just the cold.

But deep down she knew her reaction was due to more than just the arctic temperatures. The last time she'd felt so powerless in the face of a medical emergency was when her brother had overdosed. Seeing Jason lying on the floor, as unmoving as a corpse, had changed her. Something inside her had cracked, and now she could feel the fissure growing wider. Although Jim's situation was nothing like Jason's had been, the feeling of paralyzing frustration was the same.

So was the fear.

It was hard to understand Jim's mumblings, but his overall tone seemed to be one of worry for Alex. That meant Alex must have convinced Jim of his innocence—an important first step in discovering the mole in the FBI. But if Jim died, Alex would be back to square one with no one to support his claims of a traitor. And what if that had been the plan all along?

A chill that had nothing to do with the weather skittered down her spine at the thought. Alex had been so sure that the gang would find out about this meeting thanks to the mole—it was why he'd insisted on moving out of Ben's Chili Bowl in the first place. She supposed Jim could have called them, but why would the thugs shoot him if he was their source in the organization?

Perhaps they hadn't recognized him, with his face obscured by the scarf and cap. But no, she mused, recalling the scene in her mind's eye. Once the enforcers realized he wasn't Alex, they hadn't attempted to help him. If Jim was the mole, the gang wouldn't have left him there to die. That meant they had to be working with someone else, someone who may have wanted them to kill Jim so he couldn't help Alex clear his name.

If Alex is even still alive, she thought bitterly.

Seeing the gang members run after him had taken years off her life. How could one unarmed man hold up against three hardened killers? They'd already demonstrated a propensity to shoot first and ask questions later. They wouldn't hesitate to gun down Alex, and she knew they wouldn't stop at one shot, either. His earlier stunt had been like waving a red flag in front of a bull, and there was no way they would let him get away with something like that. And he'd let them get close before he'd started to run, deliberately taunting them in a foolish act of bravery. Jillian shook her head at the memory, her chest aching with a mix of pride and anguish over Alex's selfless gesture.

It all seemed so hopeless. The only person who could do anything to help Alex clear his name was lying next to her, dying by inches on the frozen ground while she buried him in coats in a futile attempt to keep him warm. Alex was gone, having served himself up as bait to draw the bad guys away from his friend and her. And she was next to useless, her efforts stymied by a lack of equipment and supplies.

Some doctor you are.

She wanted to give in to her despair, to collapse into a sniffling, crying heap on the ground, but she couldn't do that to Jim. The need to keep him alive was her driving motivation right now. No matter what may have happened to Alex, she owed it to him to help his friend. Worst case scenario...she swallowed hard and blinked back tears, then took a deep, fortifying breath. If Alex had died, Jim would make sure his memory wasn't tarnished by lies and that his killers were brought to justice. It wasn't a very comforting thought, but she clutched it to her heart like a talisman.

"You're going to be okay," she said, though she wasn't really sure if she was talking to Jim, to Alex or to herself. All of the above, she supposed.

"Hurts," Jim said quietly. He opened his eyes and really focused on her for the first time since she'd started treating him. She offered him a smile while she hugged herself and rubbed her arms with her hands in a bid to conserve what little body heat she had left.

"I hate to break it to you," she said, teeth chattering. "But pain is good. Means you're still alive."

His mouth twisted; an attempted smile that turned into a grimace. "You sound like…PT instructor…in the Academy." His words were slow and slurred, but at least he was still conscious.

"Tell me about him." She had to keep him talking, keep him awake until the ambulance arrived. If the sound of the sirens was any indication, it should be here any minute.

"Tough bastard," he said. "Like Alex. Strong."

"You know he's innocent," Jillian said.

Jim closed his eyes but mumbled, "Yes."

The ambulance roared to a stop by the curb, the back bay doors popping open with the force of an explosion. She was relieved to see the paramedics, but before she left Jim's side, she needed to know that he would help Alex.

"Promise you'll help him clear his name." When he didn't respond, she shook him gently. "Promise," she repeated, a little louder this time.

Jim's eyelids fluttered and it was obvious the effort of speaking was proving too much for him. "Dan…Dan is the traitor. Don't trust…" With that, Jim lapsed into unconsciousness.

One of the paramedics knelt by Jim's side, facing Jillian. "Ma'am, I need you to move." He peeled the jackets off of Jim and she grabbed hers, pulling it on with shaking fingers.

Jillian spoke before thinking, instinct taking over. "He's got a double GSW to the right upper quadrant.

No exit wounds visible. Slight tachycardia. Respiratory rate 20 bpm."

The medic blinked at her, but didn't waste time questioning her qualifications. "How long has he been down?"

"About ten minutes."

He placed a blood pressure cuff around Jim's arm. Jillian tried to be patient while he worked, but it was hard letting someone else run the show. Her fingers tingled with the temptation to root through the medic's bag to find the materials she needed, her confidence returning with the arrival of medical supplies.

The driver brought over a backboard and placed it next to Jim. Recognizing her chance, Jillian positioned herself so she could see Jim's back as the paramedics gently rolled him onto the board. Her heart sank when she saw the smooth, unbroken skin, pink from the cold and his position. No exit wounds. Not good.

"Do you know him?" the second medic asked while he buckled Jim onto the gurney.

Jillian thought quickly. If she said no, she'd be forced to stay here and give her statement to the police officer who'd just showed up. He was busy talking to the girl from the café, but he'd want to get her statement, as well. If, on the other hand, she said yes, she'd be allowed to ride along in the ambulance. She could make sure Jim was receiving the best care, and if he happened to regain consciousness on the trip to the hospital, she'd be there to hear anything he might reveal.

Her decision got a lot easier when the waitress pointed her way, her mouth working a mile a minute as she no doubt recounted everything she'd seen from the warm safety of the café. The cop turned his head to follow her gesture, his gaze landing on Jillian with surprising weight. There was an alarming degree of suspicion in his eyes, as if he thought perhaps Jillian had shot Jim, then run out of the café to try to save him. What exactly was that girl telling him?

Jillian opted not to stick around to find out. "He's my friend," she said. The lie triggered a twinge of guilt, but she justified it by telling herself that because Jim was Alex's friend, he was, according to the transitive property that applied to relationships as well as mathematics, her friend, as well. Or at least he would be, by the time this was all over.

"We're taking him to Howard," the medic said. Jillian nodded her approval. Howard University Hospital was a Level 1 Trauma Center, which would greatly improve Jim's chances for recovery.

"I want to ride along." She followed as the two men wheeled the gurney toward the ambulance, careful to keep hold of it so they didn't lose control on the icy pavement.

The driver started to disagree, but his partner cut him off. "Do you have some kind of medical background? You talk like a nurse."

"I'm a doctor," she replied automatically. The men shared a look that spoke volumes. "But he's your patient," she hastened to add, wanting to make it clear she wouldn't interfere with their treatment of Jim.

"Your call," the driver muttered.

They reached the back of the ambulance and the men boosted Jim into the bay. Once he was secure, the driver stepped back and closed one of the doors before heading toward the cabin. Jillian stayed where she was, waiting for an invitation to board.

"Come on up, Doc," the medic called. "Get the door behind you."

She clambered up ungracefully to land in a heap on the bench seat and then reached behind her to grab the door. She gave it a tug, but a large hand suddenly appeared, catching the door before it closed. A shadow crossed the floor of the bay as the police officer stepped into view.

"I need to talk to her." He nodded at Jillian, but didn't make eye contact with her.

The medic spared him a glance. "She'll be at the hospital. We're headed to Howard."

"I need to speak to her now."

The driver's voice crackled over the speaker. "Murph, what's the holdup back there?"

Murph pressed a button on the wall. "Two seconds." Then he returned to the process of starting an IV, his movements practiced and smooth. He didn't bother to look up when he spoke again. "Sorry, but she's a doctor. I need her with me."

The cop opened his mouth to protest, but Murph cut him off. "Close us up. We'll see you at the ER."

The man's jaw hardened and for a heartbeat Jillian thought he was going to refuse, or worse, reach into the ambulance and pull her out. Then he shot her a glare and slammed the door shut.

Murph pressed the button again. "We're a go."

The driver didn't waste any time. They took off with a lurch, the back tires sliding for a breathless second before finding purchase in the icy slush that coated the road. Jillian planted her feet on the floor and gripped the seat hard, struggling to stay on the bench when they rounded a corner.

"What's your name, Doc?"

"Jillian Mahoney."

The medic nodded, but kept his focus on Jim. "What do you do?"

"I'm in the ER at GW," she replied, using the standard shorthand for George Washington Hospital.

He whistled, long and low. "Busy place—we take a lot of patients there. You probably get a ton of GSWs."

GSW was emergency parlance for gunshot wound, a depressingly common injury in any urban setting.

"All the time."

"You did a nice job keeping him stable. He's lucky you were there." There was no accusation in his tone, but she could tell he was curious to know what had happened.

"I was in the café. Three men walked over and shot him when he tried to run. They didn't stick around for long afterward." No way was she going to mention Alex, or the real reason why Jim had been shot. Better for him to think it was a random event.

Murph was quiet for a moment, and even though he never looked at her, Jillian could tell he was weighing the truth of her words.

"Like I said," he remarked, reaching over to fiddle with the IV line. "He was lucky you were there."

The ambulance stopped, the vehicle rocking slightly when the driver closed his door. "Get ready to move," Murph told her.

She jumped out as soon as the bay doors opened, then stepped to the side to get out of the way. The medics rolled Jim out in a fluid, practiced motion. Once again, Jillian was relegated to the role of bystander,

with nothing to do but watch as they pushed Jim toward the ER.

Murph stopped at the door, letting his partner roll
Jim into the hospital. Moving quickly, he stripped off
his jacket and tossed it to her. "You're still shivering.
Zip up."

"I can't take this—"

"Sure you can. I know where to find you when I need
it back." He shot her a dimpled grin before turning to
catch up with the gurney.

She debated going after him for a split second, but
another gust of icy wind blasted through her clothes,
chilling her through to the bone. Shaking slightly, she
quickly slid into the still-warm coat, grateful for the additional layer. As an added benefit, the jacket provided
a little bit of a disguise—Grumpy Cop would be looking for her green sweater and black coat, not a navy
paramedic's jacket. To complete the effect, she pulled
her hair free of the ponytail, letting it form a sheltering
curtain around her face.

Now that Jim was safe—or as safe as he was going to
get—she had to get to Alex. The plan was to meet back
at her apartment if things went bad. While she didn't
have any experience in this kind of thing, it seemed
things had gone very badly indeed. But would Alex
be there to greet her when she got home? More importantly, if he wasn't, what could she do about it?

"Explain to me why I should continue to help you,
when all you ever do is fail." Dan felt his throat tighten
as he struggled to keep his voice down. The walls of
his office weren't particularly thin, but if he started

yelling, he had no doubt people would come running. And attention was the last thing he needed right now.

"It's not a total failure," the man on the other end of the line protested. "We shot one of them."

"The wrong one!"

"I don't think so. You told us to pop 'em both. The way I see it, the job is half done."

"And you think you deserve some kind of reward for that?"

"Be patient. We'll get it done."

"Let me explain something to you," Dan said, gritting his teeth so hard it was a wonder he didn't break his jaw. "If Jim recovers from his injuries, he'll know that I was the one who revealed his location to the gang. That means my role in all of this will be discovered. And believe me when I tell you that I will not hesitate to sell you out to save my ass."

"Relax, my man. That guy is not getting up."

"You'll forgive me if I don't believe you, seeing how nothing else has gone as planned."

"What's your beef with Malcom, anyway? Why're you so obsessed with finding him?"

Dan closed his eyes as he gripped his thigh with his free hand. It was the strangest thing, this numbness that was his constant companion. He could feel his leg, mold his palm to curve around the muscle and bone. But like a one-way street, the sensation only moved in a single direction. His leg, which should have registered the contact, was inert and unfeeling. Useless. In fact, everything below his waist was a black void of nothingness. It was as though his body had been cut in two, his legs, knees and feet—all of them gone.

To make matters worse, he was still attached to the

corpses of those once-functional limbs, a constant reminder of what he had lost. The doctors might as well have amputated them, for all the good they did him. Some days, he wished they had. Then he wouldn't feel the rage, white-hot and blinding, that came over him when he looked down unawares and was reminded of the fact that he still had those traitorous legs.

And the man who had condemned him to this shadow life had never been made to answer for his actions.

"Don't worry about my motivations," he said, unwilling to discuss something so personal with a hired thug. "Just keep looking."

Malcom may have been born under a lucky star, but that luck had to run out sometime.

And Dan was going to make sure he was there when it did.

Chapter 11

Alex paced the length of Jillian's den, his steps uneven and awkward as he tried to keep his weight off his injured leg. Her apartment wasn't very big, but the sharp, shooting pains emanating from his knee made the distance seem endless.

Where was she? Why wasn't she back yet? Had she managed to save Jim?

Or had the gang come back?

He stopped, the thought of the gang finding her making his already weak knee wobble dangerously. Moving gingerly, he lowered himself to her couch, then immediately wished he'd gone for the bathroom instead. His stomach churned in a threatening manner and his skin felt clammy and cold.

I should have made sure the cops found them.

If he'd stuck around to verify that the police officers

had apprehended the gang enforcers, he would know without a doubt that Jillian was safe, that they hadn't run back to get their car and stumbled upon her helping Jim.

It was all too easy to imagine the scene—Jillian, kneeling next to Jim, her attention absorbed by her patient. She'd be totally unaware of the approach of the enforcers until it was too late. He pictured the three men stopping, their anger overflowing to spill onto her defenseless head. Would they shoot her outright for interfering with Jim? Would they pull her away, using her as a hostage to cover their retreat? Or would she get caught in the cross fire as they battled it out with the police?

A thousand scenarios flashed through his mind, each more gruesome and horrifying than the last. How could he have left her there, alone and unprotected? What if the driver from the car had grabbed her and she was even now in the custody of the gang? A shudder racked his body and he leaned forward, gulping air while he fought to calm both his stomach and his racing heart.

Snap out of it! Panic clawed at him with sharp, digging fingers, but he forced himself to relax, focusing on each body part in isolation and consciously releasing the tension from his muscles. First his toes. Then his feet. His ankles were next.

By the time he made it up to his hips, he was breathing normally again. When he got to his shoulders, his thoughts had calmed enough that he started to come up with options. Wrapping himself in a cloak of panic was not the way to help Jillian. And while wandering the streets in search of her would satisfy his need to *do* something, it wasn't the best way to go about finding her.

First things first. He had to try to get the swelling

in his knee to subside so he could regain some mobility. Right now, he could barely walk across the room, much less run. If something had happened to Jillian, he was in no shape to help her in his current condition.

Bracing his hands on the couch, Alex pushed to his feet and headed for the kitchen before the pain made him change his mind. The bottle of ibuprofen was sitting on the counter by the sink, and he shook a few pills into his hand, washing them down with a handful of water from the faucet. He patted his face dry with the dish towel, then hobbled to the freezer and assembled an ice pack, wrapping the ice cubes directly in the towel. It would get soggy after a bit, but he didn't know where she kept the plastic bags, and he was reluctant to search through the kitchen drawers. Even though he wasn't snooping around, it seemed wrong to go through Jillian's things without her knowledge or permission. Although he was fairly certain she wouldn't begrudge his search for a sandwich bag, he hadn't known her long enough to feel comfortable making himself at home in her space.

He shook his head at the irony of the situation. Here he was, going out of his mind with worry about a woman he barely knew. In a little more than twenty-four hours, she'd gotten under his skin and was swiftly working her way into his heart. That had to be some kind of record. And yet, despite the growing intensity of his feelings, he hesitated to open a few drawers in the name of practicality.

"Don't be an idiot," he muttered. "It's the kitchen, not her underwear drawer."

Shaking his head at his own foolishness, he pulled open the closest drawer and was rewarded with the sight of the bags he sought. It took only a moment to fortify his ice pack, and he set off for the couch once again. He'd give the drugs and the ice half an hour to work their magic, and then he was heading back out into the city.

His plan was simple; he'd go back to the Civil War Memorial to try to trace Jillian's steps from there. He knew there was a hospital nearby. That was probably where they would have taken Jim, if he hadn't died on the sidewalk.

The thought made the tiny hairs on his skin prickle with unease. Not only would Jim's death make it harder for him to prove his innocence, but he considered the man to be a friend. He had few enough of those left— he certainly didn't want to lose one.

He still felt shell-shocked at the revelation that Dan was the likely mole in the Bureau. It was no secret Dan still harbored some resentment toward him for his part in the training accident, even if that part was limited to the simple fact that he had been present when it happened. But Alex had never imagined Dan's resentment would morph into hatred so deep and pervasive it would lead him to betray the very people he worked with day in and day out. Hate that strong changed a person, poisoning them from the inside out. How long had Dan been carrying around such a toxic blend of emotion? How long had he been living inside a hell of his own making?

And most importantly of all, had the destructive forces he'd set into motion touched Jillian?

He couldn't quite put his finger on the moment when she had begun to matter so much to him. But somehow she'd gone from being a stranger to a woman he cared deeply about, one he wanted to get to know better. And if his instincts were right, she felt drawn to him, as well.

Memories of last night filled his mind. The way she'd touched him, her explorations of his body simultaneously bold and hesitant, as though she was trying not to hurt him. The way she'd responded to his touch, sighing in the dark while she arched against him, silently asking for more. Physically, they couldn't be more compatible. It had taken every ounce of his willpower to stop her hands last night. But he knew now, as he had then, that if she'd continued to touch him, his desire for her would overcome his common sense.

On a rational level, he figured that some of the spark between them was due to the adrenaline of their situation. When emotions ran high, so, too, did passions. But there was more to it than that. She was a truly remarkable woman—intelligent, sarcastic, caring, with a strong practical streak. She was by turns ruthless and gentle; a contradiction that he imagined served her well in her life as a doctor. He wanted very much to spend time with her, time that wasn't weighed down by the heavy threat of discovery or violence.

A small, cowardly part of him wanted to forget about her brother, to pretend it had never happened. Alex knew she would never look at him the same way once she realized he'd been there, that he'd done nothing to save Jason as he lay dying on the dirty pavement of the alley. It was going to break his heart to tell her, but she deserved to know her brother's fate. The agony of the unknown was far greater than the pain of the truth—better for her to have closure.

Even if it meant losing her.

But now wasn't the time. She was going to push

him out of her life after he told her about Jason, and he wasn't willing to leave her just yet. Not until he was absolutely certain of her safety.

And just when will that be?

It was easy to justify keeping his secret a little while longer while they worked to clear his name with the Bureau and stay one step ahead of the 3 Star Killers. But what about after? Jillian was never going to be one hundred percent safe—she was a woman living alone in a major city that had its fair share of crime. Her job kept her on the front lines, exposing her to the aftermath of violence every day. There wasn't going to be a single moment in time that he could identify as being "safe" enough for her to learn about her brother.

It was tempting, too tempting, to imagine walking away after this was over. He could fade from her life, and she'd never be the wiser. At least then she might carry some fond memories of him, and their last moments together wouldn't be stained with anger, hurt and guilty confessions. But that was the problem. He didn't *want* to walk away from her. He wanted to be a part of her life. And that meant he had to tell her. If he kept the secret, it would eat away at his soul, much like Dan's anger had festered over the years. If he and Jillian had any real shot at being together, there was no room for a secret such as that in their relationship.

Assuming she even wants you.

He wasn't exactly a prize catch at the moment. His once-sterling reputation was tarnished, almost beyond repair. He had a gang of violent thugs after him, and his body had taken a beating. He sighed, tired down to his bones and feeling very old.

He cast a longing look down the length of the sofa,

his body crying out for rest. But the thought of Jillian in the custody of the gang sent a renewed tremor of fear down his spine, energizing him to push past his physical limitations. He stood, then gingerly moved his knee in a tentative exploration. The pain was still there, but it had gone from a fierce burn to a dull warmth. It wouldn't take long to rekindle it, but for now, he'd make do.

He had just hobbled over to the door, hand outstretched to grasp the knob, when he heard the faint sound of footsteps approaching. Jillian's apartment was at the end of a long hall, which meant there wasn't a lot of traffic by her door. Since her neighbor didn't appear to get out much, he could only assume the mystery walker was heading for him.

A quick flash of excitement tingled through his limbs and he found himself leaning forward, subconsciously pulled toward the door and the possibility that Jillian was on the other side. He held his breath as the footsteps came to a stop. He heard the faint jingle of keys, the musical tinkling cutting through the whoosh of blood thundering in his ears.

Please be okay…

The door opened to reveal Jillian standing on the threshold. She let out a startled squeak at seeing him so close, but he ignored her alarm, running his hungry gaze over her to assess her condition. There was no sign of injuries, and some of the tension left his body as relief crashed over him like a wave.

He looked back to her face then, and the sight of the tears pooling in her eyes made his stomach drop.

Oh, God, was she injured? The large blue coat she wore obscured the upper half of her body—it could be covering something. He took a step forward, reaching out for her. If she was hurt, he would need to call the paramedics.

Jillian let out a small cry. "You're here," she whispered. Then she threw herself into his arms, forcing him to take a step back to keep them both from falling.

He automatically circled his arms around her, holding her against his chest. She hugged him tightly, pressing her face into the hollow of his throat. "You're safe," she said softly, burrowing as close as she could.

It dawned on him then that she wasn't crying because she was injured or in pain—she was crying from relief. She had been scared for him. The realization filled him with tenderness, and he raised one hand to slowly stroke the softness of her hair. Had anyone ever been scared for him? He knew Jim worried about him out in the field, but he doubted his friend had ever felt fear like this on his behalf. Shannon may have worried for him, but she'd doubtless moved on with her life and didn't think of him anymore. He was so used to being on his own, he hadn't even bothered to consider Jillian might be concerned for him.

Jillian was shaking now, her body trembling as if there was a live current running through her limbs. Alex pressed his nose to her hair, making low, soothing sounds while he continued to stroke her hair, then her back.

"It's okay," he said, rocking her slightly. "I'm here. We're both safe. How's Jim?"

"Stable," she said, her voice muffled. "I think he'll be fine."

He breathed in, relishing the familiar warm vanilla scent of her. She carried other smells, too, a testament to her day—the earthy aroma of cold leaves, the metallic tang of stale blood. And the faint musk of a man's cologne, drifting up from the fabric of the mystery coat she wore.

After a moment Jillian pushed away from him. He let her go, his body immediately going cold at the loss. She stared up at him, wiping her red-rimmed eyes with brisk, impatient hands. Then she poked him, hard, though she was careful to attack his uninjured shoulder.

"Do you have any idea how worried I've been?"

Alex opened his mouth to respond, but she kept talking, apparently not interested in his reply. "How could you offer yourself up as bait for those guys? How stupid can you be?"

He didn't try to speak this time. She continued to rant, releasing all her pent-up emotion in a verbal tirade that attacked his sanity, his intelligence, his common sense—or lack thereof—and his overestimation of his own abilities. He would have been offended, had he not known she was lashing out because she cared. In fact, rather than make him angry, her words only served to underscore the fact that she had feelings for him. A warm tingling started somewhere in the vicinity of his heart, spreading outward to travel along his limbs and down to his fingers. He felt like a candle flame and glanced down at his hand, slightly disappointed to find that he wasn't, in fact, glowing.

"Are you even listening to me?" Apparently, Jillian had noticed his distraction, and if the tone of her voice was any indication, she wasn't pleased.

"Yes," he replied hastily. He stared down into her scowling face, struggling to keep his expression serious. After a few seconds he lost the battle. A huge smile took over his mouth.

Jillian's expression grew thunderous. "Do you think this is *funny*?"

He shook his head, smile still in place. "No," he said honestly. How could he explain his reaction? How could he tell her that he was punch-drunk on joy and relief and the fact that she had come back to him? He could barely articulate it to himself, much less someone else.

"You nearly killed me with your little stunt, Alex. Do you hear me? My heart literally stopped beating when you ran out to those guys." Her lips quivered and fresh tears welled in her eyes. She blinked, sending them sliding down her cheeks to drip off her jaw.

He sobered at that, the grin fading in the face of her distress. "Come here," he said, leading her over to the couch. When they'd both sat, he pulled her into his lap and held her with her head against his chest. She was stiff for a moment, but as he stroked his hand over her hair, she relaxed into him with a small sigh.

"I'm sorry," he said, keeping his voice low. "I wasn't thinking. I just wanted to get them away from you and Jim, and that was the only way to do it."

She made a low sound in her throat that could have been agreement or simple acknowledgment. He decided not to ask for clarification.

"If it makes you feel any better, I was scared, too. Not for me, but for you."

She pulled back, eyeing him incredulously. "Why were you afraid for me? You were the one getting chased by men with guns, men who had just shot your friend."

"I know, but I managed to get away from them. I ran into some cops in the Metro station and reported them, but I didn't stick around to see if the police were able to make any arrests. I've been sitting here, wondering if the enforcers made it back to their car, if they saw you helping Jim, if they stopped to hurt you or take you as a hostage." He shook his head. "It's enough to drive me mad."

Jillian rested her head against his chest again. "You have quite the imagination." She laid a hand on his arm and squeezed gently. "I guess we both do."

"Seems that way," he agreed.

They sat in silence for several moments. Alex focused on the feel of the woman in his arms—her soft curves, her warm scent. The rise and fall of her chest against his own. She was perfect. She was whole.

She was his.

Even though he had no business thinking of her in that way, his heart was all too happy to ignore the dictates of his brain. Never mind that he didn't have anything to offer her, never mind that he'd brought her nothing but trouble. She fit him like a missing puzzle piece. He felt complete when she was near, and the demons of his past—the guns, the drugs, the bloody things he'd been party to by virtue of his job—faded into nothingness. It was a heady sensation, more addicting than any drug the gang had peddled in the streets.

Jillian stirred against him, leaning back to look him in the eyes. He smiled at her, reaching up to brush a strand of hair out of her face. She smiled, her face reflecting his relief and contentment.

"Why are you limping?"

He blinked, taken aback by her question. "What?"

"You limped over to the couch. What happened?"

Alex shook his head, grinning ruefully. She didn't miss a trick, that was for sure. "I wrenched my knee pretty bad on a patch of ice when I was running. I think I just sprained it."

"Let me see." She rose to her feet, shrugged out of the coat and dropped it next to him on the couch.

"I'm sure it's fine," he protested. But he obligingly stretched out his leg to give her better access. "I've been keeping an ice pack on it."

She bent to look at his knee, tugging at the hem of his pants to raise the fabric. It got stuck about halfway up his calf, causing her to grunt in frustration as she attempted to wrestle it into submission.

Jillian straightened. "I can't look at it like this. I need you to take your pants off."

His eyebrows shot up. "Doc, if you wanted to see me in my skivvies, all you had to do was ask."

She shot him a mock glare, but the effect was ruined by twin spots of pink that appeared high on her cheeks. "I believe I just did," she said coolly.

Alex stood and shucked the pants in one motion, wobbling only a little when he stepped out of them. He straightened, waggling his eyebrows and giving her an exaggerated wink before sitting back down and extending his leg.

She leaned over again to examine his knee, and he swallowed hard, trying to control his body's reaction to her proximity to his groin. While she was several inches south of the important bits, his lack of pants intensified the intimacy of the moment.

After an endless moment of prodding and poking, her breath warm against the skin of his thigh, she leaned back, nodding in apparent satisfaction.

"Well, Doc?" His voice was surprisingly husky, so

he cleared his throat and tried again. "What's the verdict? Do I get to keep my leg?"

The corner of her mouth twitched up. "For now," she replied. She sat next to him and turned her laser-like focus on his shoulder. "Time for me to check your gunshot wound."

Keeping his gaze on her face, Alex slowly pulled his shirt off and dropped it to the floor. Jillian didn't look away, but her skin flushed a pretty rose and she swallowed hard. A small thrill of victory raced through him at the evidence of her interest. Clearly he wasn't the only one having impure thoughts at the moment.

She leaned forward again, licking her lips as she did. He braced for a flare of pain, but her fingers were gentle when she pressed around his stitches. Then she placed her other hand flush against the center of his chest, right over his heart, and he stopped worrying about his shoulder.

He closed his eyes, enjoying the comforting weight of her palm above his heart. Could she feel it beating, the way it sped up when she was near? Did hers do the same? He began to raise his hand, wanting to echo her gesture, but stopped himself just in time.

Her hand slipped away as she leaned back.

Alex opened his eyes to find her watching him. The naked yearning on her face nearly stole his breath.

"Well?" he croaked. This time, he didn't bother trying to clear his throat.

"I do believe you'll live to fight another day," she said, her voice deep and sensuous.

"Glad to hear it."

"Me, too," she whispered.

"You know, Doc, I just noticed something."

"What's that?"

"You're a bit overdressed for this party."

She cocked her head, considering him for a long moment. "You know what?" Her tone was thoughtful. "I do believe you're right." She stood and peeled off her shirt, dropping it to the floor to join his. Then she reached behind her to unclasp her bra and Alex forgot how to breathe.

Jillian kept her eyes on Alex as she let her arms fall to her sides, surrendering her bra to the forces of gravity. A surge of pure feminine satisfaction flooded her system at the look on his face—desire and surprise mixed with a touching amount of reverence. His heated gaze traced her curves, making her skin feel hot and tingly. She shivered slightly, enjoying the sensation.

"Doc." His voice was little more than a growl. "It's not nice for you to tease me like this." He fisted his hands in his lap, the muscles in his arms going taut with strain.

She stepped forward, stopping just inches away from his mouth. His eyes grew wider and a new emotion flickered across his face: hope.

"Who said I'm teasing you?" she murmured.

Before he had a chance to respond, she leaned down and kissed him. He sucked in a breath when she ran her hands through his hair, a low moan escaping his throat.

Touch me, she silently begged, wanting to feel those big hands on her skin.

As if he'd heard her unspoken demand, he grabbed her waist and pulled, dragging her down onto his lap. Another tug and she was flush against his chest. The feel of his solid, warm body pressed against hers sent electric tingles of sensation zinging through her body to settle at her core. She squirmed, fumbling one-handed at the button of her jeans in an awkward attempt to remove one of the last barriers between them. Her movements grew increasingly frantic, which did nothing to help her coordination. Alex chuckled, causing her to bite back a moan as his chest rumbled against her sensitive nipples. His warm hand covered her own, stalling her efforts.

"Patience," he admonished softly. "I've been fantasizing about this moment pretty much since we've met. I have no intention of rushing it."

"Slow is good," she agreed, running her free hand down his neck and over his chest. She flicked her index finger across his nipple, feeling a small thrill of power when he shuddered. "But slow requires self-control and I'm all out of that at the moment." He sucked in a breath when she ran her hand lower, tracing the soft line of hair that bisected his flat stomach. When she reached the waistband of his boxers, she dipped her hand underneath, her fingers brushing his velvety length. "Know what I mean?"

He made a garbled sound in reply. She stroked him once, twice, and then withdrew her hand, eliciting a groan of protest. "I'm sorry. I didn't catch that." She couldn't keep the smile from her voice, and he heard it.

He cracked open his eyes, revealing twin blue slits of disapproval. "Sadist," he muttered.

She laughed. "Not at all. I'm merely abiding by your desire to take things slow." She leaned forward to run the tip of her tongue up the side of his neck, tasting the salty tang of dried sweat on his skin. Her lips met his ear and she gently nipped his earlobe. "Isn't that what you wanted?"

"I'm starting to reconsider."

"Are you sure?" She shifted, pressing her core against him while she kissed his cheekbones, his forehead, his chin. "I wouldn't want you to feel rushed."

"Not at all," he gasped, rocking his hips in an instinctive rhythm. "In fact, I feel like we're moving at a good pace."

"Oh, good." Jillian traced his nipples with her thumbs and then leaned down to run the flat of her tongue across his skin. His low moan of pleasure was better than any caress, heightening her own arousal.

"But there is something bothering me," he confessed, his jaw clenched tight.

She paused on her journey south. "What's that?"

He waited until she met his eyes. "You're talking too much."

Without warning, Alex put his hands under her legs and pushed her off his lap, angling her to the side so she landed on the couch. Between one heartbeat and the next he covered her body with his own, his hands and mouth running over her in a sensuous assault. His touch was gentle, but she could tell he was holding back from the way his muscles quivered with barely leashed energy. It made her feel safe and cherished to know that even in the throes of passion, Alex was careful to keep her from being hurt.

But Jillian wasn't interested in careful. She wanted him to lose control, to really let go and unleash all that power. That was what she needed from him, and what he needed from her in return.

She raised her head and sank her teeth into his uninjured shoulder, biting down just hard enough to get his attention. He sucked in a breath, then dropped his head to the side of her neck and nipped her. The sting of it made her cry out and he pulled back, concern in his eyes.

"Don't hold back," she told him, raising her hands to frame his face. "I want all of you."

The heat in his gaze intensified. Silently he wrapped his hand around her wrists and lifted them above her head. The position left her even more vulnerable to him, but she wasn't afraid. She wanted this—craved it with an intensity that consumed her.

She was dimly aware of his fingers at the waist-band of her pants, felt the wash of cool air strike her skin as the fabric was pulled away. Then she felt the heat of his mouth and she was reduced to a quivering mass of nerves.

Sensations flooded her, overwhelming her conscious thought. She couldn't speak, could barely breathe. The upholstery of the sofa was rough against her palms and she focused on gripping the cushion tightly, using it as an anchor to keep herself from flying off. She tried to gather the shattered bits of her thoughts, but she couldn't concentrate enough to put the pieces back together. Alex showed her no mercy, continuing his exquisite torture with deliberation and skill. Finally, Jillian gave up and surrendered to the waves of pleasure, no longer caring if she drowned.

Chapter 12

Alex knew the exact moment Jillian let herself go. It was the sexiest thing he'd ever seen, watching this woman who was normally so composed, so poised, fall apart in his arms. Every tiny moan, every soft whimper, fed his own desire, heightening his own need until his body shook with the strain of staying in control. Her surrender made the primal, instinctively male side of him want to roar in satisfaction, but he settled for stretching out alongside her, stroking her softly as she came back down to earth.

Gradually her breathing slowed and evened out. She turned to face him, snuggling against his chest and nuzzling his neck with her nose. "That was…" she said, her voice husky and raw.

"Amazing," he finished for her. He kissed the tip of her nose and she opened her eyes to regard him with a dreamy, satiated look. Her mouth curved up in a sexy smile that shot straight to his groin, and he nearly groaned at the painful pleasure that accompanied the resurgence of his arousal.

"Amazing," she echoed. "But what about you?" She reached between them, her fingers stroking. "Don't you want to finish what we started?"

He clenched his jaw, trying hard not to give in to temptation. It would be so easy to roll on top of her, reach down and... "I can't," he said, forcing the words out with effort.

Jillian laughed softly as she caressed him. "I disagree. In my expert medical opinion, it would seem you can." She punctuated the words with a gentle squeeze that made him see stars.

"No," he gasped, trying hard to hold on to the thought before he gave up and gave in. "I mean I don't have protection."

"Oh." Her hand stalled and he was caught between relief and dismay at this end to their festivities. "Damn," she muttered, sounding almost as disappointed as he felt.

"I would have chosen a stronger word myself, but that about sums it up."

They lay silent for a moment, limbs tangled in a promising embrace that could never be realized. Alex tried to ignore his growing disappointment by focusing on the woman in his arms, on the warm vanilla scent of her hair and skin. He was humbled by her earlier surrender, and he knew just how lucky he was to have been the one to share that moment with her.

He tightened his hold on her, wanting to prolong their embrace. The real world, with all its troubles and dangers, would intrude soon enough. Now, he just wanted to be with Jillian.

She relaxed, melting against him, but then she suddenly stiffened. "I just remembered," she gasped. "I have—" She jumped off the couch and was out of the room before finishing her thought. Her footsteps pounded on the wood floor of the hall, and he heard her rummaging in the bedroom. He got up and started to follow her, picking up the pace when he heard her celebratory whoop of triumph.

He found her standing by the bed, the drawer to her bedside table open and the contents strewed across the comforter. She turned to look at him, her eyes shining.

"Look!" She thrust her hand toward him and he saw what had her so excited—three foil packets, glowing in the afternoon sunlight like small stars in her palm.

"Where did those come from?" He took the condoms from her and she turned to pile the other items back in the drawer, moving quickly to clear the bed.

"My friend Carla. I went on a date about three months ago—just dinner and a movie—and Carla dropped them in my coat pocket as a joke."

Jealousy was a bright green flame that flared to life in his heart without warning. "And did you need them?"

He realized his mistake when Jillian turned to look at him, one brow arched. "Not that it's any of your business," she said coolly, "but no. I did not need them that night. Now, are you going to waste time thinking about what didn't happen then, or shall we focus on what should be happening now?"

"I'm sorry," he said, sounding sheepish. He stepped forward and cupped her face. "I didn't mean to be that guy. I spoke without thinking, and I shouldn't have asked."

"It's okay," she said, rising to her toes to press a kiss to his forehead. "I know how you can make it up to me." She gave him a sultry smile and leaned back, holding his hand so she pulled him onto the bed with her.

God, she's incredible.

He didn't know what he'd done to merit having this woman in his bed, but he wasn't about to question his good fortune. And he wasn't about to waste any more time, either.

She arched into his touch with a sigh that made him feel like he was coming home. Then she reached out for him and he followed her into the abyss.

"He is in the hospital," Dan said, enunciating each word carefully. "He is out of surgery and he is not dead."

"He should be," said the sullen voice on the other end of the line.

"On that, we are agreed. So here's what we're going to do. You're going to meet me at the hospital and we're going to pay him a little visit."

"No way." The denial was immediate, as was Dan's anger. How dare this punk refuse *him*?

"Excuse me?"

"No way am I meeting you in person. For all I know, you could have the cops waiting just outside to arrest me. I'm not gonna walk into an ambush."

Dan rubbed his brow, trying hard to keep a grip on his patience. "Why would I involve the police, when my goal is to handle this situation as quickly and quietly as possible?"

The line went silent as the other man considered his words. "How do I know I can trust you?"

"You don't. Just like I can't be sure I can trust you." He hardened his voice, leaning forward while he tightened his grip on the phone. "But the fact remains there is a loose end that needs to be taken care of. It would be very damaging to both of us if he is left alive to testify."

"I can't just walk into a hospital and shoot him. The cops would be all over me!"

"You're not going to shoot him. Or stab him, or do anything else that would make people realize he's been murdered. We're going to be a lot more subtle about it."

"How come I gotta be there, then? Why can't you do this yourself?" He sounded put-upon, like a child told to take out the trash.

"Because this is your mess," Dan informed him. "And you will clean it up."

There was a loud sigh, then a muttered, "Fine."

"Meet me in the parking lot of Howard University Hospital in two hours. And for God's sake, wear a suit."

"Tell me about Jim."

Jillian opened her eyes, the question cutting through her drowsy satisfaction like a surgeon's scalpel. Guilt pricked her conscience as she realized she hadn't spared a thought for the injured man since arriving home and finding Alex safe. Even though Jim wasn't officially her patient, she had worked on him, and the fact that she'd put her own pleasure above her concern for him was mildly disconcerting. She'd never allowed herself to be so distracted before, and certainly not by a man.

But then again, she'd never met a man like Alex.

She rolled off his chest and onto her side, and he

turned to face her. "Jim was shot twice in the gut. Right about here," she said, reaching out to touch Alex just below the slope of his rib cage. "When I got to his side, the entrance wounds had pretty much stopped bleeding. His belly remained soft, which means he probably wasn't bleeding into his abdomen. But I didn't see any exit wounds when the paramedics moved him, so they'll have to go in and find the bullets."

Alex was silent for a moment, digesting her words. "Was he conscious?"

"Yes. He spoke to me. He knows you're innocent. Said something about a man named Dan—do you know who he's talking about?"

"I do." His lips tightened at the mention of the name. "Dan is the traitor in the FBI. He's the one I have to stop."

"Ah."

He waved his hand, dismissing the other man. "What are Jim's chances?"

Jillian pursed her lips and exhaled slowly, considering his question. "It depends," she said finally. "They took him to Howard, which is a Level 1 trauma facility—that fact alone improves his odds. We got him to the ER during the 'golden hour,' which is another point in his favor."

Alex frowned at her. "'Golden hour'?"

"It's what we call the hour just after a traumatic event. If we can start treating a patient within that time, their chances of survival go up. In Jim's case, the hospital was practically around the corner. I didn't go into the ER with him, but they'll have ordered scans to try to find the bullets, and they'll have sent him to surgery."

"I see."

She reached out and placed her hand on the side of his face. "I think Jim's chances are good, but you need to understand that abdominal injuries can be tricky. There are a lot of vital organs that can be damaged by a bullet. If the surgeons were able to find and repair the injuries, then I think he'll pull through. But there's always a chance…" She trailed off, knowing that she didn't have to finish her thought. From the look on his face, Alex got the message loud and clear.

"I can call the hospital," she offered. "I can tell them he's one of my patients and get an update on his condition. Would that make you feel better?"

Alex shook his head slightly. "I think it's better if I go to the hospital myself. I'll say he's my brother. They'll let me see him if they think I'm family, right?"

"They should," Jillian responded, alarm making her voice higher than usual. "But why do you need to go there in person? Won't the place be crawling with FBI agents who think you're the traitor?"

"It's a chance I'm going to have to take. Once Dan realizes Jim is still alive, he's going to send someone after him to finish the job. He can't risk Jim waking up and telling the world what he knows. And since Jim is the only one who believes I'm innocent, I have to protect him."

His words made a sick kind of sense, even though they flew in the face of her desires. She had just gotten him back and now he was going to put himself in harm's way again. Part of her admired his dedication to his friend, but another part worried that he was tempting fate. He'd already had more narrow escapes than anyone had a right to—was this going to be the end of his lucky streak?

"I'm going with you." She sat up, kicking the covers free of her legs so she could scoot to the edge of the bed.

"Jillian—" he began, clearly unhappy with her announcement.

"Don't even start," she said, moving toward the attached bathroom. "You need me in case they refuse to let you see him. If he's in the recovery room, you can only stay for a minute. You won't be allowed to spend any time with him until they assign him a room, and that could take a while."

"And how will that change if you're with me?"

"You're going to pretend to be his brother, right?" He nodded. "Well, I'll be his sister-in-law, the doctor. A lot of times, a hospital will allow a relative who is a doctor more access to a patient and their medical records as a professional courtesy."

A muscle in his jaw flexed. "I don't like it."

Jillian shrugged, stepping onto the cool tile of the bathroom. "Face it—you need me. The way I see it, we became a team when you told me the truth in that crappy motel. You're stuck with me now."

"I never wanted this for you!"

She turned to face him then, and her heart thumped hard at the look of anguish on his face. "I know," she said softly. "But here we are. Let's make the best of it, okay?"

Chapter 13

Why was it, Alex mused while he and Jillian walked down the hall, that hospitals always smelled the same? It didn't matter what hospital he walked into, they all shared a particular odor that was instantly recognizable. He'd smelled it on Jillian that first night, when she was fresh off her shift. It was a combination of disinfectant and soap, but with an underlying organic note that made it clear there were sick people inside.

It was a scent that was so strongly associated with illness he felt an instinctive revulsion, as if to be near the smell put him at risk of getting sick, too. He didn't know how Jillian could stand it. He glanced at her from the corner of his eye. She was striding along, full of confidence and competence, seemingly unaffected by the pervasive stink of the place. Of course, she was probably used to it; she was, after all, constantly exposed to it.

He'd had the same reaction to the scent of drugs at first, his initial disgust gradually replaced by acceptance and eventual dismissal as he'd spent more time with the gang and their wares. Now, the pungent stink so common to habitual meth users didn't even register as foreign to his acclimated nose. It still reeked, though—a sharp combination of ammonia and body odor that was enough to make his eyes water. Some days the horrible smell seemed baked into his sinuses and he feared he'd never be able to take a normal breath again.

I am so tired of this.

When he'd first joined the Bureau, the prospect of undercover work had seemed so exciting, so glamorous. Raised on a steady diet of James Bond movies, Alex's inner twelve-year-old had thrilled at the opportunity to infiltrate a dangerous street gang, to take them down from within. He had trained hard, and he'd had a good understanding of the risks involved. What had really knocked him for a loop, though, were the gray areas he encountered once he was living the life. No amount of classroom time, no amount of physical training or debriefings or seminars had prepared him for what it was really like to be confronted with a million tiny decisions every day, each one seemingly insignificant, but all of them holding the power to expose him if he made the wrong move.

Before he'd joined the Bureau, he had viewed the world in terms of black and white, right and wrong. Now, he recognized how naïve he'd been. Life was all about the gray.

Still, he'd fought hard to stay on the lighter side of that shade, trying to pick the lesser of two evils. For the past several years he'd been walking a tightrope, trying to fit in with some very bad men while still retaining his own humanity. It was a delicate balance, and one that had left him exhausted and drained.

At least I don't have to try anymore. The thought made him smile grimly. If there was one good thing about this mess, it was that his cover had been blown sky-high. He would no longer have to associate with the gang, pretending to be friends with men who made his skin crawl. He didn't have to fake enjoyment from ripping off tweakers, didn't have to pretend to look the other way when an enforcer got rough with a user who couldn't, or wouldn't, pay. He was done with that life and he couldn't be happier about it.

He cast another glance at Jillian as they made their way through the maze of hospital corridors. Was there a place for her in his new life? He shook his head—of course there was. There was no point in him denying the connection he felt anymore. Making love with her had cemented his feelings, and he knew that even if nothing came of their interlude, he would never forget it. Or her. A pang speared his chest at the thought of her walking away when this was over, but he brushed it aside. While he wanted very much to be a part of her life, the real question was, did she feel the same way about him?

"We should be coming up on the nurses' station soon," Jillian said, stepping aside to make room for a man in a wheelchair.

"How do you know?" Alex hadn't seen any signs indicating where they were in the hospital, but then again, he hadn't exactly been paying close attention.

She shot him a quick grin. "My medical spidey-sense is tingling," she said dryly.

He shook his head, trying not to laugh. She winked at him. "I did a few rotations here when I was a resident. Most of the floors have the same basic layout."

"I liked the idea of you having superpowers better."

"Me, too."

They rounded a corner and he could see the nurses' station up ahead. A few women sat behind computer monitors, while a steady stream of people walked around, their movements brisk and businesslike. The atmosphere surrounding the place was very no-nonsense, and Alex got the feeling these people were used to saying no. He felt his stomach tighten as they approached and glanced at Jillian. "Are you sure we shouldn't have called first?"

"Don't worry," she murmured. "Nurses love me."

She walked right up to an older woman in navy scrubs. "Excuse me? My husband and I got a call that his brother had been shot and was here. Can we see him?"

"Name." The lady didn't even bother to look up.

"Jim DeWinter," Alex said. He didn't try to keep the anxiety from his voice, knowing his worry for his "brother" would help them get in.

She typed away for a moment, then nodded. "He's here, but he's not allowed visitors right now."

"Please," Jillian said. "I'd really appreciate it if you let us see him. We won't stay long, and we won't bother him."

The woman did look up then, clearly ready to refuse Jillian's request. Then she saw Jillian's scrubs and her eyebrows shot up. "Do you work here?"

Jillian shook her head. "I'm over at GW, in the ER. I came straight from work after getting the call."

The nurse nodded, her expression softening. "Tell you what. You can head on back, but we really don't allow visitors on this floor, so try not to stay too long."

"Thank you," Jillian said. Alex echoed her words. "We really appreciate it."

The other woman waved off their gratitude. "He's in room 427. Just down the hall, then take a right. Door is on the left."

Jillian nodded and reached out to grab his hand. "Come on, honey. Let's go say hi."

Alex spent the short walk trying to brace himself for what he might find in Jim's room. Would Jim be awake? Would he be happy to see him or angry because of what had happened earlier? What if he wasn't awake? What if he was unconscious, hooked up to machines keeping him alive? Would his friend recover or would he forever feel the effects of his injury?

His thoughts whirled like the flakes in a shaken snow globe, spinning around but getting nowhere. It was his nature to plan, to try to see every possible outcome of a situation or a problem. To try to control things as much as he could. But recent events had knocked down his carefully constructed reality, and he was beginning to realize control was just an illusion. He would have to take things as they came, rather than waste energy wishing circumstances were different.

They paused outside the door and Jillian turned to look at him. "Ready?" she asked.

He nodded. He was as ready as he'd ever be. He took a deep breath, bracing himself to shoulder the blame for Jim's current condition. Even though he hadn't sent the gang after Jim, even though he hadn't pulled the trigger, he knew that Jim wouldn't be lying in a hospital bed if it wasn't for him.

Jillian seemed to sense his thoughts. She placed her hand on his arm and squeezed gently. "This isn't your fault," she said, keeping her voice low so they wouldn't be overheard. "You saved his life. If you hadn't gotten those guys to chase you, he would have died at their feet."

Alex nodded mechanically. He didn't bother trying to explain. There wasn't time and they had more important things to do. Such as making sure Jim stayed alive so he could expose Dan as the traitor he was.

She gave his arm a final fortifying squeeze, then turned and pushed open the door. It was dim inside the room—apparently someone had turned off most of the lights so it would be easier for Jim to sleep. He was taking full advantage of the low light, dozing peacefully in the bed. His face was relaxed, with no lines of strain or pain. It was so different from Alex's last glimpse of Jim that for a moment he just stood at the foot of the bed, absorbing this new reality. Then he exhaled slowly, relief overtaking his earlier anxiety.

Jim was going to be okay. He didn't need to look to Jillian to confirm it. The last time Alex had seen his friend, his skin had been the color of old milk. Now he was a healthy pink. His chest rose and fell in a regular rhythm and a quick glance at the monitors by his head confirmed his heart was beating, steady and sure.

"He's looking good," Jillian said softly. Alex nodded, pleased to hear her echo his thoughts.

"Is he asleep or sedated?"

Jillian tilted her head, considering him. "Probably just asleep. He's only been out of surgery a few hours, so he's likely still sleeping off the anesthesia. Do you want to wake him?"

"I think we'd better." Although he hated to interrupt his friend's rest, it was important Alex spoke with him. Their earlier conversation had been interrupted before he'd been able to confirm Dan's involvement, and he needed to make sure Jim still believed he was innocent.

A thought occurred to him. "Will he be lucid?" There was no need to wake Jim up if he wouldn't understand or remember what was said.

Jillian shrugged. "Hard to say. Some people are able to shake off surgical anesthesia quickly and can have a normal conversation soon after. Others are more affected and it takes several hours, sometimes a day or two, for them to feel normal again. The only way to know which camp Jim falls into is to talk to him."

He nodded and Jillian approached the bed. She called Jim's name, but when he didn't respond, she reached out and put her fist just above his heart.

"Jim," she repeated, rubbing his skin with her knuckles. "Wake up for me. C'mon, buddy, I need you to wake up now."

Jim stirred, shaking his head. He lifted his hand to bat weakly at Jillian, trying to push her hand off his chest.

"Are you hurting him?" Alex stepped forward, guilt rising. He only wanted to talk to Jim—he hadn't meant to put the man in more pain.

"It's more uncomfortable than painful," Jillian explained, not letting up. "It's a surefire way to rouse someone. See?" she said, smiling down at Jim. "It worked."

Jim stared up at her, blinking slowly, like a nearsighted owl. "What—? Who—?" He seemed to focus on Jillian, and he let out a groan. "Oh, no, you're back. No more pain, okay, lady? Gimme a break."

Alex shot her a questioning look, but Jillian just grinned in reply. "When Jim and I were waiting for the ambulance, I explained to him that pain is a good thing. I think he took exception to my logic."

"Damn right I did," Jim muttered. "I was the one in pain!" He squinted up at her. "Who are you talking to?"

Alex stepped forward, catching Jim's attention. "Alex! Thank God you're alive!" Jim held out a hand and Alex stepped forward to grab it.

"I'm so sorry, Jim. This is all my fault."

Jim frowned up at him. "Things are still a little fuzzy, but I do remember getting shot. And I don't remember you pulling the trigger. So quit beating yourself up."

"Roger that." Alex smiled, feeling some of his worry lift away. If Jim remembered getting shot, there was a good chance he remembered their earlier discussion about the real mole in the Bureau.

"Do you recall our conversation on the bench? Before all hell broke loose?"

Jim closed his eyes and leaned back against the pillow. "Mostly. I think the gist of it was you're innocent and Dan is the bad guy. Do I have that right?"

"Pretty much," Alex said simply.

"Where are my clothes?"

Thrown by the sudden change of topic, Alex glanced at Jillian. Jim seemed lucid, but perhaps this was a side effect of the anesthesia? He raised a brow at her in question and she shrugged in reply. Whatever was going on here, she couldn't explain it, either.

"Um, I'm not sure. Do you need them for something?"

"Yes." Jim tried to sit up, winced, then relaxed back onto the bed. "Find my jacket. It has a recorder in it."

Alex glanced around the room, the tension in his muscles mounting when he didn't see any clothes. Jillian walked over to a cabinet, pulled open the door and removed a white plastic bag with a drawstring top. "His personal items should be in here," she said, handing him the bag. Alex loosened the strings and reached inside. His fingers closed around the rough tweed of Jim's jacket and he pulled, shaking it free of the bag.

"Which pocket?" He began patting the jacket, searching for telltale bulges that would indicate a concealed recorder.

"Inside right," Jim instructed.

The recorder was small and thin, a dull black that seemed even darker in the dim light of the room. Alex pressed it into Jim's hand. "Here you go."

Jim fumbled with it for a moment, pressing buttons with a careful exaggeration that made Alex think he was still under the influence of the surgical medication. Then the playback started, faint at first, but growing louder as Jim toggled the volume controls. He'd recorded their conversation, and he hadn't stopped the device after they'd been discovered. Jillian jumped when the gunshots rang out and they heard the muffled thud as Jim hit the ground. There was the crunch of feet on snow, then a curse.

"That's when they realized I wasn't you," Jim interjected with a rueful smile.

Alex tried to smile back, but he couldn't quite manage it. Bad enough his friend was in a hospital bed;

reliving the accident and hearing these men talk so casually about killing Jim twisted his gut into knots.

"Should we finish him?"

"Nah." Alex recognized the voice as the leader of the group. "He won't last long."

"The man said no survivors."

"Look at him. He won't survive. We need to move."

"Who's that?"

There was more cursing, then the gunmen took off. Jim moaned in pain and there was a scratching sound, as though he had tried to move. Quick footsteps, growing louder, then Jillian's voice, clear and strong. "Don't move."

Jim switched the recorder off, letting silence fill the room. In a way, it was almost worse than the sounds of Jim's shooting because now Alex had no distraction from his thoughts.

"My God." Jillian spoke softly, but her voice cut through the heavy stillness like a cracking whip. "It was bad enough watching all this happen through the window of the coffee shop. Hearing the soundtrack makes it even worse." She shuddered, wrapping her arms around her stomach like she was cold. She took a step closer to Alex and he hooked his arm around her shoulder, pulling her snug against his side. She relaxed, her body warm against his, and he felt a quiet joy at the knowledge that she had sought comfort from his touch.

Jim's eyebrows shot up, but he didn't comment on the cozy scene they made. "Yeah, well. It wasn't much fun for me, either," he grumbled. He held the recorder up and Alex leaned forward to take it. "Get this to Parker," Jim instructed. "I'll call him, let him know you're coming. He can help you."

"Are you sure?" He tucked the device into his pocket, but it was too long and it stuck out awkwardly. Afraid it might fall out, he searched for another place to keep it. Jillian saw his dilemma and held out her hand. Without any hesitation, he dropped the recorder into her palm and she tucked it away in one of the huge front pockets of her coat. The information that little recorder contained was the key to proving his innocence, but he trusted Jillian completely. She was his one constant in this whole mess.

"What do you mean, am I sure?"

Jim sounded offended so Alex rushed to clarify his earlier question.

"It's nothing personal. But it was hard enough getting you to trust me again, and we've been friends for years. I barely know Parker. Will he take your word that I'm clean?"

Jim relaxed on the bed, looking appeased. "He will," he said simply. "Especially once you give him the evidence." He nodded at Jillian's pocket. "Hand me my phone, please."

Alex dug around in the plastic bag and removed Jim's phone. The other man dialed, then conducted a short conversation, presumably with Parker. He hung up and regarded them again. "He's waiting for you."

"Where?"

"Coffee shop just off 10th and E Street. Across from work." Jim yawned, his eyelids drooping. "I'll do what I can from here, but I'm not going to be much use to you, I'm afraid." His voice grew fainter, the words beginning to slur a bit as fatigue dug in.

Alex patted his friend's hand. "You've done more than enough. Just get well. I'll see you soon."

"Hope so," Jim mumbled. "Be safe, buddy." He dropped back into sleep, his body going limp on the mattress.

"Will he be okay?"

"I'm almost positive," Jillian said, snaking her arm around his waist. She laid her head on his shoulder and he tilted his head to press his cheek against her hair.

"Why almost? Why not absolutely?"

"I don't deal in absolutes," she said, squeezing him. "But his color is good, he was lucid, and he seems to have the spirit needed for recovery. Barring any unforeseen events, I think he'll be fine."

"I hope so," Alex murmured.

They stood there for a moment, holding each other close, watching Jim sleep the peaceful slumber of the medicated. There was a faint sound in the hall outside the room—probably the nurse coming by to kick them out—and Alex pulled away from Jillian.

"What now?" she asked.

"That, Doctor," said a smooth male voice from the doorway, "is a very good question."

Alex stiffened, inhaling sharply with an audible hiss. "Dan," he said softly, his jaw clenched so tightly it was a wonder he'd gotten that single word out.

Jillian felt her eyes widen, disbelief warring with dread. They were so close to clearing Alex's name—why, oh why, did this have to happen now? All they needed was a little time, no more than a half hour, and Alex would be safe. But it couldn't be that easy.

Alex turned to face his foe and she caught a glimpse of his expression while he moved. He looked nothing like the man she'd come to care about, and she had to force herself to stand still, resisting the instinctive impulse to take a step back. Gone was the handsome man who looked at her with concern, with affection, with desire. In his place was a hard man, eyes bright with anger and the promise of violence. With his brows drawn down and his mouth set in an angry slash, he looked like an avenging angel, ready to unleash his vengeance on those who had wronged him.

Jillian turned with him, caught up in the terrible beauty of Alex preparing to do battle. She'd never seen him this way before, and she realized with a sudden jolt that this was the side of him the gang had known. He hadn't revealed his humanity to those men, knowing that mercy would be mistaken for weakness. Instead he'd worn this mask, this awful armor of protection that he donned so quickly now. He moved to stand in front of her, a menacing step that was no less threatening for the fact that it was to the side and not toward his enemy. For a heartbeat Jillian was caught in a dizzying cyclone of emotions—pity for the life Alex had been forced to lead, admiration for his strength of character, pleasure that he had allowed her to know him, to see the *real* him, and a thrill of feminine shock at the fact that he'd put himself between her and danger. Then she blinked and the moment was gone.

"Why are you here?" Alex said softly.

"Just tying up some loose ends," Dan replied. Jillian peered over Alex's shoulder and got her first glimpse of the man responsible for turning her life upside down.

He was smaller than she'd imagined, and not just because he sat in a motorized wheelchair. His narrow shoulders, long arms and legs, and slim torso reminded her of a stork, all thin, lanky lines, folded into a tidy package. With sandy-brown hair and light brown eyes framed by wire-rimmed glasses, he was not a man who would stand out in a crowd. Rather, he had the look of an everyman, someone who would blend in with his surroundings. It was likely one of the reasons no one had suspected him of being the mole—his appearance was so average it was hard to imagine him capable of such treachery.

"It's good to see you, Alex," he continued. "Saves me the trouble of finding you later."

Dan hadn't looked at her yet. Neither had the man who had stepped inside the room to stand next to him. They were both totally focused on Alex, watching him as if he was a wild animal they had just cornered.

Jillian slipped her hand into her front coat pocket, running her fingers along the recorder. The buttons were marked with raised symbols and she pressed the one stamped with a circle, hoping the device would start recording. She didn't know if the device was even capable of picking up sound through a layer of fabric, but it was worth a shot. The more evidence they could gather against Dan, the stronger Alex's case would be.

"If you wanted to talk to me, all you had to do was ask." Alex's voice was even, almost pleasant, but she heard the underlying rage. He was doing a good job of keeping his emotions in check so far, but how long would that last?

"But I don't want to talk to you. I want you gone."

"And so you killed innocent people in your attempts to get rid of me? Sloppy of you. Of course, I wouldn't expect anything better. You've always been careless—that's what landed you in the chair in the first place."

Jillian held her breath, shocked at the cruelty of Alex's words. Why was he provoking him in Jim's hospital room? Was he hoping Dan and his friend would make a scene, attracting security? Or was he simply venting his anger and frustration, lashing out against a man he so obviously hated?

Dan stared at him, a dull red climbing up his neck and cheeks as he held Alex's gaze. Neither man spoke and after a moment the color faded from his face. He smiled, almost pleasantly. "We shouldn't talk about these things here."

Alex made a show of looking around, turning his head back and forth in an exaggerated search of the sparse room. "I don't see an alternative."

"And that's your problem," Dan replied, a bite in his voice. "You never could think past your current situation. You only react to what's in front of you, rather than plan for what could be. That's why you'll never be more than a foot soldier."

Alex's jaw tightened, but he gave no other outward sign of being upset by Dan's words. "At least I never betrayed my friends. I never had innocent people killed."

Dan laughed, a rich, flowing sound that under other circumstances would have been pleasant. "Didn't you? Come now, Alex, I know you're not that naïve. You may not have pulled the trigger yourself, but I know for a fact you have blood on your hands."

Alex did flinch then, his gaze sliding over to Jillian before flicking back to Dan. He looked guilty and she could have sworn she'd seen a flash of apology in his eyes. But why? He hadn't done anything to merit such a reaction, at least not in front of her. She knew he'd seen some dark things in his time as an undercover operative, but she didn't blame him for the things he'd had to do to survive. And while she hadn't known him long, she knew him well enough to recognize that he was a good man. If Dan was right, and Alex had seen someone killed, it went a long way toward explaining the haunted, pained look that she sometimes saw in his eyes.

Her heart ached for him and she longed to touch him, to offer him reassurance. He needed to know that no one blamed him for the actions of others. But more importantly, he needed to forgive himself.

"You haven't told your lady friend?" Dan asked, sounding amused. "My, my. This will be an interesting conversation." He turned to her then, extending a hand. "We haven't been properly introduced yet. Dan Pryde."

Jillian made no move to take his hand.

After a few seconds he dropped it. But he continued to hold her gaze, clearly expecting her to respond.

"I know who you are," she finally said.

Alex made a sound low in his throat and took a half step forward. "You don't talk to her."

"Down, boy," Dan replied. He raised a brow at Jillian. "Are you going to let him speak for you like that?"

The man standing next to Dan had been growing increasingly restless, rocking back and forth on his heels while he monitored the conversation. Now he stepped forward, tugging at the neck of his shirt as though he was uncomfortable with the fabric.

"C'mon, man," he said. "We need to wrap this up and move." He pushed up the sleeves of his suit jacket, exposing part of the stars tattooed on his forearm. Jillian felt the fine hairs on the back of her neck rise when she saw the color. Black.

Black is for enforcers. The guys who do the wet work.

Dread coiled in her stomach, writhed in her belly like a nest of snakes. While she wasn't surprised that Dan would bring along someone to do his dirty work, she didn't expect him to be so bold as to kill Jim in his hospital bed. Even the busiest hospital ward would take notice if a visitor tried to kill a patient, especially in a violent manner. And while she had no doubts as to the second man's willingness to hurt Jim, she didn't think he was well-versed in the more subtle ways of ending someone's life.

But maybe Dan didn't care about attracting attention. After all, this was a man who had sold out his co-workers for a shot at revenge. It was entirely possible he'd planned to have his enforcer kill Jim, and then he would turn on the man, disposing of him and deflecting suspicion over Dan's involvement in the whole thing.

Alex made eye contact and she could tell by the look on his face he was thinking the same thing. If Dan turned his enforcer loose, Jim was as good as dead. They had to distract him. But how?

"He's right," Jillian said. Both Dan and his friend turned to her, wearing identical looks of surprise. "We need to go. The nurse is going to come by to kick us out soon, and if we don't leave, she'll get security involved. I assume you don't want that to happen?" She directed this last bit at Dan, who was watching her with his head tilted to the side, like a bird eyeing a potentially tasty bug.

"We do need to go, yes," he agreed, the words slow and measured. "But I have a few loose ends to tie up first. Kyle." He motioned to the second man, who stepped forward.

"I wouldn't bother if I were you," Jillian said, trying to sound bored. "He's dying anyway."

Dan held up a hand and the man stopped, almost as if he were a puppet on a string. "What do you mean?"

"I saw his chart at the nursing station—his internal injuries are extensive. He's already got a fever and the antibiotics they've put him on aren't working. He's not going to make it past morning." She shrugged, as if the matter was of no consequence. "Not all that uncommon for a gut injury, really."

Alex rounded on her, fists clenched. "You lied to me," he said, the words full of betrayed outrage. "You said everything was going to be fine!"

"I tell that to all my patients," she explained, hating the lies that fell so easily from her lips. "It keeps them calm so they die in peace."

Alex continued to play his part to the hilt, staring at her with horrified disgust that looked all too real. But she'd seen true horror in his eyes before and could tell this was just an act. He was good, though, and his performance gave her a flash of insight into what his life had been like for the past few years. *God, no wonder he's exhausted!* Her lies weren't nearly as extensive, and she was already finding it difficult to keep up the facade of cool detachment.

Dan watched her intently, his eyes bright with suspicion. "Why should I trust your analysis?"

She pointed to the monitor. "Look at his heart rhythm. See that bump at the end of every beat? It's a sign of early cardiac distress." *Please, please, please don't have any medical knowledge…* She knew from experience that an authoritative tone and an air of self-confidence went a long way toward bluffing someone.

But if Dan had any clue about medicine, it was all over. She might be able to throw some complicated words at him, but how far would that really get her?

Not waiting to give him a chance to respond, she forged ahead. "And his respiratory rate—" She gestured to a number on the monitor. "It's gone up since we've been talking." Which probably meant Jim was awake and listening to their conversation. *Keep your eyes closed!* She willed the thought in his direction, hoping an instinctive sense of self-preservation would overcome any residual grogginess from the anesthesia.

"What does that mean?" Dan was still suspicious, but she could tell by the way he hung on her every word that he was considering what she said.

"When a patient goes into congestive heart failure, their breathing rate goes up because they feel like they're suffocating. The sign on his EKG, combined with his increased respiratory rate, indicates he's in the early stages of heart failure." She could have bitten off her tongue for such blatant lies, and she was sure that her old medical physiology professor was rolling in his grave, but it had to be said.

"Why is his heart failing if the damage is to his intestines?"

"The organ systems all work together." In for a penny, in for a pound. "Damage to one means the other organs have to work harder. In Jim's case, one too many cheeseburgers and a career spent behind a desk means his heart is already weak. Now that it's being asked to do more, it can't handle it."

"How long?"

She shrugged. "I've seen patients decompensate in

a matter of hours. It won't take long—the process has already started."

Dan narrowed his eyes as he considered her and she realized, rather belatedly, that trying to bluff a man who had made lying his profession was probably not one of her better ideas. She was banking on his ignorance of medicine, but he wasn't a fool.

A cough sounded from Jim's bed. Deliberate or not, it punctuated her words, lending credence to her predictions. She held her breath, hoping Jim wouldn't make another sound. One cough lent an air of realism to her tale. Two or three coughs were laying it on a little thick, and Dan would likely suspect something.

Jim apparently realized the same thing as he fell silent once again. That seemed to be the deciding factor for Dan. "Fine," he said, nodding at her. "I can wait. In the meantime—" he gestured to the door "—let's take this conversation elsewhere."

"And if I don't want to?" Alex asked.

Kyle pulled a gun from his jacket and pointed it at Jillian. "Then I shoot her, your friend in the bed and you. In that order."

Dan held up his hands, as if to absolve himself of any coming violence. "I don't think there's any need for that, do you?"

"All right," Alex said, the words forced. "Put the gun away."

The enforcer looked from Alex to Jillian, realization slowly dawning on his face. "Come here, sweetheart." He beckoned her toward him, and when she didn't move, he pointed the gun at Alex's head. *That* made her step forward, her heart racing like a scared rabbit's.

Kyle grinned at Alex, revealing stained teeth. "I think I'll keep her close, just to make sure you behave." He clamped his hand around her upper arm, squeezing so tightly she choked back a yelp. If Alex thought she was being hurt, there was no telling what he'd do, and she didn't want him to get killed over something as insignificant as a bruise.

"Off we go, then," Dan said, looking at Alex. "They won't be far behind," he said with a nod in her direction. "So don't get any ideas about hurting me, or overpowering me." He turned his attention to the man holding her. "If he tries anything, shoot her."

The man smiled cruelly and tightened his grip.

"You got it."

If I stay behind, maybe they'll let her go...

The trouble was he didn't think she'd leave him behind. The thought was warming and exasperating in equal measure. It was all too easy for him to imagine a situation where Jillian had an opportunity to leave, but chose to stay with him. After all, she'd been doing just that since they'd first escaped the gang at the motel.

Dan led them through the hospital parking garage, stopping at a black van. "Your behavior has a direct correlation on how I will treat the woman." Alex glanced back to see Jillian and her escort approaching, still several yards away. Dan kept his voice low, apparently wanting this conversation to be private. "If you continue to behave, I'll kill her quickly. If you try anything…" He trailed off, shrugging. "You'll just have to imagine the things I'll have done to her before she dies. Maybe I'll even let you watch some of it before I dispose of you."

Alex nodded, not trusting his voice. He knew Dan wasn't making an empty threat. And if there were more gang members where he was taking them, he'd have no shortage of volunteers ready and willing to step in and administer pain, even to a woman they didn't know.

Jillian and Kyle caught up to them and Dan opened the back door, gesturing Alex forward. He climbed inside to find the interior had been modified. Two bucket seats sat by each door, but the entire back of the vehicle was open, providing a flat, stable surface for Dan to ride in his chair. While he was happy to see Jillian wouldn't be far away from him, he had hoped to sit next to her. Even though neither one of them had a weapon, he would have liked to touch her during the ride.

Apparently Kyle pulled double duty as Dan's enforcer and chauffeur. After everyone was inside, he climbed into the driver's seat and started the van. Seated behind him, Alex was perfectly positioned to reach forward and strangle the man. He moved the barest inch, his body wanting to take action before his mind had finished contemplating the best strategy. Then he felt the tap on his shoulder and turned around to find Dan pointing a small, snub-nosed pistol at Jillian.

"None of that," he warned, correctly guessing Alex's thoughts. "I may not be an expert marksman, but at this distance, I can hit anything."

Jillian held his gaze, her brown eyes wide with fear. But he saw anger and determination there, as well, and while he knew there wasn't anything either of them could do now, she wasn't giving up. Neither would he.

The drive didn't take long. Within minutes the van pulled into an alley off R Street, and the driver climbed out. He opened the back door for Dan, who reversed down the wheelchair ramp, leaving Alex and Jillian alone.

He turned to face her, determined to take advantage of their brief isolation. "When I cause a distraction, I want you to run."

She shook her head. "I'm not leaving you," she whispered fiercely.

"Listen to me," he hissed. "I need you to get out. I love you for wanting to stay, but I won't let you get killed for me."

Jillian blinked at him. "You love me?" She sounded incredulous and just a little breathless.

Real smooth, Malcom. He'd wanted to share his feelings when they were both safe, and they could talk about what to do next. Instead, he'd blurted out the most important words of his life when they were both in grave danger. One more thing he'd messed up. "Say you'll leave. Please." He let some of the desperation he felt creep into his voice.

She opened her mouth to respond, but the door next to him opened, putting an end to their conversation. He gave her a meaningful look and after a second's hesitation she nodded once.

"Let's go." Kyle reached in and clamped a hand on Alex's injured shoulder, squeezing hard. White-hot pain flowed down his arm and into his chest, making his vision blur. He bit down hard on his tongue to contain the moan fighting to escape the confines of his clenched teeth. He would not show weakness in front of this man, or any other. The gang operated under the laws of the jungle, and vulnerability was seen as an invitation to do more harm.

Jillian emitted a cry of distress and he glared at her, shaking his head subtly. *No*, he mouthed, hoping she would stay quiet. If she revealed his injury, it would only make things worse.

"What's your problem?" The man glanced at Jillian, but kept a tight hold on Alex. "I haven't even touched you. Yet." A slow smile spread across his face and he licked his lips suggestively.

Jillian shuddered, her revulsion clear.

"That's enough." Dan wheeled around to the side of the vehicle, coming to a stop a few feet away. "Bring them inside. Then you can have your fun." He beckoned to Jillian and, after a moment's hesitation, she climbed out of the van.

They moved up a ramp and through the front door of the row house. The entry hall was wide and bright, with light streaming in from the tall, narrow windows on either side of the door. Tarps covered the floors and walls, and the lingering smell of paint hung in the air. Dan led them into a room off the right side of the hall, the wheels of his chair making the plastic covering crackle as he moved.

The room was empty, the walls and floor lined like the hall. A knot formed in Alex's stomach as he took in the sinister draping. Every surface was covered, including the windows, which would make cleanup easy.

"I'm curious," he said, trying to fake a confidence he didn't feel. "How, exactly, are you going to get rid of our bodies? You seem to have thought of everything else." He waved a hand, encompassing the room and its macabre decoration.

"Don't worry about that," Dan replied. "We have other things to focus on." He glanced at the enforcer, who stepped forward, plastic cuffs in hand. Kyle fastened them around Alex's wrists, not bothering to be gentle about it. He pulled, and Alex moved reluctantly across the room, being led like a lamb to slaughter.

A long metal chain hung from the exposed ceiling beams, a lethal-looking hook swaying gently at the end. The thick metal links gleamed dully in the filtered light of the room. Alex tensed, but it was no use. His arms were forced above his head, the cuffs captured on the hook. The strain on his shoulder was almost unbearable, but he refused to make a sound. He stood on his toes to take some of the pressure off the joints, making him lurch precariously. He was forced to watch, helpless, as the man restrained Jillian with another set of the cuffs.

"Go fetch the others," Dan instructed. "You know where to park."

"You sure?" Kyle asked. "I don't like leaving you alone with them."

"Please," Dan scoffed. "They're hardly a threat. Besides…" He pulled out his small gun and pointed it at Alex. "She's not going to do anything to me while I'm pointing this at her lover. Now go."

Kyle left the room and a few seconds later the front door slammed. Alex felt the vibrations of it travel through the chain and down his arms, a strange, almost pleasant sensation.

"Now." Dan smiled up at him. "It's just us."

Yes, indeed, you bastard.

Dan didn't realize it yet, but he'd just made a fatal mistake. He was outnumbered, and although his gun gave him a false sense of security, it wouldn't provide the protection he needed. Guns only worked if the person on the other side was afraid of getting shot. And Alex wasn't, especially not if it meant protecting Jillian.

"Got something on your mind?" Alex said. He glanced at Jillian. She was standing very still, her eyes wide and unblinking. She hadn't made a sound since they'd been taken from the van, and he hoped that she wasn't going into shock. He needed her to be ready to run.

As if she felt him looking at her, Jillian turned and met his gaze. He offered her what he hoped was a reassuring smile, gritting his teeth as a tear slid down her cheek.

"Are you expecting me to explain this to you?" Dan asked. He moved closer, his expression almost comical.

"You're the one who brought me here," Alex replied.

Just a little closer… He just needed Dan to get in range. A few more feet and he'd be able to kick him in the face. He might even be able to kick him hard enough to knock him out, if his shoulders could stand the stress. It was going to hurt like hell to throw his legs out, but it was the best chance they had.

And he'd only get one shot at it.

"Do I look like a Bond villain to you?" Dan scoffed. "You really think I'm going to sit here and tell you everything before you die?"

"Sounds fair to me," he said. His gaze snapped back to Jillian when she stirred, her hands slowly dipping into her front coat pocket. What was she doing? She wore an expression of fierce concentration, her eyes flicking to Dan and back to him, her meaning clear.

Distract him!

"You did go to all this trouble," Alex continued, nodding as best he could at their surroundings. "I figured you'd want to gloat a little. You know, brag about how you got the drop on me. Like how did you make your connections with the gang? It took me years to work my way in. How'd you do it so quickly?"

"Flatter me all you want. I'm not going to spare your life."

"Then telling me shouldn't be a problem." He wiggled his fingers, trying to stave off the numbness creeping down his arms. "If I'm going to die soon, why do you care if I know your secret?"

Dan eyed him appraisingly and then shrugged. "Fine. We do have a little time before the others arrive. I might as well tell you now." An evil smile spread across his face. "Besides, once we get started, the only thing you'll be able to hear is the sound of your own screams."

* * *

Jillian's heart stuttered at Dan's announcement. She'd known Dan planned to kill them, but the thought of torture made her knees tremble alarmingly. *Don't fall down...* Right now, Alex was doing a decent job of holding Dan's attention, but if she collapsed, it would wreck her plan.

She fumbled through her front coat pocket, trying not to make any sudden moves that would remind Dan of her presence. Her fingers connected with the cool plastic of Jim's recorder, but she pushed it to the side, digging deeper. She didn't remember taking it out of her pocket, so it should still be there...

Yes! Right there! Buried at the bottom of the pocket was the syringe she'd filled in the motel bathroom, the one she'd thought to use on Alex. She brushed against the cylinder, trying to get a grip on the smooth barrel so she could pull it out. She bit her lip as she worked, determined not to make a sound.

Finally, after what seemed like ages, she caught the top of the plunger with her fingernail. In one smooth motion, she pulled up, withdrawing the syringe and repositioning her hands for a better grip.

Alex gave no indication he'd seen the syringe, but he continued to antagonize Dan. He was careful though, poking at Dan just enough to hold the other man's attention, but not so much that Dan might snap and start shooting at them. It was a fine line he walked and, once again, Jillian marveled at his ability to manipulate the situation, even when he was tied up and incapable of fighting.

Slowly, so slowly, Jillian moved back and to the side, positioning herself behind Dan. She would only get one chance at this, and she had to do it right. If she missed, or if Dan caught her, he would shoot her and then Alex. Not exactly the outcome she was hoping for.

Jillian put the needle in her mouth, biting down on the plastic cap. A quick jerk forward and the needle was unsheathed, ready to administer the drug. She didn't remember what, exactly, was in the syringe, but it should knock Dan out. She just hoped it wouldn't kill him. Dan needed to spend the rest of his life rotting in prison for the things he'd done. She didn't want to deny Alex the justice he so richly deserved.

Dan leaned forward, waving his arm as he made a particularly forceful argument. Seeing her chance, Jillian darted close and aimed for the side of Dan's upper thigh. The needle passed easily through his clothes, sinking into his flesh with a satisfying resistance that was at once familiar and gratifying. She pushed down on the plunger, injecting the solution as quickly as she could. Then she stepped back, leaving the syringe still in place.

Alex kept his gaze on Dan's face, but she saw the corners of his mouth twitch and knew he'd seen everything. She fought the urge to whoop in triumph and grinned back at him instead. She'd done it.

"What's so funny?" Dan asked. Jillian stepped to the side a split second before he turned to search for her, putting a bit of distance between them. He narrowed his eyes and pointed the gun in her direction. "What are you doing back there?"

Jillian swallowed hard, trying to look innocent and scared. The scared part was easy, but innocent? She'd never been a very good liar. "I'm n-not doing anything," she stammered. She held up her hands, still bound by the plastic cuffs, as proof. Dan relaxed a bit at the sight, but kept the gun trained on her.

"Move over there." He indicated a spot closer to Alex, but still far enough away that she couldn't touch him. "I want you both in my sight."

She glanced at Alex while she moved, wincing in sympathy. His hands had turned the dark reddish-purple of a ripe plum, and she could only imagine how painful the stretched position was for his injured shoulder. But he showed no signs of distress, and if she didn't know better, she'd say he looked bored.

"Getting a little paranoid, don't you think?" Alex asked. "What exactly do you think either one of us can do to you, tied up like we are?"

Dan shook his head, as though he was trying to clear his ears. "I don't trust you," he said slowly, the words slurring together. His arm slowly drooped, the gun lowering to point harmlessly at the floor. Then his head tilted down, making him look like he was taking a nap.

Jillian took a step forward, intent on taking the gun away from Dan. She stopped when Alex uttered a sharply whispered, "Not yet!" Sure enough, Dan's head snapped back up to loll on his neck and he blinked at them, clearly trying to process what was happening to him.

"What—what did you do to me?"

Jillian could barely understand his mumbling, but his meaning was clear enough. He yanked his arm up, the gun waving wildly in her general direction. She stepped back, but it was no use—there was no place for her to hide, and Dan had no control over the gun. His shot could go anywhere. She stood stock-still, heart pounding hard, hoping Dan didn't use the last of his muscle control to pull the trigger.

"She didn't do anything to you," Alex said, his voice soothing and soporific. "Nothing's wrong. Just calm down."

Dan shook his head again, but the drug was too powerful and he was starting to lose the battle for consciousness. He made a few more incoherent sounds before surrendering, his body going lax in the chair. Jillian let her breath out in a sigh and glanced at Alex.

At his nod, she moved toward Dan, approaching him from the side. If he wasn't fully under yet, she had a better chance of not getting shot if she wasn't directly in front of him.

She reached for the gun, surprised to find it was warm. She had expected cold metal, but the plastic grip had absorbed the heat from Dan's hand. Sliding it free from Dan's grasp, she placed the gun on the floor, several feet away from his chair. Then she walked back to Alex and used her shoulders to prop him up a few inches so he could unhook his hands.

He brought his arms down slowly, grimacing while he moved. The fabric of his shirt smoothed out as he stretched his arms back into position, revealing a reddish-brown stain on his shoulder.

"You're bleeding," Jillian said, stepping forward and raising her bound hands. She couldn't do much with her hands tied together, but she wanted to look at the wound to get a sense of how badly he'd reinjured his shoulder.

Alex waved her off. "No time. I'm fine." He turned, presenting her with his back. "There's a small knife in my pocket. Can you reach it?"

"Shouldn't we be going?" Now that Alex was free,

there was no reason for them to stick around. Especially not with gang reinforcements due to arrive any minute.

"I'm going to need my hands first." She pulled the pocketknife free and unfolded the small, lethal-looking blade, then set to work sawing at Alex's bindings. Her nerves made her movements frantic and hurried, and more than once, she came dangerously close to cutting the pale, smooth skin of his inner wrists. Wouldn't that just be the perfect end to this day?

"It's okay," he said, his deep voice rumbling through her and leaving a sense of calm peace in its wake. "You're doing great. I'm going to cut you free next, and then we'll get out of here."

She nodded, keeping her attention on the task at hand. "When do you think Dan's bodyguard will be back?"

"Long after we're gone," Alex replied. She didn't know if he was lying to make her feel better, or if he knew something she didn't. Either way, Jillian chose to believe him, using his confidence to battle back the fear trying to claim her.

The plastic gave way with a satisfying snap and Jillian didn't try to contain her cry of relief.

Alex dropped his hands, shaking them out as he sought to regain the feeling in his fingers. The color of his skin was fading, but his fingers would likely be stiff and sore for several days. Not to mention his wrists—hopefully, the position hadn't done any lasting damage to the joints.

He gestured for the knife and Jillian passed it to him. She held up her arms, careful to keep her wrists pulled as far apart as the cuffs allowed while he worked to free her. Despite his recent ordeal, Alex's movements were more controlled than hers had been and he cut through the cuffs much faster.

Jillian started moving toward the door before the plastic cuffs had even hit the floor. It took her a few steps to realize Alex wasn't with her, and she turned to find him holding the gun, his expression thoughtful.

"Alex?" She felt a sudden frisson of unease at the way he looked at the gun, then at Dan, then back to the gun in his hands. It didn't take a mind reader to know what Alex was considering.

She stepped closer, careful not to make any sudden movements. While she knew without a doubt that Alex would never hurt her, she didn't want to startle him into shooting Dan accidentally.

"I should do it," he said softly. "It would be so much easier. And it's what he deserves."

"Yes," she said carefully. "It would be easier."

"I just want it to end. How many times has he gotten away with it? How many people died because of him?"

"Too many."

Alex stared at Dan for a long moment and then turned his gaze to Jillian. Anger, confusion and hurt danced across his features, and her heart broke for him and the pain he was in. "So why can't I pull the trigger?"

"Because you're not that kind of man," she said, infusing all the love she felt for him into those words. "You are not a murderer, Alex. And despite the justice of it, this would be a murder."

He laughed; a sharp bark of sound that was devoid of humor. "I may not have pulled the trigger, but I am responsible for deaths," he said, echoing Dan's earlier statement. Alex nodded at the unconscious man in acknowledgment. "He did get that part right."

"I'm sure you only did what you had to in order to survive." She had to make him understand, make him realize that she didn't judge him for the things he'd had to do to stay alive while working undercover. She couldn't begin to imagine the difficulties he'd faced living a double life, knowing that one wrong step would be his last.

Alex shook his head. "Don't you see? That makes me just as much of an animal as the guys I tried to put away."

Jillian was silent for a moment, considering his words. "I don't know what you did, but I know who you are now. The choices you've made since I've met you have showed me that you are a good man, no matter what your past holds. You can't spend your life looking back, Alex. You need to forgive yourself and move on."

He blinked at her and then nodded slowly. "Maybe you're right," he muttered. He glanced down at the gun in his hand, looking mildly surprised to find that he still held it. He started to put it on the floor but halted midway and tucked it into the waistband of his pants instead.

Jillian's stomach twisted as she processed the implications of his action. Did he think they would encounter the gang on their way out? Would one small gun be enough to protect them? And could he even fire it, with his fingers still stiff and swollen?

"Let's go," he said, cutting through her increasingly frantic thoughts.

He held his hand out to her and she took it, grateful for the contact.

"I've kept us here long enough."

Jillian reached up and touched his cheek, gently

stroking her fingers across the rough stubble. "Are you all right?" she said softly.

He smiled at her, then leaned down and pressed a quick yet sweet kiss to her lips. "I'm always fine when I'm with you."

She squeezed his hand and they moved together to the door. After a quick glance showed the hall was empty, they headed for the front door. "We need to find a phone," Alex said, speaking softly even though they were alone in the house. "I want to call the Bureau and leave an anonymous tip about Dan."

"Do you think they'll get here in time to find him?" She had no idea how long he'd be out, but hopefully the effects of the drug would last long enough for the FBI to apprehend him.

Alex approached the front door and gestured for Jillian to get behind him. He opened the door a crack, then stepped back as it was pushed in from the outside. Several men dressed in black tactical gear entered, their weapons drawn and pointed at Alex. He raised his hands in surrender and Jillian quickly followed suit.

"FBI," the lead man barked. "Get on the floor now!"

Relief was an overwhelming sensation that flooded her system and made her knees weak. Jillian hit the floor and dropped forward to lie on her belly, offering no resistance as one of the other men patted her down. They did the same to Alex, who caught her eye before they put cuffs on him.

"How's that for timing?" he said wryly.

Chapter 15

She was going mad.

It had been three days since the FBI had stormed the town house, arresting Dan and hauling her and Alex in for questioning. They had separated her from Alex, taking her to a stuffy, windowless room in the bowels of the J. Edgar Hoover building. There, she'd been subjected to a marathon interrogation session, culminating with her questioner frowning down at her and proclaiming that if she had been anything less than truthful, the entire force of the U.S. justice system would be brought to bear on her fragile little head. She had narrowly resisted the urge to roll her eyes at him, instead opting for the more diplomatic route. She assured him that she'd told him the truth, the whole truth and nothing but the truth, which had earned her a snort. She had meant it, though. Mostly.

She hadn't told him about the fact that she and Alex had slept together, and she certainly hadn't told him that she'd grown to care for him, very deeply. In fact, if she were really being honest with herself, she loved him. While she recognized his impromptu declaration of love had been made in a moment of crisis, she still held the words close to her heart, feeling a warm tingling in her chest when she remembered his deep voice saying them to her. It was a far cry from candles and roses, but she wouldn't have it any other way.

Eventually she'd been released with a sternly worded warning that she was not to leave the city without telling them first. As if. She'd returned to work the next day, part of her grateful for the distraction, the other part anxious to take off and comb the city for any sign of Alex. It was the same desperation she'd felt when Jason had disappeared the last time, but now, it was tinged with a frantic sense of panic. Jason had left because he'd wanted to. Alex had been taken from her.

It didn't help that she had no way of getting in touch with him. His real address, phone number, email—she didn't know any of them. How could she love a man and not have any idea how to find him? It was a strange world indeed when she knew the important things about Alex's character and personality, but didn't know something as basic as his contact information.

She'd tried calling the FBI, but quickly realized that was an exercise in futility. To say they had been less than forthcoming would be a massive understatement—the people who worked there could make a brick wall look like Swiss cheese. She'd finally given up that approach, not wanting to give them any more ammunition against Alex. She wasn't well versed in FBI rules and regulations, but she was pretty sure that kidnapping someone and then sleeping with them was a big no-no. He'd probably been questioned extensively on the nature of their relationship, and if she kept calling to inquire after him, it would only make them more suspicious.

She'd tried to see Jim, heading back to the hospital in the hope that he could give her a means of reaching out to Alex. But by the time she'd gotten there, he'd been released to complete his recovery at home. Since his personal information was protected, she had no way of knowing how to find him. Not unless she wanted to break protocol and access his records, which would cause her to lose her job, a decidedly unattractive option.

So here she sat, alone in her apartment. Christmas was a day away, a holiday she normally enjoyed. But she couldn't get into the holiday spirit, not when she was still so worried about Alex.

Her friend Carla had noticed her change in mood. "What's going on with you?" the other woman had asked, cornering Jillian at the nurse's station earlier in the day. "You've been really quiet since you came back from your three days off."

Jillian had offered her a faint smile. While she appreciated Carla's concern, she really didn't want to get into the story of what had happened over her break. "I'm just tired," she said. "I spent most of my break doing laundry and cleaning the apartment. Not really much of a vacation."

"I know how that goes." Carla eyed her thoughtfully. "But something seems off about you. Are you sure you're okay? You normally love the holidays, but I haven't seen you wear any of your pins yet."

Jillian had a collection of holiday pins that she wore on the lapel of her white coat. She normally enjoyed the small bit of flair, and her patients seemed to like it too, often commenting on the snowman, reindeer, holly branch or Santa on her coat. The staff got a kick out of seeing what she picked every day, and it was a fun way to get into the holiday spirit. She normally started wearing them about two weeks before Christmas, but the holiday was tomorrow and she'd hadn't worn one yet. She made a mental note to put on one tomorrow, if only to deflect more questions.

"It totally slipped my mind," she said, injecting a cheerfulness she didn't feel into her voice. "The days are going by faster and faster—the holiday is really sneaking up on me this year."

"I hear you," Carla affirmed. "I barely have time to get any Christmas shopping done. If it wasn't for the internet, none of my family would have any presents!"

Carla had seemed content to leave her alone after their conversation, but her friend's concern had made her realize how much Alex's absence had affected her. Never in her wildest imaginings would she have dreamed that she'd fall in love with a man in a little more than two days' time, but that's exactly what had happened. And while the logical part of her felt she should be concerned that things were moving too fast, her heart understood that they had packed a lot of living into those few short hours. She had seen Alex at his worst, laid bare and exposed, and she still wanted him.

If she could only find him.

Were they still questioning him? Her interrogation had taken hours, and she'd only played a peripheral role in the drama. She could only imagine how long it would take to get the full story from Alex, to unravel the knot of details surrounding the failed operation and everything that had happened since then.

But more importantly, did they believe him? Her stomach tightened at the thought of Alex in a prison cell. He'd run because his own coworkers had turned against him—had they changed their minds? Did they realize Alex wasn't to blame, and that Dan was the traitor? She had no idea if Jim's recorder had picked up anything through her pocket, but surely they had people who could enhance anything that was there? And Jim had said he believed Alex and knew the truth— was that enough?

She stared down into her bowl, pushing the chocolate puffs around with her spoon. They bobbed lazily on the surface, moving along the current she created in the milk. She wasn't hungry. Ever since the FBI had released her, there was a tightness in her throat that made it hard to swallow. Still, she knew it was important to eat. Cold cereal wasn't ideal, as far as dinners went, but it was better than nothing.

After a few minutes she gave up pretending and rose from the table to carry her bowl into the kitchen. She turned on the faucet to rinse out the bowl, but turned it off after she heard a soft knock at her door. She paused, unsure if the sound had been real or just a product of her imagination. After a few seconds she heard it again, a little louder this time.

She debated ignoring it, as she wasn't in the mood for company. But it might be Mrs. Rodriguez. While most of her neighbor's issues were insignificant, she could be having an emergency, and Jillian would never forgive herself if something happened to the older woman because she'd failed to answer the door.

She grabbed a dish towel, drying her hands as she walked to the door. She pulled it open and froze, the damp towel landing softly at her feet.

"Hi."

He looked good, she noted, running her eyes over him in instinctive appraisal. Dressed in dark jeans with a hunter-green sweater pulled over a white button-down shirt, he looked nothing like the desperate, hunted man who had forced her into a car almost a week ago.

Jillian swallowed hard, not trusting her voice. "Hi."

Alex offered her a dazzling smile and held out the bright red poinsettia he was carrying. "I noticed you didn't have any holiday decorations up," he said by way of explanation. "So I decided to help you out."

"Thanks." She accepted the plant with numb fingers, still shocked at the drastic turnaround in his appearance. She'd gotten used to seeing him in rags, his hair too long and his face covered in stubble. Seeing him now, all clean-cut and presentable, made it hard to reconcile this man with the one she'd known.

"Uh, come in." She stepped back, brushing a hand over the front of her scrub top as he moved past. It was silly, she knew, but the new and improved Alex made her feel underdressed, and she was very aware of the fact that she hadn't showered in more than eighteen hours. She sniffed experimentally at her top, hoping she didn't reek of the hospital.

She shut the door and turned to find Alex watching her, his gaze soft and tender. Her breath caught in her throat and she blinked to clear the tears that had suddenly appeared. Without breaking eye contact, she carefully set the plant on the floor. Then she took three quick steps forward and flung herself into his waiting arms.

"God, I've missed you." His voice was a low rumble in her ear, his hands fisting in her top as he gripped her tight and crushed her to his chest.

"I know," she murmured. She breathed in, the clean, musky scent of him—new, but yet somehow still familiar.

"Are you all right? They wouldn't let me talk to you."

"I'm fine. Better, now that you're here."

His chuckle vibrated through his chest and into hers, making her smile. "Were they nice to you?"

She shrugged, still holding him close. "I wouldn't say 'nice' exactly, but they weren't horrible, either."

"How long did they question you?"

"A few hours. What about you? I've been going out of my mind, worried that they didn't believe you, or that they threw you in some dark hole where I'd never be able to find you."

He laughed, stroking his hand down her hair. "No, the dungeon is full. It took me a couple of days, but I managed to get the whole story out. Jim corroborated the details."

"And Dan?"

He sighed, shifting slightly. "Dan swore up and down that I was lying. But since you managed to record him—" he squeezed her gently for emphasis "—his protestations of innocence didn't go far."

"Oh, good. I was hoping the recorder would pick up his voice through my coat pocket."

"Jim always buys the best," Alex said, a smile in his voice.

Jillian leaned back to look at him, enjoying the view. "Is Jim okay?"

Alex nodded. "He'll be fine. In fact, he's the reason the squad found us so quickly."

She tilted her head to the side. "How so?"

"The recorder you had in your pocket? It has a tracking chip. Jim woke during our conversation with Dan in his room. Once we left, he called in reinforcements and they were able to pinpoint our location thanks to the signal from the device."

"Amazing," she murmured, shaking her head. "When we were right in the middle of things, I had a hard time imagining we'd make it through. But we did, and now we can put all of that behind us and move on with our lives."

Alex stiffened against her and a tremor of unease shot down her spine. Had she said something wrong? Was he upset at her use of the word "we"? Maybe she was moving too fast, pushing him toward something he didn't want. Her stomach tightened, a familiar sense of dread washing over her. The last time she'd tried to get serious with a man, he'd turned out to be a lying cad. But although she trusted Alex completely, had she made another mistake? Did he not want to get involved with her?

"I'm sorry," she said, releasing her grip on him and stepping back. "I shouldn't have assumed. I mean— I didn't mean to imply that we—" She gestured between them, feeling her face heat.

Alex stared down at her, his expression serious. "That's why I came here," he said softly. "We need to talk."

Jillian shook her head, embarrassment a hot wave that crashed over her head and made her skin burn.

"No, really, it's okay. You don't need to explain. I understand." He opened his mouth to respond, but she held up a hand. "I get it. We came together in the heat of the moment, and now that things have calmed down, it's time we returned to real life. It was just the adrenaline— I'm sure it happens all the time." She couldn't meet his eyes, so she focused on his broad shoulders instead. Had his injury healed? She didn't want to ask him a personal question while he was clearly trying to let her down gently.

"Well, it's been a long day and I'm sure you're still catching up on rest after everything that's happened." She moved to the door, her hand on the knob. "I'm glad everything turned out well for you, and I wish you the best."

Please just leave. It hurts too much to look at you.

Alex didn't move but he kept his eyes on her, his gaze unreadable. "Are you done?"

She blinked, taken aback by his question. "Uh," she said, stalling. "Thank you for the plant?"

"You're welcome," he replied solicitously. "Is it my turn to talk now?"

Jillian let go of the doorknob, her brows pulling together in puzzlement. Did he really think he had to spell it out for her?

Apparently so. He gestured for her to sit on the couch, and she gingerly lowered herself to the cushion, bracing for the words that would remove him from her life forever.

"Okay." He took a few pacing steps, stopped and sucked in a deep breath. "There's something I need to tell you, and I'm not sure how to start." He ran a hand through his hair, breaking her gaze to stare down at the floor.

Jillian sat forward, his uncharacteristic distress making her nervous. Even when Dan had pointed a gun at him, Alex hadn't broken a sweat. For him to be so discomposed now told her he had something troubling to share.

"Why don't you start at the beginning?" she asked softly. "I think that's probably the easiest approach."

He sent her a half-smile and nodded. "I suppose you're right," he replied. "Here goes, then.

"I know what happened to your brother."

She felt as though a bucket of ice water had just been dumped over her head. Her body went completely numb and for a few seconds her mind was blank, like a computer going through a reboot process.

Her brain finally kicked back on with a small shock that ran through her system, making her arms jerk slightly. Jillian shook her head, certain she had misunderstood. What was he talking about? Jason had disappeared from her life two years ago. How could Alex possibly know him? She opened her mouth to speak, but she couldn't force the words out. Swallowing hard, she tried again. "What do you mean?"

"I saw him once. A couple of years ago."

"Were you his dealer?" She hadn't meant the question to sound so harsh, but Alex flinched like she'd slapped him.

"No." He shook his head emphatically.

"Then how—?"

Alex held up his hand, cutting her off. "I was meeting with another dealer, trying to bring him into the gang.

Tony, the kid you patched up, was keeping watch outside in the alley. Your brother came along and wanted
to see the guy, needing a fix. I guess he was agitated,
and he and Tony got into a scuffle." He swallowed, then
continued, the words growing quieter as he went on.
"Tony shot him. I stepped out into the alley to see what
had happened, but by the time I found your brother, he
was already gone."

"And then what happened?"

"I checked his pockets for identification, but didn't
find anything. I reported it to Jim as soon as I could,
and his death was added to the growing list of gang
crimes. But I don't know if the local police ever really
investigated."

"I see." An aching heaviness settled in her chest as
she pictured Jason, drug-thin and desperate, dying in
a dirty alley surrounded by strangers. He'd never been
violent—not when he'd been high, not when she'd seen
him in withdrawal. The idea that he had somehow attacked Tony, provoked the kid into shooting, was ab-
surd. No way would Jason ever do that. It was likely an
excuse Tony had come up with to explain his twitchy
trigger finger.

She thought back to the dingy motel room and Tony,
lying helpless on the bed in front of her. He had the body
of a young man, but he was no innocent. She'd caught
a glimpse of his cold, desensitized nature when he'd
talked about torturing Alex. She shivered at the memory of his expression, the feral light in his eyes and the
pleasure in his voice as he'd contemplated killing Alex
slowly. Tony enjoyed causing pain. She had no doubt
he needed very little provocation to inflict it.

And she had saved his life, pulling him from the jaws

of death to act as grim reaper to the ones unfortunate enough to get in his way.

Her numbness was fading quickly, replaced by a bright, fierce anger that flowed through her like lava.

"Did you know?" she asked, her voice sounding dangerous, even to her ears. "Did you know who I was when you took me?" She stood and stalked toward Alex, who took a reflexive step back. "Did you make me save my brother's killer?"

"No!" Alex tried to put his hands on her shoulders, but she shied away, glaring at him. "I swear, Jillian, I didn't know. I had no idea who you were the other night. You were a stranger to me."

She studied him for a long moment, trying to gauge the sincerity of his words. His tone was earnest, appealing even, and he held her gaze without flinching or shifting. He bore her scrutiny without comment, as if sensing that additional protests wouldn't help to convince her. Finally she sighed, turning away from him. It was all too much. She needed a minute to think, to process what was happening.

A thought occurred to her, accompanied by a small thrill of hope that made her gasp. Perhaps Alex was mistaken, and the man who had died in the alley wasn't Jason, after all. How could he be sure after two years? That was a long time, and if he'd only seen the man for a moment, had he really gotten a good look at his features?

"How did you know?"

"What?" She could tell he had moved to follow her, but he made no move to touch her again. "How did I know what?"

"If you didn't know Jason, and you didn't know me, how did you link us together?"

"Oh." He sounded uncomfortable again, and she turned to face him, wondering if this was the moment his story was going to fall apart.

"Maybe you're wrong," she challenged.

He shook his head. "I'm not," he said sadly. He walked over to her bookshelves and reached for a framed picture. "As soon as I saw this, I knew."

"This" was a picture of Jason, his arm around Jillian after her graduation from medical school. He looked happy and proud, if a little pale.

Jillian took the frame from him, tracing her fingertip across her brother's face.

"That's why you were upset. The night I brought you here." It all added up—Alex's sudden withdrawal, his desire to leave, to get away from her.

He nodded. "I almost threw up when I saw that picture. I couldn't believe it."

Moving carefully, Jillian set the picture back on the shelf. "Why didn't you tell me that night?"

"You had already been through so much…" he began, but she shook her head.

"I am not a child. You don't get to treat me like one."

He reached for her, but she stepped away. "I brought you into my home. I treated your injuries, fed you, gave you my brother's clothes, for God's sake!" And wasn't that the height of irony? She had shared Jason's clothes with the man who'd had a hand in his death—some sister she was.

"I slept with you," she whispered, the words thick in her mouth. "Only to find out you used me." She shook her head. What was it about her that told men they could lie to her and use her for sex? First Mark and now Alex. She was better off alone, and she needed to remember it.

"It wasn't like that!"

"Wasn't it? From where I'm standing, it seems like you kept the truth from me because you were afraid I wouldn't help you if I found out about Jason."

"From where I'm standing," he snapped back, "it seems like that was a correct assumption."

She narrowed her eyes at him. "So you admit it?"

"No!" He thrust a hand through his hair, clearly searching for words. "Was I afraid you'd kick me out if I told you about your brother? Yes. But that wasn't the only reason I kept it from you. We needed time to talk about it, and if you recall, time was something we didn't really have. Not while we were in the middle of things. So I decided to tell you later, after we were safe." He spread out his hands, encompassing the two of them. "And here I am."

"You were worried about time?" she huffed. "You certainly had time to sleep with me!"

Alex took a step forward, his eyes glinting dangerously. "As I recall," he said coldly, "you were very willing to sleep with me, as well."

Jillian felt her face heat and turned away, but he grabbed her arm, holding her in place. "Don't try to cheapen what we did, or what was between us. That meant something to me." He released her and stepped back, giving her room. "It still does."

The couch was a few feet away and she staggered over to it, dropping onto the cushion and putting her head in her hands. It hurt to breathe. Her chest felt tight and constricted, and it seemed as if all the oxygen had been sucked out of the room.

How could she have been so wrong? She'd allowed herself to fall in love with this man, thinking he was a good guy, that he would never hurt her. But he'd been lying to her all along.

Just like Mark.

It's not that surprising, a cynical voice inside her head commented. *He's an undercover agent. He lies for a living. Why should you be any different?*

Why, indeed? Thinking back, the signs of his deception had been there all along. His reaction to the photo, which she'd assumed had been due to the pain of his injury. His reluctance to talk about his past with the gang and the things he'd done. The way he'd squirmed when he'd told him about Jason. Seemingly innocent actions that took on a new terrible meaning now that she knew the truth.

"I know you blame me for Jason's death," Alex said softly. "And I can't tell you how sorry I am for it. I'd give anything to be able to go back and stop Tony from shooting him."

Jillian stared at him in disbelief, then shook her head. "I don't blame you for that."

"You don't?" He sounded puzzled and the slightest bit relieved, as though he'd just been granted an unexpected reprieve. His expression brightened and he moved to kneel next to her. "Then we can move on?" He sounded almost shy, but his eyes were shiny with hope.

Jillian's heart crumpled at the sight. Moments ago she would have gladly said yes, would have thrown herself into his arms and cried tears of happiness at the thought of their future together. But now she couldn't look at him without seeing Jason, without hearing the echo of Mark's voice. And while a small, foolish part of her would always love this man, his betrayal had cut too deeply, leaving a wound that couldn't be healed with pretty words and apologies.

"You lied to me," she said, hating the way her voice shook. "You lied to me about Jason's death. What else have you been keeping from me?"

"Nothing. I swear to you." He wrapped his large hands around her smaller one, squeezing gently. "What can I do to prove it to you? I'll do anything—just tell me what I need to do to make this right."

She shook her head, ignoring his pleading tone. "It doesn't work that way." She pulled away from his touch, growing colder as she withdrew deeper into herself. "I can't trust you, Alex. And that's the truth."

Chapter 16

"Okay, spill it."

Jillian looked up from her salad as Carla slid into the chair across from her. The hospital cafeteria wasn't crowded, and she made a show of glancing at the empty chairs nearby while she continued to chew. Carla merely raised a brow at her, unimpressed.

"I don't mean to be rude, but I'm not really in the mood for company right now." Jillian returned her focus to her plate, hoping Carla would take the hint.

She didn't.

"You've been working almost nonstop over the past few days. You volunteered to work on Christmas Eve and Christmas Day, and I know you tried to get on the schedule for tomorrow, even though tonight is New Year's Eve. While I've never thought of you as lazy, that schedule is pretty extreme. Makes me think you're trying to avoid something. Or someone." She took a healthy swig from her water bottle.

"You might be able to fool everyone else, but you can't fool me. I know something happened to you, missy, and I want you to tell me about it." The crinkle of cellophane punctuated her words as Carla unwrapped her sandwich and crumpled the malleable film into a ball.

"I'm fine. Really."

Her friend snorted and set to work opening a single-serve bag of chips, popping one into her mouth with a crunch. "I don't think so," she said. "I let you off the hook once before, but I'm not going to do it again."

"Carla…" Jillian set her fork down with a sigh.

"Jillian." Carla's brown eyes were wide and beseeching. "You're my friend. I can see that something is eating at you, and it worries me. Won't you please talk to me?"

Jillian blinked hard, trying to rein in her wayward emotions. She was not the kind of woman who cried at work, and certainly not in the cafeteria! But Carla's obvious concern soared over the protective wall she'd built around her heart, and in that moment she felt less alone.

It had been a week since Alex had dropped his bomb and destroyed her hopes regarding both him and her brother. She had always known that the silence from her brother was a bad sign, but having his death confirmed wrecked her illusions. Over the years she had taken comfort in pretending that Jason had moved to a new city and started a fresh life, free from his addictions and troubles. Now, she could no longer hide from the truth, and she grieved the loss of Jason all over again.

To make matters worse, every time she closed her

eyes she was assaulted by a host of horrible images, a movie reel of Jason getting shot and bleeding out playing on constant loop thanks to Alex's description. He hadn't been graphic by any means, but her imagination filled in all the gaps with a prize-winning director's attention to detail. It made sleep almost impossible, and what rest she did manage to get was fitful and sporadic.

And then there was the problem of Alex himself. His lies cut her more deeply than Mark's ever had. Even worse was the fact that even though she couldn't trust him, she still wanted him. Being separated from him felt unnatural, wrong even. She moved through her days feeling like an amputee, the phantom pain of Alex her constant companion. But no matter how much her heart cried out for him, her mind held strong. For a relationship to last, it had to be built on a foundation of trust. And as much as it hurt her to say it, she couldn't trust Alex.

In her darker moments she wondered which was worse: the pain of losing her brother or the burning sting of betrayal she felt every time she remembered Alex had deliberately kept that information from her.

"You still with me?" Carla waved a chip in front of her face, pulling Jillian out of her reverie.

"Yeah. Sorry about that." She glanced down at her plate and poked halfheartedly at a cherry tomato. It didn't look very appealing, but she still had several hours left to go on her shift.

"S'okay," Carla replied through a mouthful of sandwich. She washed it down and fixed Jillian with her take-no-prisoners stare. "I'm sure you were just deciding how to tell me what's going on."

"Something like that," Jillian muttered. How could

she tell her friend? *Yeah, the other night I was kidnapped by an undercover federal agent and we spent forty-eight hours on the run from a psychopathic gang and the traitor in his organization. And while all this was going on, I kind of fell in love with him. But then I found out he was keeping the truth about my brother's death from me, so now I don't trust him anymore.*

As if Carla would believe that! Jillian would dismiss it herself, if she hadn't actually lived through it all. No, perhaps total honesty was not the way to go.

But she couldn't deny that Carla deserved some kind of explanation. The woman was her closest friend, and she didn't want to sour their relationship by pushing her away.

Choosing her words with care, Jillian sketched out the basic problem. She didn't go into details about Jason, or the circumstances that had led to Alex finally telling her the truth. Instead she explained she was seeing a guy who worked undercover in law enforcement and she was having trouble trusting him.

"He kept something really important from me," she explained. "And since he lies for a living, I'm not sure I can trust him."

Carla studied her for a moment, chewing thoughtfully. "Has he given you reason to doubt anything else he's said?"

Jillian frowned. "Well, no," she said slowly, replaying conversations in her mind. "But how can I be sure?"

"You can't," Carla said. "But that's no different from any other relationship. No matter who you're with, you have to decide to trust them or you'll drive yourself crazy second-guessing their every move. That's no way to go through life."

"Yeah, but in this case, he lies all the time. That means he's especially good at it."

"He's in law enforcement, right?" At her nod, Carla continued. "Well, there you have it. He lies to the bad guys to stay alive. That doesn't mean he's automatically going to lie to you." She paused for a moment and then added softly, "He's not Mark, honey."

How many times had she thought the same thing, before Alex had told her about Jason? Coming from Carla, it sounded so simple, so obvious. But while she couldn't deny the truth of her friend's words, she couldn't let go of the pain of knowing Alex had deliberately kept the news of her brother a secret.

"Maybe you're right," she said. "But I'm so angry with him for the way he acted. I don't know if I can get over that."

"I understand. But are you being fair?"

Jillian bristled, her eyebrows shooting up. "What do you mean?"

"I don't know what he kept from you. But I'm sure he had his reasons for it."

"Whose side are you on?"

Carla shot her an exasperated look. "Yours, of course. I'm just playing devil's advocate here."

"Humph."

"I just want you to consider his side. Maybe he was scared to tell you. Maybe he hadn't had a chance to bring it up because he was waiting for the perfect moment. Maybe he couldn't figure out how to tell you." She shrugged. "From what you've told me, he sounds like a good guy. I don't think you should automatically cast him out for making a mistake, especially if his heart was in the right place."

Dammit. Jillian's anger faltered in the face of Carla's argument. Thinking back, she was forced to admit that perhaps she wasn't being fair to Alex. Given the nonstop action of their first meeting, there really hadn't been an ideal time for him to share the news of Jason's death. Hadn't he said as much, when he finally did tell her? But once the danger had passed, and their lives returned to normal, he hadn't hesitated to talk to her. That took courage, something she hadn't acknowledged until now.

She knew better than most how hard it was to deliver bad news. As a doctor, she'd lost her share of patients. Notifying the surviving family was never an easy task, no matter how she tried to soften the blow. She closed her eyes, recalling the creeping dread that accompanied her steps down the endless hospital corridor. A trek to the waiting room to deliver bad news always made her feel like she was walking in quicksand.

Had Alex felt the same way? Had his feet slowed when he'd approached her door, responsibility and reluctance warring for dominance? Had he drawn a fortifying breath before lifting his hand to knock?

He didn't have to tell me, she realized with a small shock. Jason had been gone for two years, and she had stopped looking for him around every corner. Alex knew he was dead, and knew his family had never been notified and likely never would be. It would have been much easier for Alex to keep her in the dark. They could have moved on with their lives, with her none the wiser about her brother's fate. The fact that he had stepped up and shared that information, despite the consequences to himself, spoke volumes about his character.

She'd been spending so much time comparing Alex to Mark, but they were nothing alike. Mark had used her for sex, and had never intended to tell her the truth about his wife. He was a liar and a cheat, and he would never confess to any wrongdoing unless confronted with evidence. He was nothing like Alex, and she'd done Alex a disservice by lumping the two of them together.

"You may have a point," Jillian muttered, feeling slightly foolish. Perhaps she had overreacted a bit after hearing the news, but in her defense, it had been a huge shock.

"Just talk to him," Carla suggested. "Give him a chance to explain why he did it. If you don't like his reasons, you can move on. But I think you still care for him. Otherwise, you wouldn't be pushing yourself to exhaustion." She polished off the rest of her sandwich, looking a little too pleased with herself.

"Maybe I enjoy my job," Jillian said, unwilling to give in so easily.

"I know you do," Carla replied evenly. "But you're not working nonstop because you love it here. You're doing it so you don't have to think about Mr. Secret Agent Man."

Jillian felt a smile tug at her mouth and she glanced at Carla, hoping her friend hadn't noticed. She had.

"Uh-huh," Carla muttered. "That's what I thought."

"Okay, okay." Jillian raised her hands in surrender. "I'll talk to him."

"Today."

"Tonight, after I get off."

Carla raised a brow, unimpressed.

"You can't expect me to call him in the middle of my shift," Jillian said, exasperation creeping into her voice.

"I suppose not," Carla said. "But you better be out the door as soon as your shift ends. No hanging around looking for extra stuff to do so you don't have to go home like you've been doing the past few days."

"Yes, Mom."

That bit of sarcasm earned her the patented Carla death stare, and she leaned back, chastened. "Sorry."

Before Carla could respond, the pager at Jillian's belt buzzed insistently. She grabbed it, checking the coded display. Inbound emergency. Carla's pager buzzed a second later and the two women rose as one, tossing trash on their way out the door of the cafeteria.

It was a short walk to the ER, and they made it just as the ambulance pulled into the bay.

"What have we got?" Jillian called out, tugging on a pair of gloves.

"Multiple stab wounds, chest and abdomen. Stable during transport," a nurse yelled back.

Jillian stepped out to meet the paramedics, who were tugging the gurney out of the ambulance. She caught a brief glimpse of long, lanky limbs and a face covered by a plastic breathing mask, and then they were moving, wheeling the patient inside while the EMT updated her on the kid's vitals and injuries.

A quick count and the team slid him off the gurney and onto the bed. His clothes were cut away with brisk, efficient movements, and Jillian began her perusal of his body, checking for any visible wounds. The skin of his chest and abdomen was slick with blood, and she wiped most of it off with gauze to clear her field of vision.

"Can you tell me what happened to you?" she asked, her attention focused on his chest while she spoke. There appeared to be multiple shallow cuts along his ribs, indicating someone had tried to stab him but the blade had glanced off the bones of his rib cage. A few deeper wounds appeared low on his abdomen, angled to the side as if the victim had almost gotten away from his attacker.

The young man lifted his hand and pulled at the oxygen mask. Jillian reflexively moved to stop him, then caught a glimpse of his face and froze, her hand stalling in midair.

Tony cast her a slanted grin, his dark eyes glittering in the fluorescent lights of the ER bay. "Hey, there, Doc. Nice to see you made it out alive."

Alex missed Jillian with an aching fierceness he felt in his bones, the kind of lingering soreness that followed a car accident. And wasn't that an apt metaphor for the way their relationship had ended? Crash and burn, with no recovery in sight.

He doubted Jillian missed him, or even thought of him. After all, she hadn't contacted him in the days since she'd kicked him out of her apartment. He had hoped that after a little time had passed, Jillian would reach out to him so they could continue to talk about her brother and why Alex had kept the news of his death from her. But as the days marched on with no sign of her, Alex realized that Jillian had no intention of speaking to him and likely didn't want to hear from him. It was a bitter pill to swallow, especially because his feelings for her hadn't waned.

He had relived their conversation a thousand times, trying to figure out where things had gone so wrong. Could he have said something, done something differently to make her understand that he hadn't kept his secret to hurt her, but because he'd simply wanted to wait for the right moment to tell her? Maybe he should have told her right away, as soon as he realized the connection. But he'd been desperate for a safe place to sleep, and by the time an opportunity presented itself, his feelings for her had developed to the point that he hadn't wanted to just share the news and walk out of her life. He had hoped—still hoped, if he was being totally honest with himself—that she would forgive him and they could move on with their lives.

Now he realized she didn't share that desire.

He stared into space, hands still gripping the steering wheel. The sun was setting, the last weak rays of light casting a soft glow over the cars in the hospital parking lot. Alex had tried to find Jillian at her apartment, but for the past several days, she hadn't answered his knock. He felt like the worst sort of stalker to seek her out at work, but he had news to share and he wanted to deliver it in person. Then he would walk away and not bother her again.

Hopefully she would be happy to hear that the DC police and the FBI were searching for Tony so that he could be charged for her brother's death. Maybe she'd even smile at him as she thanked him for telling her. That would be a nice way to remember her, he mused. He'd much rather their last encounter end with a smile, so that it could replace the memory of her tear-stained, grief-stricken face as she'd pushed him away.

"Time's wasting," he muttered, shaking his head to clear it. He wasn't sure when her shift ended, but he figured she had to have some kind of dinner break. He reached for the brown bag in the front seat, careful not to jostle it. The sandwich should be fine, but he didn't want to spill the soup. He'd stopped at the fancy deli across the street from the hospital, figuring she hadn't taken the time to eat a good meal today. Hopefully the food could act as a sort of peace offering, and would help break the ice between them.

At this time of day the ER was relatively empty. A few sniffling souls sat in the plastic waiting room chairs, but to his untrained eye, they appeared to be fine. He approached the sign-in desk, pasting on a friendly smile for the benefit of the nurse behind the Plexiglas.

"I'm looking for Dr. Mahoney. Is she here?"

The woman regarded him suspiciously. "Who wants to know?"

"Special Agent Alex Malcom," he said, pulling out his badge. He wasn't above using his position to cut through a little red tape, especially if it meant he'd get to see Jillian.

One of the nurses standing a few feet away snapped to attention and turned to stare at him, her dark brown eyes alight with a speculative gleam. She approached the Plexiglas barrier, coming to stand behind the receptionist. "Are you Jillian's friend?" she asked, eyeing him up and down.

He nodded, sensing this woman knew him somehow. He racked his brain, trying to come up with a connection, but gave up after a few seconds. "Do I know you?"

She snorted, apparently finding his question amusing. "Nope. But I know all about you, Mr. Secret Agent Man."

His stomach dropped as he realized Jillian must have talked to this woman about him. *Great. Now I'll never get to see her.* Not with her friend running defense. He may as well go back to her apartment and camp out in front of her door. Maybe her elderly neighbor would take pity on him and invite him in for dinner.

"Is Jillian here?"

The nurse tilted her head and tapped a finger to her lips while she considered his question. "Maybe. It depends. Why are you here?"

"I need to speak with her. I have some important news."

"Does it come with an apology?"

None of your business. It was on the tip of his tongue, but Alex bit his lip, recognizing he would have to pass this test if he wanted to see Jillian. He settled for a nod instead, hoping that was enough.

"All right. Come on back. She's with a patient now, but she should be finishing up. I'll see if she's available." At her nod, the receptionist pressed a button and the door to the left of her station swung open. The nurse met him as he walked through, and pointed to a chair just past the reception station. "Stay there. I'll be back in a minute."

Alex sat and arranged the bag on his lap, surprised to find his palms were damp. He wiped them on his pants, ignoring the flutter of nerves in his stomach. Would she see him? How would she greet him? What if she told her friend to send him away?

I'll leave her a note if she doesn't want to talk to me. He patted his pockets for a pen in case one was needed.

A muffled shriek sounded from somewhere down the hall and he heard the slam of a door followed by rapid footsteps coming his way. The nurse was back, looking distressed.

He stood, but she moved past him, reaching for the intercom system near his head. "Code Green. I repeat,

Code Green. Dr. Strong to the ER. Dr. Strong to the ER, stat!" She replaced the mouthpiece and turned to face him, alarm written across her face.

"What happened?"

She shook her head. "You can't be here now. You need to leave."

Alex put his hands on her shoulders and shook her gently. "Is it Jillian?"

The nurse bit her lip, clearly torn. She glanced down the hall, then looked back at him and nodded. Tears pooled at the corners of her eyes. "Her patient is using her as a hostage."

His gut twisted at her words and a cold fist gripped his heart, squeezing hard. "What room?"

"You can't—"

"What room?" he repeated, trying to keep his voice down. He wanted to roar in frustration, but yelling at this nurse wasn't going to help the situation.

"Three B. Down the hall. Third on your left."

"Does he have a weapon?"

"He's using the scalpel as a knife."

"Tell the police a federal agent is on the scene," he said, already moving. He grabbed his badge with one hand and pulled his gun from his shoulder holster with the other.

The nurse's announcement had triggered some kind of rehearsed response and people streamed past him, apparently moving to a pre-arranged muster station. He held his badge up as he walked against the flow of traffic, identifying himself and ensuring he wasn't stopped on his way to Jillian's room.

He paused outside the door, pressing his ear against the cool wood. Faint scuffling sounds reached him, as though someone was being dragged across the floor. Then he heard Jillian's voice, muffled but strong.

"I'm telling you, it isn't him."

"Then who's your visitor?" Was that Tony? Alex flattened against the door, straining to hear.

"It could be anyone," Jillian said. "My dad. My brother. Who knows?"

"Nah, it's him. That nurse lady was too excited for it to be one of your relatives."

"I haven't seen him since that night at the motel. I promise you, he hasn't showed up here."

"Then he will," Tony said, sounding confident. "Once your boyfriend finds out we're in here, he'll come."

"He's not my boyfriend," Jillian replied, but she sounded unsure.

Tony laughed; a harsh sound that grated on Alex's already frayed nerves. "I know what I saw, lady. And me and him, we've got some unfinished business."

Alex kept his ear against the door, but heard nothing else. If he was right, and it was Tony holding Jillian hostage, he hoped the kid would keep hold of his temper. It killed him to stand outside while she was trapped, but he needed to come up with a plan. Barging into the room wasn't the best idea, especially since he had no idea what he'd be walking into.

Could he try to approach from above? He glanced up at the institutional ceiling tiles. Were the heating and cooling tunnels large enough to accommodate his frame? Could he even get access to them from here? He looked around in search of a mechanical access room, but saw nothing. It was probably at the end of the hall, and he wasn't willing to leave his post by the door for a wild-goose chase.

"You need to call him." It was Tony. Apparently the kid had figured out that Alex would not automatically be notified and realized either he or Jillian would have to make contact. "He needs to get here now."

Alex was pleased to hear that Tony wanted to talk, but his growing impatience was a bad sign.

"I don't have his number."

"Do you think I'm stupid?" Tony's voice rose along with his agitation. "I know you can talk to him. Now do it!"

He heard Jillian whimper and his budding plans went out the window. Keeping her safe was the only thing that mattered.

"Tony, I'm here," he said, speaking loudly so his voice would travel through the door. "It's Alex. Can I come in?"

"You got a gun?"

Alex moved carefully, tucking the gun in the waistband of his pants at the small of his back, so it would be hidden. Then he grabbed a clipboard off the neighboring door and slid it across the floor, hoping the sound would convince Tony he had given up his weapon. "Not anymore," he replied.

"Open the door slow," Tony instructed. "And keep your hands where I can see them, or I'm gonna cut her."

"There's no need for that," Alex said. "I'm here to talk. No one needs to get hurt."

Alex pushed the door open a crack and stuck his hands through, fingers splayed wide. Careful not to make any sudden movements, he used his toe to widen the opening until he was standing in the doorway, his hands held up by his head.

At first glance, Jillian seemed unharmed. The tension in his chest relaxed a bit and he took a deep breath as he ran his gaze over her body. No sign of blood or other injury. Maybe Tony really didn't want to hurt her, but had just used her as bait to get to him.

After assuring himself that Jillian was fine, at least for the present, Alex scanned the rest of the room, searching for other potential threats. Aside from Jillian and Tony, the room was empty.

Tony shifted, forcing Jillian to move with him or risk getting cut by the scalpel he held to her throat. The blade was bright in the fluorescent lights, gleaming with lethal potential against the pale column of her neck. Alex forced himself to stay rooted to the spot, knowing that if he rushed in, Tony wouldn't hesitate to slice her up. And although they were in an emergency room and had immediate access to medical care, he couldn't risk her safety like that.

"Told you he was close," Tony said, his voice low in Jillian's ear. She shuddered slightly and he tightened his grip. "Come on in, man," he said to Alex. "We need to talk."

Alex stepped into the room, keeping his hands up. "This is between us. Why don't you let her go?"

Tony grinned and shook his head briefly. "You know that's not how this works. But nice try."

"How do you think this is going to end?" Alex moved closer, taking small, slow steps. If he could get within arm's reach, he could make a grab for Jillian and pull her away from Tony. It might not be too difficult, given the way Tony was swaying slightly on his feet. A small puddle of blood had formed on the floor underneath him, and he heard a steady plop as more drops were added. If Alex could keep him talking, it might not take long for Tony to pass out, which would be the safest way of dealing with him. He met Jillian's eyes, which had gone wide and round with shock and fear.

Trust me.

"That's far enough," Tony said, taking a step back and tugging Jillian with him. Her gaze never left his face, and Alex tried to look reassuring, hoping she had gotten his message.

"Now what?"

"Now you're both gonna die."

Chapter 17

Jillian's heart stalled at Tony's words and she braced herself for the cold bite of the scalpel. Would it hurt? Would she even feel it? Or would the shock of the situation keep her numb, so that she died feeling muffled and cold?

Was that how it had been for Jason?

Anger swelled, pushing aside her fear. This was the man who had killed her brother, and now he was threatening her. She would not—could not—allow him to win. He'd taken enough from her already; he wasn't about to take her life, as well.

Jillian closed her eyes, embracing her fury and stoking it into a blazing inferno, preparing for the moment when she could use it against him.

She'd been so shocked when she'd seen him, she hadn't thought to call the police. After all, what could he do to her, lying injured on her exam table? So she'd moved on autopilot, ordering tests and scans to determine the extent of his injuries. She was determined to fix him, so that he could pay for his crimes. Luckily for him, the wounds were superficial. She'd felt a perverse satisfaction in knowing Tony would make a full recovery so he could rot in jail for what he'd done to her brother. In fact, she'd been so busy silently gloating that she'd allowed herself to become distracted and that's when Tony had made his move.

She cursed herself again for taking her eyes off Tony to talk to Carla, for letting the news of Alex's visit fluster her. Tony was injured but he wasn't stupid, and he'd seized the opportunity to gain the upper hand. But what Tony didn't realize was that he'd lost a lot of blood. He was still standing, but she could tell by the way he rocked slightly that he was feeling dizzy. A few more minutes and he'd probably be leaning on her for support.

Unless he killed her first.

"How are you going to kill me, Tony?" Alex asked. "You have one weapon, and it's not a great one. Besides, you're too busy holding it up to her throat to reach me."

Tony stiffened against her, sending a flare of panic through her limbs. *Don't move,* she pleaded silently. The last thing she needed was for Tony to slit her throat as a demonstration of his prowess.

"I don't have to do anything to you, man," Tony replied. "I called my boys. They're on the way. Just like last time." He made a sound that might have been a laugh, his breath a little wheezy.

Alex glanced at Jillian, apparently seeking confirmation. She shrugged slightly. While Tony hadn't made any calls since coming to the ER, she had no idea who he may have talked to beforehand. It was possible he had phoned his friends and told them where he was going. This time, though, the police would keep any gang members from accessing the ER. She caught Alex's eye again.

Stall him.

Alex cleared his throat and slowly lowered his hands. "Well, since we have some time to kill until your buddies arrive, why don't you tell me how you found out who I really am?"

"None of your business."

Alex shrugged and rested his hands on his waist. He seemed normal, but there was something a little *too* casual about the way he moved his hands. Did he have a weapon behind his back?

"Just trying to make conversation," he said, his gaze flicking back to her. He read the question in her eyes and nodded once.

Tony's hand grew heavy on her shoulder and she realized he was starting to fade. Adrenaline flooded her system, making her tremble slightly. If Tony noticed, he didn't respond.

"I don't wanna talk to you," Tony said. "We're going to wait for them to get here, and then we'll take care of you. Her, too," he added, turning his head to sniff her hair.

Bile rose from her stomach, scalding the back of her throat. It was time to end this. She'd rather take her chances with the scalpel than stay in Tony's arms a minute longer.

She looked at Alex and saw the rage in his eyes. He, too, had had enough. She kept her gaze locked on his, drawing comfort from the knowledge that if this didn't work, if Tony cut her throat, at least Alex would be the last thing she saw before she closed her eyes forever. The thought both calmed her and gave her strength, and she tried to let all the emotion she felt for Alex show on her face. *I love you*, she mouthed.

He blinked and fear danced across his face when she started to count down.

One...

He shook his head, lifting a hand to stop her.

Two...

Tony noticed Alex's distress. "What the hell—?"

Three...

Jillian raised her arm and drove her elbow back into Tony's abdomen with all the force she could muster. He doubled over, his breath whooshing out in a pained grunt. She dropped to her knees and scooted away as fast as she could, trying to get out of his reach before he recovered enough to stab her.

Everything seemed to happen at once. Shouting voices, a rush of feet, the sounds of weapons being cocked.

From her vantage point, Jillian couldn't tell who had stormed into the room. Was it Tony's friends? *Please, no,* she thought, curling up into a ball on the floor. If she kept her head down, she wouldn't get shot.

Strong hands pulled her up and she opened her eyes to see Alex, his face creased with concern. "Are you all right?" he asked, running his hands over her neck, turning her head from side to side so he could inspect the skin of her throat.

"I think so," she answered, feeling a little uncertain. The numbness was back, creeping across her body and making it hard to tell how she felt.

"You took ten years off my life just now," Alex said, pulling her close and squeezing her gently. "Don't ever do that again."

Jillian closed her eyes, savoring the contact with Alex's broad chest. She felt complete for the first time in days and wanted to stay in his arms for hours, making up for lost time. Unfortunately the police had other ideas.

"Ma'am? Sir? I need you to step over here, please." A policewoman gestured for them to move and Jillian reluctantly surrendered her hold on Alex to comply. She kept her hand on him, though, wanting to maintain some connection, however tenuous. She had made the mistake of letting him go once. She wasn't going to do it again.

Hours later Jillian walked out of the hospital hand in hand with Alex.

It had taken some time to explain all the whos, whats and whys of tonight's events, but once the police learned of the FBI's ongoing investigation into the gang, they settled for taking everyone's statement and calling it a day. Jillian suspected Alex and his mysterious phone calls had played a part in their sudden acquiescence, but she didn't ask and he didn't volunteer.

"Never a dull moment with you around," she remarked. She'd meant for the remark to be teasing, but he flinched. "I'm sorry," she said, pulling them to a stop. "I didn't mean that in a bad way."

He shook his head. "It's okay. I deserved that."

She studied him a moment, her heart softening as she watched emotions play across his features. "No, you don't," she said softly. "And I'm the one who should be apologizing, not you."

He frowned at her, clearly confused. "What are you talking about? What have you got to apologize for?"

Jillian reached up and brushed the hair off his forehead. He closed his eyes briefly at her touch, making her want to pull him down so she could hold him. "I'm sorry for the way I reacted when you told me about Jason. It wasn't your fault, and I shouldn't have pushed you away like that."

Alex shrugged, the tips of his ears going pink. "It's okay," he replied, his voice gentle. "I don't blame you for that. I just hate that I hurt you."

She shook her head. "You didn't. Tony did. I took the anger I felt for him and directed it at you. I realize now why you told me when you did, and I shouldn't have punished you for it."

"I'm just glad you're talking to me now. I was scared you wouldn't want to see me again."

"Why were you here tonight? Not that I'm upset— you definitely saved the day. But what made you find me at work?"

He ducked his head, looking unaccountably shy. "I've been trying to reach you for the past several days, but you were never home. I wanted to tell you that the FBI and police were looking for Tony so he could be charged for Jason's death, among other things."

Tears sprang to her eyes and she blinked, forcing them back. "Good. I'm glad he'll finally pay for what he did to Jason."

Alex nodded. "He'll never hurt you again."

"Or you," she replied, rising to her tiptoes to press a soft kiss to his mouth.

He sighed her name; a whisper of sound. "Jillian."

"Do you still want me?" she asked quietly. She placed her hand against her stomach to quell the nervous fluttering, but it didn't help. So she settled for holding her breath, waiting for his response.

His dark blue eyes glowed in the light of the streetlamps, and she flashed back to their first encounter, when he was a big, dark, mysterious stranger. He was still physically powerful, but she knew now he wasn't dark or sinister. He was hers, and she wanted desperately to be his.

If he would still have her.

"You know I do."

Excitement bubbled up into her chest, making her feel like she'd just swallowed a huge gulp of champagne. "Then I need you to do something for me," she said, trying to tamp down the giddy lightness that threatened to carry her away.

One dark brow rose as he considered her. "What's that?"

Jillian laid her hand against his chest, over his heart. It thumped reassuringly against her palm, grounding her in this moment. "Promise me you'll try to forgive yourself for the things you've had to do."

He looked down, shaking his head. "It's not that easy," he murmured.

"I didn't say it would be. But I'm asking you to try."

Alex took a deep breath and then nodded. "Okay. I can do that."

"Good." She stretched up to kiss him again.

"Will you do something for me?"

"Anything," she replied automatically.

"Love me?"

It was such a simple request, and she could tell he was trying to appear strong while he waited for her answer. But vulnerability shone in his eyes, along with something else. Hope.

Jillian pulled him close, snuggling against him as the boom of New Year's firecrackers echoed in the cold night air. "You couldn't stop me if you tried."

* * * * *

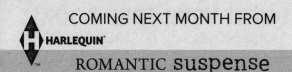

REQUEST YOUR FREE BOOKS!
2 FREE NOVELS PLUS 2 FREE GIFTS!

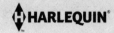

ROMANTIC suspense

Sparked by danger, fueled by passion

YES! Please send me 2 FREE Harlequin® Romantic Suspense novels and my 2 FREE gifts (gifts are worth about $10). After receiving them, if I don't wish to receive any more books, I can return the shipping statement marked "cancel." If I don't cancel, I will receive 4 brand-new novels every month and be billed just $4.74 per book in the U.S. or $5.24 per book in Canada. That's a savings of at least 14% off the cover price! It's quite a bargain! Shipping and handling is just 50¢ per book in the U.S. and 75¢ per book in Canada.* I understand that accepting the 2 free books and gifts places me under no obligation to buy anything. I can always return a shipment and cancel at any time. Even if I never buy another book, the two free books and gifts are mine to keep forever.

240/340 HDN F45N

Name _____ (PLEASE PRINT) _____

Address _____ Apt. # _____

City _____ State/Prov. _____ Zip/Postal Code _____

Signature (if under 18, a parent or guardian must sign) _____

Mail to the **Harlequin® Reader Service:**
IN U.S.A.: P.O. Box 1867, Buffalo, NY 14240-1867
IN CANADA: P.O. Box 609, Fort Erie, Ontario L2A 5X3

Want to try two free books from another line?
Call 1-800-873-8635 or visit www.ReaderService.com.

* Terms and prices subject to change without notice. Prices do not include applicable taxes. Sales tax applicable in N.Y. Canadian residents will be charged applicable taxes. Offer not valid in Quebec. This offer is limited to one order per household. Not valid for current subscribers to Harlequin Romantic Suspense books. All orders subject to credit approval. Credit or debit balances in a customer's account(s) may be offset by any other outstanding balance owed by or to the customer. Please allow 4 to 6 weeks for delivery. Offer available while quantities last.

Your Privacy—The Harlequin® Reader Service is committed to protecting your privacy. Our Privacy Policy is available online at www.ReaderService.com or upon request from the Harlequin Reader Service.

We make a portion of our mailing list available to reputable third parties that offer products we believe may interest you. If you prefer that we not exchange your name with third parties, or if you wish to clarify or modify your communication preferences, please visit us at www.ReaderService.com/consumerschoice or write to us at Harlequin Reader Service Preference Service, P.O. Box 9062, Buffalo, NY 14269. Include your complete name and address.

HRS13R

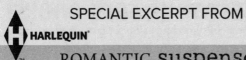
UNDERCOVER HUNTER

Calvin Sweet knew he was taking some big chances, but
taking risks always invigorated him. Coming back to his
home in Conard County was the first of the new risks. Five
years ago he'd left for the big city because the law was closing in on him.

Returning to the site where he had hung his trophies was
a huge risk, too, although he could claim he was out for a
hike in the spring mountains. There was nothing left, anyway. The law had taken it all, and the sight filled him with
both sorrow and bitterness. Anger, too. They had no right
to take away his hard work, his triumphs, his mementos.

But they had. After five years all that was left were some
remnants of cargo netting rotting in the tree limbs and the
remains of a few sawed-off nooses.

He could close his eyes and remember, and remembering
filled him with joy and a sense of his own huge power, the
power of life and death. The power to take it all away. The
power to enlighten those whose existence was so shallow.

They took it for granted. Calvin never did.

From earliest childhood he had been fascinated by spiders and their webs. He had spent hours watching as insect after insect fell victim to those silken strands, struggling mightily until they were stung and then wrapped up helplessly to await their fate. Each corpse on the web had been a trophy marking the spider's victory. No one ever escaped.

No one had escaped him, either.

He was chosen, just like a spider, to be exactly what he was. Chosen. He liked that word. It fit both him and his victims. They were all chosen to perform the dance of death together, to plumb the reaches of human endurance. To sacrifice the ordinary for the extraordinary. So he quashed his growing need to act and focused his attention on another part of his life. He had a job now, one he needed to report to every evening. He was whistling now as he walked back down to his small ranch.

A spiderweb was beginning to take shape in his mind, one for his barn loft that no one would see, ever. It was enough that he could admire it and savor the gifts there. The impulse to hunt eased, and soon he was in control again. He liked control. He liked controlling himself and others, even as he fulfilled his purpose.

Like the spider, he was not hasty to act. It would have to be the right person at the right time, and the time was not yet right. First he had to build his web.

**Don't miss UNDERCOVER HUNTER
by *New York Times* bestselling author
Rachel Lee, available January 2015 wherever
Harlequin® Romantic Suspense books and
ebooks are sold.**

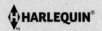

ROMANTIC suspense

Heart-racing romance, high-stakes suspense!

HIGH-STAKES PLAYBOY
by *New York Times* bestselling author
Cindy Dees

Available January 2015

Who will get this Prescott bachelor first— the girl or the killer?

To help his brothers, marine pilot Archer Prescott goes undercover to find out who's sabotaging their movie set. But the die-hard bachelor isn't ready for what he finds in the High Sierras: his doe-eyed girl-next-door camerawoman is the prime suspect.

Marley Stringer isn't as innocent as she seems. As Marley turns irresistible and the aerial "accidents" turn deadly, Archer begins to wonder who's more dangerous—the perfect woman who threatens his heart...or the desperate killer who threatens his life.

Don't miss the first exciting installment from Cindy Dees's *The Prescott Bachelors* series:

HIGH-STAKES BACHELOR

Available wherever Harlequin® Romantic Suspense books and ebooks are sold.

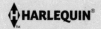

HARLEQUIN®

ROMANTIC suspense

Heart-racing romance, high-stakes suspense!

BAYOU HERO
by *USA TODAY* bestselling author
Marilyn Pappano

Available January 2015

One family's scandal is responsible for a rising body count in New Orleans's Garden District...

Even for an experienced NCIS agent like Alia Kingsley, the murder scene is particularly gruesome. A man killed in a fit of rage. Being the long-estranged son of the deceased, Landry Jackson quickly becomes a person of interest. But does Landry loathe his father as much as the feds suspect?

It's clear to Alia that Landry Jackson has secrets, but his hatred for his father isn't one of them. Alia feels sure Landry isn't the killer, but once more family members start dying, she's forced to question herself. What if the fierce attraction she has developed toward Landry has compromised Alia's instincts?

Don't miss other exciting titles from
USA TODAY bestselling author Marilyn Pappano:

UNDERCOVER IN COPPER LAKE
COPPER LAKE ENCOUNTER
COPPER LAKE CONFIDENTIAL

Available wherever Harlequin® Romantic Suspense
books and ebooks are sold.

www.Harlequin.com

HRS27902